PRF
by Anton I

The three young Britons who, in the summer of 1880, set out on a hunting and fishing expedition in the mountains of Jotunheimen, could hardly have imagined that their simple tale – so full of humour, ridicule and ironic self-criticism, and yet so rich in perceptive observations – would become such a treasured classic of generation after generation of Norwegians. Certainly, Norwegians like to be provoked by so-called typical English humour (especially when it is so clear to see that they actually think Norway is wonderful!), but it is not only Norwegians who like the book. It is a classic, irrespective of Norwegian pride, as can be seen by the fact that it has been published three times in Tauchnitz's *English Library*.

But who were they, these humorous, nature-loving, knowledgeable, fit and literary young gentlemen? And how did they find helpers in the remote, exotic Vågå? In the book, they conceal the names of the authors, helpers and the people they meet, preferring to use nicknames, first names, or just an initial. Let us take a closer look at some of them.

THE AUTHORS

The three Britons did not remain anonymous for long. Many people in both England and Norway knew about their expedition. Then, in a book about a similar trip to Canada seven years later – *B. C. 1887* – two of them admitted to being the authors. *Three in Norway* has always been published as the authors intended, however; *by two of them* is undoubtedly just as well known by the public as any author's name.

James A. *Lees* (1852–1931) and Walter J. *Clutterbuck* (1853–1937) do not rank amongst the most famous of authors in England. They were first and foremost hunting, fishing and wildlife enthusiasts. Yet, they wrote about the kind of life they loved, and in a way that set a new standard for such accounts. The reviewers at once remarked on the novelty in their approach: the humour and lack of all sentimentality, combined with precise observations, graphic wildlife descriptions and a totally unrestrained joy of living on their own surrounded by nature. *Three in Norway* was their first book, but they had immediately found their own specific style.

Both J. A. Lees ("Esau" in the book) and W. J. Clutterbuck ("The Skipper") wrote subsequent books. These are mentioned in English reference works, and in 1938, the magazine *Fiskesport* ("Angling") published an article by H. L. Larssen who, one year earlier, had been in touch with Clutterbuck and with Lees' widow. We know considerably less about "John". We do know, however,

THE JOTUNFJELD

Showing various Routes to it.

English Miles.

1 2 3 4 5 · · · · · 10

To Throndhjem

Vaage
Sörum
(Last Posting Station)

Snerle (Station)

Flatningen'

Otta R.

Laagen R.

Aasören
(Station)

Lemond
Lake

Bjölstad
(First Posting Station)

t. Sinclair's Monument

Ransvœrk

Hedalen

Bredevangen (Station)

Sjoa R.

Sjoa River

Storklevstad
(Station)

Laagen R.

Mu
Lake

To Lillehammer

Vinstra R.

Laagen R.

Fœton
Lake

Colaan
Lake

Camp
Sikkildals
Horne
Aakre
Kampen
Aakre Sœter
Aakre
Lake

als Lakes
Sikkildals
Sœter

Hy Sœter

Hinögelid
Slangen

Olstappen L.

3rd Camp
Dals Sœter

Finböle

Waterfall

2nd Camp

Böle

Oiang
Lake

Bred Sjö

Espedals Lake

Megrunden

ER LAKES

als Lakes

1st Camp

Dalbakken

Kvisberg
(Last Posting Sta)

To Lillehammer

THREE IN NORWAY

Running the Rapids below Gjendesheim.

THREE IN NORWAY

by

TWO OF THEM

WITH MAP AND FIFTY-NINE ILLUSTRATIONS ON WOOD

FROM SKETCHES BY THE AUTHOR

ANDRESEN & BUTENSCHØN

Three in Norway by Two of them
was written by J.A. Lees and W.J. Clutterbuck
First published in London 1882
By Longmans, Green & Co.

This edition is published by
Andresen & Butenschøn AS
Box 1153 Sentrum, 0107 Oslo

The preface to this edition is translated by Kevin M.J. Quirk

Production Consultant: Arne E. Olsen
The illustrations in this edition
are reproduced by Cappella AS, Tønsberg
Printed and bound in Latvia 2001 by Preses Nams

Published in cooperation with *Ferd*

ISBN 82-7694-095-1

ISBN 82-7694-104-4 (Ferd)
ISBN 82-7694-105-2 (Leather bound)

"A man is at all times entitled, or even called upon by occasion, to speak, and write, and in all fit ways utter, what he has himself gone through, and known, and got the mastery of; and in truth, at bottom, there is nothing else that any man has a right to write of. For the rest, one principle, I think, in whatever farther you write, may be enough to guide you: that of standing rigorously by the fact, however naked it look. Fact is eternal; all fiction is very transitory in comparison. All men are interested in any man if he will speak the facts of his life for them; his authentic experience, which corresponds, as face with face, to that of all other sons of Adam."

THOMAS CARLYLE

CONTENTS

that his real name was Charles *Kennedy*, that he was Irish, and that he was well known for his "wonderful spirits". In *B. C. 1887*, the authors recount that they had to find a new third man as John had decided to marry and establish himself (while Esau was "married, but *unestablished*"). Later on, John broke his thighbone and this put an end to his wildlife adventures.

The two main authors were *gentlemen of independent means* who could realise their ambitions of adventure by taking long holidays in far-away places. When they visited Norway in 1880, they were young and unestablished, and without any form of obligations. They had, in fact, completed their education (at Eton and Cheam, Oxford and Cambridge) only a short time before.

J. A. Lees began practising as a lawyer after his trip to Norway. He married in 1882. However, by 1889, he had already given up his legal practice, partly due to medical reasons, and had decided to settle down on his family estate in Lancashire, where he became a country magistrate. He did not give up his travelling, however. Following his trip to Canada in 1887, he returned to Norway in 1898 and 1907, and also travelled to various other European countries and to Morocco. After his Norwegian tour in 1898, he wrote, this time on his own, *Peaks and Pines* (republished in English by Nortrabooks in 1968). "The Skipper" and "John" each took a separate part in this expedition, together with Lees' only son (who was killed in the First World War) and a nephew. They fished in the valley of Sirdal, and hunted reindeer in places he chose to conceal behind names such as "Ingenstad", "Nord Vann" and "Nordmannshø" (Nowhere, North Lake and Norseman's Mountain) – presumably areas around Lesja. Lees also wrote travel accounts for a number of magazines, and regularly contributed humorous poetry and other texts to *Punch*.

W. J. Clutterbuck appears to have had no form of permanent employment. His interests in wildlife and the countryside took him to the Arctic Ocean, America, Asia and Australia. All the time, he continued to write. He married in 1896 and his wife accompanied him on many of his trips. They were "wonderfully interesting, but pretty unorthodox", she once explained. He was always wandering into the remotest parts of the countryside and into the unknown. After *B.C. 1887*, he wrote, as sole author, *The Skipper in Arctic Seas* and *Ceylon and Borneo*. He also became a top-class landscape photographer and had some of his photographs hung on the walls of the exclusive *London Salon of Photography*. It may well be his artistic skills that contribute to our enjoyment of *Three in Norway*.

We still do not know, however, who actually drew the pictures. Both Lees and Clutterbuck illustrated their books, but it is difficult to distinguish their style in *Three in Norway* as the engraver has left *his* mark on them. All three authors practised drawing, and it may well be that the engraver, G. H. Ford, made use of some of the sketches of all of them.

J. A. Lees is often attributed the title of principle

author. His widow told H. L. Larssen that the other two merely contributed notes and sketches. Certainly, the style of the book has a lot in common with Lees' *Peaks and Pines*. Even so, *The Skipper in Arctic Seas* also conveys much of the same tone, and since Lees and Clutterbuck agreed to share the honours for the book, it is reasonable to assume that W. J. Clutterbuck's contribution was important. The book also makes it clear that all three kept a diary. The rather indefinite expression "by two of them" may therefore well have been more than just a humorous riddle. Each of them produced their own observations, comments and antics. It is impossible to know who was behind each contribution.

CONNECTIONS

The three adventurers were pioneers – they were, for example, the first to use Canadian canoes in Norway. But many people had been here before them. They were able to read up on the country in books such as *Norway and its Glaciers* (1853) and *How to see Norway* (1871). Then, in 1875, Cooks, the travel agents, started offering tours to Norway, taking English tourists to the Sognefjord. From there, some went east. So, by 1880, the sight of Englishmen in the Jotunheimen mountains was a common occurrence, whether climbers, hunters, or anglers. The network of contacts was already well established.

One of the first travellers who really knew the Norwegian countryside well, was the Englishman

John *Blackwell*. He joined the legendary hunter and sharp-shooter Jo Gjende, Theodore Rathbone (Rathbone's hut is still standing at Gjende) and a Swiss mountain guide to spend the whole summer and autumn of 1855 in Jo Gjende's hut at Gjendeosen. When he finally left the mountains towards Christmas, he stayed on at the coaching station at Svee, in Vågå. Later, he married Mari Svee, bought a farmstead called "Klones" and settled down there. It is hardly a coincidence, therefore, that *Ola*, assistant to the three Britons, was Mari's cousin, Ola Ivason *Viste* (1844–1917). "A big, handsome man, and rather too much of a gentleman, we fear," was their reaction on meeting him the first time – a fear they were to find well founded, as they time and again found him too lazy for their tastes. Ola, in turn, seems to have found the English gentlemen very energetic – calling Clutterbuck "Klatterbakkjen" (*the hill climber*).

The Blackwell circle probably also established contact with *Petter Tronhus* at Bessetra, and with his son, *Jens*. Jens was a reindeer hunter they often praised and after the tour, they even left their tent and caps to him. Blackwell died in 1866, only 33 years of age. His private doctor, however, W. D. *Crotch*, subsequently married his widow, Mari. Another person who may have put them in touch with helpers, is *Lord Bamford*, who owned an estate near Cambridge. He also owned Bessetra until 1874 and leased the fishing rights at the lake of Russvann.

Petter Tronhus (born 1816) used to go hunting with Blackwell and became a legendary figure that many would look to for information on the locality. Theodor Caspari described him as a Peer Gynt who got "Bessleiken" to resound "in the old backroom at 'Bessun' [...] with Ola or Per on the floor doing a wild spring dance while the townsfolk and village folk lined the walls in awe".

His son, Jens, who was born in 1846, had taken part in many climbing expeditions. One of these, in 1878, took him from Memurubu to Surtningssue and then down across Surtningssubreen and over to Russvann. This was the precise area where he subsequently led "Esau" and "the Skipper" on hunting expeditions. He later became the local guide for Crown Prince Gustav, who went on several hunting trips to Jotunheimen.

John Blackwell's brother, the general, also went to the Jotunheimen mountains. He built a stone hut at Russvann (you can still see the ruins) and bought the lake. But the seller changed his mind and cancelled the sale. Blackwell did not want to own "a freshwater lake that had been made salty with the tears of the remorseful seller".

Since this time, Russvann has only ever been leased, even though our friends believed that "Mr. Thomas" owned it. They had heard a lot about the lake, were keen to get permission to fish, and knew all about the Blackwell hut where "the Skipper" had stayed two years previously during a reindeer hunt with Jens.

Mr. Thomas was Thomas *Fearnley* (1841–1927), later to be appointed *hoffjegermester* (literally: the court's chief huntsman). He was the son of the

15

famous artist, an enthusiast of the outdoor life, a hunter and a prominent member of society. Characteristically, he not only sponsored, but actually took on the practical shipowner responsibilities for Nansen's ship, "Fram". Both he and his son leased hunting and fishing rights on their beloved "Russboden" estate for the rest of their lives.

A strange and rather intriguing person appears in the book under the name of Coutts. He can readily be identified, however, because we are told that he was the third person ever to climb Store Skagastølstinden. This was *Johannes Heftye* (1850--1907). (The first was the Englishman William C. Slingsby.) Heftye made several other spectacular climbs and is regarded as the first Norwegian to practise mountain climbing purely as a sport. His route to the top of Store Skagastølstinden, which the authors of the book refer to with great admiration, has been named after him -- "*Heftye's Route*". Johannes Heftye was born of one of Norway's most well-known men in the last half of the 19th century, *Thomas Heftye* (1822--86) -- a businessman, benefactor and highly important member of society. Thomas Heftye was also the founder of the Norwegian Tourist Association and donated the forest around Tryvann -- today acclaimed as the jewel of the capital -- to the city of Oslo. (His house is now the residence of the British ambassador.) Johannes, however, seems to have been pretty much the solitary eccentric described in the book.

One man who has really become a legend -- who appears, as it were, as the very embodiment of the region where our three friends spent most of their time – was Jo Tjøstelsson, called Jo *Gjende* (1794–1884). They did not meet him, but he was in fact the hunter that they said placed a windmill on a mountain top to scare the reindeer down to more manageable areas. This windmill, with the inscription "J. T. 1844" marked on it, was carried away to an unrecorded destination in 1902, but was rediscovered in 1974. Jo Gjende built stone huts at both ends of Gjende Lake and spent most of his time hunting in the mountains. He shot around 500 reindeer, almost exclusively large bucks, and was considered an unparalleled marksman. He also became a great friend of several very highly placed Norwegians, and of the two Englishmen mentioned above (John Blackwell and Theodore Rathbone). It seems to have been largely due to him that they chose to spend a whole year around Gjende in 1855.

Another person who can be identified is "The Professor" who stayed in a hut beside Lake Gjende. This was professor Julius *Nicolaysen* (1831 – 1909), a pioneer in surgical medicine. He, too, was a well-known personality in Norwegian society at the time, and was often called "The Emperor" by his students. He was to use the Leirungsbu hut, bought in 1880, for many, many years. Leirungsbu still exists today as a privately owned hut.

Passing Christiania on their way home, our three British friends wished to see "the Viking's ship recently unearthed somewhere on the fjord". This was the Gokstad ship, which had been excavated that very year – the much-applauded achievement of the antiquarian *Nicolay Nicolaysen* (1817–1911), a half-brother of the professor they met at Gjende. It is not known whether the "Professor" who showed them around was Nicolaysen, or whether it was the actual university professor at that time, Oluf Rygh (1833–99).

A few words remain to be said about the place names in the book. As we have chosen to reproduce the original edition unchanged, the spelling of these names might make it a little difficult for the reader to locate them on a modern map. We shall therefore point out the most important differences. *Vaage* is today Vågå; *Gjendeboden* = Gjendebu; *Tykningshø* = Surtningssue; *Hinaakjern* = Hinnotetjønn. As for *Besse Sæter,* it is unlikely to be found on modern maps. But the *seter* (which is today a privately-owned group of huts) was very close to what is now called *Bessheim.* The latter, however, is a tourist resort which evolved from a neighbouring *seter,* situated further north on the other side of the road.

Such a tourist resort is not an altogether modern phenomenon; as we learn in this book, the one at Gjendesheim existed already. But the Besse Sæter of *Three in Norway* was something different: Although they did not stay in the *seter* itself, they lived in the atmosphere of Petter Tronhus' personality, as alluded to above, and more or less as his personal guests. So the difference in names may well be taken as symptomatic of different times.

ACKNOWLEDGEMENTS
In my research for this preface I was provided with valuable, kind and patient help from people who know the area and the local conditions around Vågå and Jotunheimen. I should particularly like to thank Mathias Øvsteng, Kåre Lund, Tor Ekre, Ove Collett and Tore D. Christiansen. Other excellent source material was found in A. Engen *et al*: *Sjodalen frå fangst til fritid (Sjodalen – From Hunting Society to Leisure Life.)* (Vågå 2000) and Ben Johnsen: *Jotunheimens stortopper (The Peaks of the Jotunheimen Range)* (Oslo 1991).

My thanks also go to *Ferd* who took the initiative to publish a new edition of the book and thus provided the incentive for a new translation and for the work that went into this preface.

INTRODUCTION.

'CANADIAN canoes are the only boats that will do' was our conclusion after a thorough inspection of every existing species of boat, and long consultation with 'Sambo' of Eton about a totally new variety, invented but fortunately *not* patented by one of our number.[1]

Our party consisted of three men, who shall be briefly described here. First 'the Skipper,' so called from his varied experience by land and sea in all parts of the world, but especially in Norway, whither we were now intending to go in search of trout, reindeer, and the picturesque. The Skipper is lank and thin, looking as though he had outgrown his strength in boyhood, and never summoned up pluck enough to recover it again. His high cheekbones and troubled expression give one the idea of a man who cannot convince himself that life is a success, which is perhaps pretty nearly the view he actually takes of existence.

Secondly, 'Esau,' who received this name in consequence of the many points in which his character

---

1   Our canoes were built by Herald of Rice Lake, Canada, and supplied by Rowland Ward, the well-known taxidermist.

and history resemble that of the patriarch who first rejoiced in it: for our Esau, like his prototype, is 'a cunning hunter and man of the fjeld;' and we are sure that if he ever had such a thing as a birthright, he would willingly have sold it for a mess of pottage. Esau is short and joyous, and is one of those people who never indigest anything, but always look and always are in perfect health and spirits. It is annoying to see a man eat things that his fellow-creatures cannot without suffering for it afterwards, but Esau invariably does this at dinner, and comes down to breakfast next morning with a provoking colour on his cheek and a hearty appetite. His office in this expedition was that of Paymaster; not because he possessed any qualifications for the post, but because the Skipper had conclusively proved that such employment was too gross and mundane for *his* ethereal soul, by constantly leaving the purse which contained our united worldly wealth on any spot where he chanced to rest himself, when he and Esau went to spy out the land two years before this.

Lastly, 'John,' so called for no better reason than the fact that he had been christened Charles: he had never yet visited the wilds of Scandinavia. John is an Irishman, whose motto in life is 'dum vivimus vivamus:' he is tall and straight, with a colossal light moustache. He generally wears his hat slightly tilted forward over his forehead when engaged in conversation; and the set of his clothes and whole deportment convey an idea that he is longing to tell you the most amusing story in the world in confidence.

He is no gossip, and the anecdotes of his country-men, of which he has an inexhaustible supply always ready, are merely imparted to his listeners from philanthropic motives, and because he longs for others to share in the enjoyment which he gleans from their mental dissection.

The general idea of the campaign was that the Skipper and Esau should leave England in the early part of July; fish their way up a string of lakes into the Jotunfjeld, getting there in time for the commencement of the reindeer season; establish a camp somewhere; and then that John, starting a month later, should join, and the three of us sojourn in that land until we were tired thereof. How we accomplished this meritorious design we have tried to relate in the following pages.

GEOGRAPHY.

The map of Norway, apart from Sweden, presents an outline something like a tadpole with a crooked irregular tail. The Jotunfjeld is an extensive range of the highest mountains which are to be found in Northern Europe: before 1820 A.D. they were totally unexplored, and at the present time they are still perfectly wild and desolate, their summits covered with eternal ice and snow, and even their valleys uninhabited. That part of the Jotunfjeld which we intended to make our goal and headquarters is situated about the middle of the tadpole's body, and nearly equidistant from Throndhjem and Christiania.

LANGUAGES.

It is customary when writing a book on any foreign country to scatter broadcast in your descriptions words and phrases in the language of that country, in order to show that you really have been there. We propose to depart from this usage in the course of this work but if at any time the exigencies of narrative seem to demand the use of the foreign tongue, we have little doubt that the English language will provide an equivalent, which shall be inserted for the benefit of the uninitiated.

MATHEMATICS.

Foreigners have a curious prejudice which leads them to adopt different systems of coinage and measurement from those in favour in England. But shall a Briton pander to this prejudice by making any use of their ridiculous figures. Decidedly not. What matters it to us that a Norwegian land-mile contains seven of our miles, and a sea-mile four? we speak only of the British mile. What care we that the Norwegian krone is worth about 13 $1/2$ d.? Shall that prevent us from always calling it a shilling? Never! And shall the fact that it is divided into 10-öre pieces (which are little nickel coins worth about five farthings each) restrain us from alluding to them as the 'threepenny bits' which they so much resemble? Not while life remains.

EXTRA SUBJECTS.

Some of the statements that will be found in these pages may strike the reader as being, to say the least of it, improbable. We therefore wish to explain that all the incidents of sport and travel are simple facts, but that here and there is introduced some slight fiction which is too obviously exaggerated to require any comment.

THREE IN NORWAY.

CHAPTER I

THE VOYAGE.

July 8. – At ten P.M. on the platform of the Hull station might have been seen the disconsolate form of Esau, who had arrived there a few minutes before. To him entered suddenly an express train, with that haste which seems to be inseparable from the movements of express trains, adorned as to the roof of one of its carriages by a Canadian canoe. From that carriage emerged the lanky body of the Skipper, and general joy ensued.

Then in the hotel the Skipper related his perilous adventures; how he had crossed London in a four-wheeler with the canoe on the quarter-deck, and himself surrounded by rods, guns, rugs, tents, and ground-sheets in the hold, amid the shouts of 'boat ahoy!' from the volatile populace, and jeers from all the cabs that they met (there are many cabs in London); how the station-master at King's Cross – may his shadow never be less! – had personally superintended the packing of the canoe on a low carriage which he put on to the train specially; and how the G. W. charged four times as much as the G. N. He had seen John the day before, and on being asked to 'wander about, and get some things with him,' the Skipper had replied that it was quite impossible, as his time was occupied for the whole day: but when John said, 'I wanted your advice chiefly about flies, and a new rod that I am thinking of buying,' he replied, 'Sir, I have nothing of the slightest importance to do; my time is yours; name the moment and place of meeting, and I will be there.' Then they twain had spent a happy day; for decidedly the next best thing to using your own rod is buying one for another man – at his expense.

Poor Esau had no charming experiences to relate; he was a little depressed because an intelligent tyke at Doncaster had looked into the horse-box in which his canoe was travelling, hoping no doubt to see some high-mettled racer, and had asked if 'yon thing were some new make o' a coffin.'

July 9. – We walked about Hull and made a few last purchases. In the course of our wanderings we chanced to come to a shop in the window of which many strawberries, large and luscious, were exposed for sale. We immediately entered that shop without exchanging a word, and the Skipper said to the proprietress, 'This gentleman wants to buy a quantity of strawberries for a school feast;' while Esau remarked, as he fastened on to the nearest and largest basket, 'My friend has been ordered to eat strawberries by his doctor.' After this a scene ensued over which it were best to draw a veil.

At six o'clock we were safely aboard the good ship 'Angelo,' and saw our baggage stowed. It consisted of three huge boxes of provisions, weighing more than 100 lbs. each, two portmanteaus, two smaller bags, a tent, a large waggon-sheet intended to form another tent, a bundle of rugs and blankets, a large can containing all cooking utensils, four gun-cases, seven rods, a bundle of axes, a spade and other necessary tools, and the canoes with small wheels for road transport. Those wheels were the only things in the whole outfit that turned out to be not absolutely necessary. We did use them, but only once, and might have managed without them.

When the aforesaid was all on board, there did not appear to be much room for anything else in the steamship 'Angelo,' registering 1300 tons; yet this vast pile was destined to travel many miles over a desperately rough country in the two little canoes.

We were warped out of dock about eight o'clock, and steamed down the Humber with a west wind and a smooth sea. It was showery up to the moment of our departure, but as Hull faded from our sight it became fine, and with the shores of England we seemed to leave the cloud and rain behind.

July 10. – The day passed as days at sea do when the weather is all that can be wished, and the treacherous ocean calmly sleeps. The passengers were as sociable as any collection of English people ever are, and we spent the time very pleasantly chatting, smoking, eating enormously, and playing the ordinary sea games of quoits and horse-billiards.

The Skipper was much exercised in spirit because Esau had told him that he believed a certain passenger to be an acquaintance of a former voyage, named, let us say, Jones, and that he was a capital fellow. So the Skipper went and fraternised with

Jones, and presently, trusting to the 'information received,' remarked, 'I believe your name is Jones?' and was a little annoyed when Jones replied, 'No, it's not Jones; it's Blueit, and I never heard the name of Jones as a surname before.' Then the Skipper arose and remonstrated with his perfidious friend, who with great good temper said, to make it all right, 'You see that man by the funnel? That is a Yankee going to see the midnight sun; go and talk to him.' Now the Skipper has been in America a good deal, and likes to talk to the natives of those regions, so he sailed over to the funnel and tackled the Yankee. Presently, with that admirable tact which is his most enviable characteristic, he observed, 'I understand that you have come all the way from America to see the midnight sun: it is a very extraordinary phenomenon. Imagine a glorious wealth of colour glowing over an eternal sunlit sea, and endowing with a fairy glamour a scene which Sappho might have burned to sing; where night is not, nor sleep, but Odin's eye looks calmly down, nor ever sinks in rest.' As he paused for breath the Yankee saw his opportunity and said, 'No, I was never in America in my life. I am a Lincolnshire man, and am going over to Arendahl to buy timber. I have seen the midnight sun some dozen times, and I call it an infernal nuisance.' Here the Skipper hastily left, and came over and abused Esau until he made an enemy of him for life.

CHAPTER II

CHRISTIANIA.

Sunday, July 11. – We reached Christiansand about six, and set sail again at eight. There was what the mariners called a nice breeze with us. Esau declared it to be a storm, and was prostrate at lunch, owing as he said to attending church service, which was conducted under considerable difficulties, members of the congregation occasionally shooting out of the saloon like Zazel out of her cannon, or assuming recumbent postures when the rubric said 'Here all standing up.' However, we came along at a great pace, and arrived at Christiania about nine at night, after a first-rate passage.

The Fjord was not looking as beautiful as usual, as there had been a great deal of rain, and the storm-clouds and mist were still hovering about the low hills, so that no glories of the northern sunset were visible.

We arranged that the Skipper should go straight to the Victoria Hotel for rooms, as we heard that the town was very full, and Esau was to follow with the luggage. Now there was a young Englishman on board, very talkative, extremely sociable, remarkably kind-hearted, and overflowing with the best advice. He had gone round the whole ship entreating everyone to go to the 'Grand,' as he intended to do, because it was by far the best hotel.

Just as the Skipper had engaged our rooms at the 'Victoria,' in rushed this guileless child of Nature, panting from the speed at which he had come from the quay, and the Skipper had the gratification of witnessing his discomfiture and listening to his apologies for having lied unto us, which of course he had done in order to get rooms for his own party at the 'Victoria.'

We say nothing against the 'Grand,' because we know it not, but any one who has once tried the 'Victoria' will go there again: the man who is not at home and happy there must be a very young traveller.

This hotel possesses a spacious courtyard, surrounded by galleries from which bedrooms and passages open, very much like that historical hostelry in the Borough at which Mr. Pickwick first encountered Sam Weller.

These galleries, and indeed most portions of the hotel, are made of wood, and the building is not of recent date, for now no houses in Christiania are allowed to be constructed of timber only.

In the centre of the court is a fountain which keeps up a gentle plashing, very pleasant to listen to on a day when the thermometer is at 90° in the shade, as it generally is about this time of year in Christiania. All round the fountain are small tables and chairs, ready for the little groups who will assemble at them after dinner for the cup of coffee and glass of cognac which form an indispensable part of a Norwegian dinner. The dinner itself is, during the summer months, always served in a large oblong tent in the same courtyard at 2.30, and a very pleasant meal it is, if you are not too much wedded to English habits to be able to secure an appetite at that hour. At short intervals down the table large blocks of ice are placed, which perform excellent service in helping to keep the tent cool.

Then there is another delightful resort, the smokingroom, which is upstairs on an extension of the gallery overlooking the courtyard. It also is covered by a sort of tent, in the roof of which divers strange and gruesome birds and beasts disport themselves, or seem to do so: we have reason to believe that they are stuffed, as we notice that the flying capercailzie never seems to 'get any forrader;' the fox stealing with cautious tread upon the timid hare unaccountably delays his final spring, but perhaps he is right not to hurry, for the hare does not appear to be taking any measures for her safety, but sits calmly nibbling the deeply dyed moss which it were vain to inform her is not good to eat. But there are other birds which we *know* are stuffed, for we helped to stuff them, and these are the sparrows, which come gaily flying in at the open side of the smoking balcony; hopping on the chairs and tables, peeking at the crumbs on your plate, and behaving generally in that peculiarly insolent manner which can only be acquired, even by a sparrow, after years of study, and the most complete familiarity with the subject. These birds are a source of endless delight to Esau, who certainly gives them more than can be good for them; they eat twice as much as the capercailzies, though the latter are considerably larger. And if the sparrows are not enough entertainment, there are tanks of gold-fish and trees of unknown species in pots; but neither of these perform very interesting feats.

In this room it is the custom of the ordinary traveller to have his breakfast and supper. Breakfast is very much like a good English one, except the coffee, which is not at all like English coffee, being perfectly delicious; but the supper is a meal peculiar to Norway, and is generally constructed more or less on the following principles:–

Caviare, with a fresh lemon cut up on it.

Norwegian sardines, garnished with parsley and bay leaves.

Cray-fish boiled in salt water.

Prawns of appalling magnitude.

Bologna sausage in slices.

Chickens.

Slices of beef, tongue, and corned beef.

Reindeer tongue.

Brod Lax (spelling not guaranteed), meaning raw salmon smoked and cut in thin slices.

Baked potatoes.

Good butter, and rolls which no man can resist, so fresh are they, and light, and crisp.

Drink: 'salon öl,' which is the best Norwegian beer.

This supper does not come in in courses, but the whole of it is placed on the table at once; not spread out all over the surface of the board as at home, but

Norwegian Arrangement of Dishes at Table.

arranged in small oval dishes all round the con-
sumer, and radiating within easy reach from his
plate, making his watch-chain the centre of a semi-
circle, and thus entirely dispensing with that creak-
ing-booted fidget the waiter. Such an arrangement
cannot fail to coax the most delicate appetite. There
is no coarse *pièce de résistance*; no vast joint to disgust
you; but, like the bee, you flit from dish to dish,
toying, now with a prawn, now with a merry-
thought, till you suddenly discover that you are
unconsciously replete, and you rise from the table
feeling that it was a good supper, and that existence
is not such a struggle after all.

Altogether the 'Victoria' is a most charming inn,
either to the wave-worn mariner wearied by the
cruel buffetings of the North Sea, or to the weat-
her-beaten sportsman returning straight from the
bleak snowfields of the interior of Norway. We

never stayed there for more than two days, but for that time it is an uninterrupted dream of delight.

July 12. – We had a very hard day, buying all sorts of things to make our stores complete: jam, butter, whisky, soap, and matches, Tauchnitz books, and several other necessaries. The butter is most important, as the best variety that can be got up country is extremely nasty; the worst is unutterably vile, though it is quite possible to acquire almost a liking for the peculiarities of the better kind after starvation has stared you in the face. We were much put out at not being able to get a small keg of whisky, as we fear that the bottles will fare badly in the rough travelling we shall have.

Accounts of Christiania may be found in many excellent guide-books, with which this simple story cannot hope to compete, so we will not attempt to describe the town, since, though our knowledge of all the grocers' shops is voluminous and exhaustive, we are totally ignorant of the interior arrangements of either the churches or police stations.

The Skipper was very anxious to get some violet ink, because he is firmly convinced that it is the only sort fit for a gentleman to use. 'A man,' he said, 'is known by his ink;' so we went into many shops and asked for that concoction, always in the English tongue. Then we arrived at a shop where they did not speak our language; and here suddenly, to the intense surprise of Esau, the Skipper broke forth into a long harangue in Norse, concluding with an extremely neat peroration. The shopkeeper listened with respectful admiration, and then said, 'No, this is a stationer's shop, we do not keep it.' Then Esau gave way to irreverent laughter, and the shopkeeper concluded that we were attempting a practical joke, and we had to fly. The Skipper was not angry, but very much hurt. It afterwards transpired that he had got up the whole of that magnificent burst of eloquence out of 'Bennett's Phrase Book,' and then it had failed for want of two or three right words; truly very hard.

We took our canoes to the railway station, and despatched them to Lillehammer this afternoon; they had been a source of great interest to all beholders since our arrival, especially to the Norwegians, who have all a sort of natural affinity with any kind of boat, and seemed very much pleased with the combined lightness and strength of their build. As far as we can learn, they are the first of the kind that have yet been brought to this country.

At the station they were surrounded by a crowd of inquiring Norsemen, all of them wondering much what the name of 'Nettie' on the bows of the Skipper's craft could mean, and spelling it over very slowly and carefully aloud. When we came away, one of them, evidently a linguist, had just translated it into his own language, and was proceeding to conjugate it as an irregular verb.

CHAPTER III

BY RAIL AND LAKE.

July 13. – We were engaged till late at night putting the finishing touches to our packing. The last thing we did was to put our most gorgeous apparel, and any articles not likely to be needed during our camp life, into two portmanteaus, with strict orders to the Boots to keep the same until our return. This morning, after an early breakfast, on descending to the courtyard we found these portmanteaus roped down on the roof of the omnibus which was to take all the luggage to the station *en route* for Lillehammer. This we rectified, and then set off to walk to the station ourselves.

Now Esau is possessed by an insensate craving for anchovy paste, which he considers a necessity for camping; he said, 'It imparts a certain tone to the stomach, and aids digestion;' and added that 'no well-appointed dinner-table should ever be without it,' which sounds a little like an advertisement, but which he asserted was a quotation from the rules laid down for his diet by Dr. Andrew Clark. In Christiania these rules are not strictly adhered to either by Esau or the inhabitants of the place, for anchovy paste is not to be obtained there: this we know, because we went into every shop in the town, and asked for it without success. And in this supreme moment, when we were walking to the station with only a few minutes before the train should start, he insisted on diving into a wretched pokey little shop, which had escaped our notice yesterday, and demanding 'anchovy paste' in a loud English voice. The Skipper devoutly thanked Providence it could not be bought, as he declared the smell of it alone was enough to put a man off his breakfast, and that he had such a morbid longing for hair grease, that he could not have prevented himself from putting it on his head.

We got our baggage safely booked, and ourselves also, after a scene of riot that was nothing like a football match, but something like Donnybrook Fair, and at last found ourselves in a compartment with five other passengers, all of whom had a most inconsiderate amount of luggage with them in the carriage, while we contented ourselves with four guns, seven fishing-rods, two axes, one spade, four hundred and fifty cartridges, two fishing-bags, and a pair of glasses. We calculated that we saved at least one and fourpence by taking these things with us; and although our fellow-passengers were rather profane at first they soon settled down, and we had time to digest the fact that we were one and fourpence to the good. It was very warm in there; outside the thermometer was 92° in the shade; but we survived it, and after that no mere heat has any terrors for us.

Two of our fellow-passengers were an Englishman and his wife, who had a maid travelling with them through to Throndhjem; and when getting the tickets the booking clerk informed them that there were no second-class through tickets issued, 'but,' he added, 'this will do as well,' and handed them one first and one third through ticket, which we thought an extremely ingenious way out of the difficulty.

A railway journey is not interesting anywhere, and less so in Norway than other countries, as there is not even the sensation of speed to divert your mind, and keep you excited in momentary expectation of a smash. Uphill the pace is slow because it cannot be fast; downhill it is slow for fear of the train running away.

There are only two trains a day, one very early, one rather late, but timed to arrive at its destination before dark, for there is no travelling by night. Directly darkness comes on the train is stopped, and the passengers turned out into an hotel, where they remain to rest till dawn. From Christiania to Eidsvold is about a three-hour journey, and during that time the guard came to look at our tickets 425 times. He wanted to incite us to commit a breach of the peace, or to catch us offending against some of his bye-laws, and was always appearing at a new place; first at one door, then the other, anon peeping at us through the hole for the lamp, and again blinking from the next carriage through the ice-water vessel. But we were aware of his intention, and did nothing to annoy him, and always showed the same tickets till they were worn out, and then we produced strawberry-jam labels, which seemed to be quite satisfactory.

We reached Eidsvold at twelve, and went aboard the steamer 'Skiblädner,' where we found the canoes already nicely placed, lashed on the paddle-boxes.

We had a delightful voyage up the Mjösen, on the most beautiful of Norwegian summer days, in the best of Norwegian steamers. The Mjösen is the largest Norwegian lake, about fifty-five miles long, and the guide-books say it is 1440 feet deep, but we had not time to measure it, as we were busy admiring the scenery on the saloon table most of the way. This steaming up the Mjösen is a very pleasant way of spending a fine day: the shores are nowhere strikingly beautiful, but always pretty and charming; the steamer goes fast, so that there is a sensation of getting on and not losing time. There are intervals of mild excitement whenever we come to a village, and take up or disembark passengers; generally speaking they come out in boats, but occasionally we come to a larger and more important place where there is a pier, or even a railway, and at these the excitement is greater and the crowd quite worthy of the name. The folks all take off their hats directly we get within sight, and continue to do so till they fade away or sink below the horizon; and we in the steamer all do the same. But the great attraction is undoubtedly dinner, which is uncommonly well served in the saloon, every luxury that can be obtained being placed before us, concluding with wild strawberries and cream of the frothiest and most captivating appearance.

Both on this boat and her sister the 'Kong Oscar' they take great pride in doing things well, very

41

much as the old mail-coaches which occupied a parallel position in England used to do. The 'Kong Oscar' is rather the faster boat, but we consider the captain of the 'Skiblädner' to be lengths ahead of his rival, being a first-rate old fellow; on the other hand, the 'Skiblädner' handmaidens are not comely, whereas they of the 'Kong Oscar' are renowned for their beauty, not only in Norway, but in certain stately homes of England that we wot of. Esau lost his heart to one of them two years ago, and still raves about her, though the only way in which he endeavoured to win her affection was by sitting on a paddle-box with his slouch hat tilted over his eyes, gazing at her with mute admiration from a respectful distance, while she, alas! was totally unconscious of his passion. He never told his love, because he could not speak Norse.

We arrived at Lillehammer about eight o'clock, and went to the Victoria Hotel, from the flat roof of which, after an excellent dinner, we enjoyed a pipe and one of the prettiest views, in a quiet homely style of prettiness, that any one could wish to see; just at our feet the wooden village, with its many-coloured houses and their red roofs; then some green slopes, and 100 feet below the vast extent of the Mjösen lying calm and still and looking very green and deep, with the landing-stage and deserted steamers apparently quite close below us. On the opposite side of the lake highish hills covered with fir-trees, and to the right the river Laagen with its green waters hurrying down from the mountains in a broad and rapid stream as far as the eye could reach. Just across the road in front of the hotel there is a nice little stream which turns a saw, and rejoices in a cool splashing waterfall, the soothing sound of which refreshes us by day and night. The same torrent can be seen higher up the mountain in a place where it makes some rather fine falls, which only look like a long white rag fluttering amongst the trees at this distance. This was the view we had at midnight, when it was, apparently, no darker than immediately after sunset, and a good deal lighter than it generally is in London at midday; the while the sky was covered with the rich glow of colouring which can only be seen in the Northern summer.

There were two Englishmen with us on the roof, with whom, aided by coffee, we roamed over the greater part of the civilised and uncivilised world – Australia, Canada, Japan, Turkey, and Ceylon, and we all agreed that none of them can 'go one better' than a summer night in Norway.

CHAPTER IV.

BY ROAD.

July 14. – We arose pretty early, wishing to get over thirty-eight miles of ground before evening, which with the canoes would be a long day's work; as we had the natives to contend with, who by reason of their dreadfully lazy habits are most difficult to 'bring to the scratch.'

We have decided, after long experience, that nothing that you can do has any effect in hurrying them; but that it is quite possible to make them slower by losing your temper, or taking any vigorous measures of acceleration. They seem to get more deliberate and aggravatingly slow as they grow older.

Norwegian boys are distractingly restless and full of energy, and look as if they have had nothing to eat, which is generally the actual fact, judging by an English standard of what constitutes food. At the age of fifteen they become better fed, and their energy departs altogether, and after entirely disappearing it keeps getting less every year. A full-grown man does not seem to need much food, certainly not as much as an Englishman, and prefers that of the worst kind, conveyed to the mouth at the end of a knifeblade. We have never noticed any des-

44

cription of food which he does not make sour, rather than eat it when sweet. Bread, milk, cream, and cheese, jam and cabbages, for instance, are articles which he prefers fermented or sour. He reminds one of the Cockney who complained that the country eggs had no flavour, or of the Scotchman who, replying to the apologies of a friend in whose house he happened to get a bad egg, said, 'Ma dear freend, ah *prefair*'em rotten.'

But his laziness and love of nasty food are almost the only bad qualities that we have discovered in him. He is ridiculously honest,[1] and his kindness and hospitality are beyond praise. This morning, however, the laziness was the quality chiefly conspicuous, and though we ordered our conveyances last night and got up early (for us), we did not succeed in starting till twelve o'clock.

We first despatched the canoes and baggage packed on a kind of low waggon, and then got into a double cariole (which is something like a gig) ourselves, and drove gaily off along the Throndhjem road. We did not, however, follow it far, but turning to the left down a steep hill, we crossed the Laagen by a long and rather handsome bridge, and then up a winding road on the further side, all looking very pretty on such a glorious day. The road became more picturesque the further we got from Lillehammer, every turn bringing us to some fresh combination of mountain, pine-trees, rock, and

1 Save, perhaps, on three points — fishing tackle, strong drinks, and straps or pieces of cord; which may be committed to memory as 'a fly, a flask, and a fastener.'

waterfall – especially rock. There are so many tracts of country in Norway entirely composed of rock, that, as Esau remarked, 'probably no one will ever find a use for it all.'

We lunched at a nice little station called 'Neisteen;' a delicious meal off trout, strawberries and cream, and fladbrod, for which they charged us a shilling each.

'Fladbrod' is the staple food of the country folk in Norway; they make it of barley-meal, rye-meal, or pea-meal, but the best and commonest is that composed of barley-meal. It is simply meal and water baked on a large, flat, circular iron, and is about the thickness of cardboard, of a brownish colour, and very crisp. The taste for it is easily acquired in the absence of other food, and with butter it becomes quite delicious – to a *very* hungry man.

At Neisteen there was a little shop where the Skipper at last obtained his violet ink, but Esau was foiled in his dastardly attempt at retaliation with anchovy paste.

After this our road lay along a lovely river for fishing, and we were much tempted to stop and try a cast in it, especially as we saw natives luring fish from their rocky haunts by the time-honoured Norwegian method. They first settle how far they want to cast – say thirty feet. Then cut down a thirtyfoot pine-tree; take the bark off it; tie a string to the thin end, and a hook to the string; stick a worm on the hook, and go forth to the strife. When the fish bites, they strike with great rapidity and violence, and *something* is bound to go; generally it is the fish, which leaves its native element at a speed which must astonish it; describes half of a sixty-foot circle at the same rate, and lands either in a tree or on a rock with sufficient force to break itself.

But we had no time to spare, especially as for this stage we had a bad, shying, jibbing horse, and a perfect fool of a driver..

Near the last station we passed three English people on the road, who our driver informed us lived near there. He told us their name was Wunkle, but the man at the next station said it was Punkum, and we could not decide which of these two common English names it was most likely to be.

Kvisberg, the last station on this road, was reached at 9 P.M., but before this the road, which had gradually got worse all the way from Lille-hammer, had faded away and disappeared: and as the road got worse, so did the hired conveyances; so that we were gradually reduced from the gorgeous double cariole with red cushions with which we started, and a horse that could hardly be held in, to a springless, jolting stolkjær (country cart), and a pony that required much persuasion to induce him to boil up a trot.

Kvisberg is situated, with peculiar disregard for appropriateness of position, on the side of an almost unclimbable hill, about a quarter of a mile from the place where the road departs into the Hereafter. No English horse would take a cart up such a hill, but Norwegian ponies are like the Duke's army, and 'will go anywhere and do anything,' only you must give them plenty of time. We mounted to the station, a wretched little place, and being hungry ordered coffee and eggs, for which repast we paid two-pence-halfpenny each, and then at ten o'clock got a man to carry our few small things the last six miles to Dalbakken, where we intended to sleep the night. The walk was delightful, through a precipitous thickly wooded gorge, at the bottom of which the river which we had followed all day went leaping and foaming along, though it was now reduced to a mere mountain torrent.

About a mile from our journey's end we were overtaken by a Norwegian student on a walking tour, who spoke a little English and walked with us the rest of the way, as he too was bound for Dalbakken.

We reached it at midnight, and were not much gratified to find that it was a very small poor building, and that our luggage had not arrived. We had been hoping against hope that it might have done so, as we had not seen it anywhere on the road. The next pleasant discovery was that four other travellers had arrived before us and taken all the rooms. This fact was first conveyed to our minds by seeing four pairs of socks hanging out of the upstair windows to dry; at which sight we began to suspect that things were going to turn out unpleasant for us; but at last we got a room with one very small bed between us. We tossed for this bed, and the Skipper won; so Esau passed the night on the floor, on a sheepskin, and was very comfortable – at least he said so next morning. The natives here were much impressed by

Midnight Study of Stockings at Dalbakken

all our habits and belongings, but especially by our sleeping with the window open; wherefore the old woman of the Sæter[1] below kept bouncing into the room at intervals during the night to see us perform that heroic feat; and though it was flattering to be made so much of, still fame has its drawbacks.

The general appearance of the place caused us to expect nightly visitations from other foes, not human, but to our surprise there were none.

---

1 A Sæter is a mountain farm, to which all the cattle are driven during the summer, so that the Lowland pastures can be mown for hay.

Dalbakken is only three-quarters of a mile from a lake called Espedals Vand, where we propose to commence our cruise. It is beautifully situated on a small flat bit of ground halfway up the north side of the gorge: the hills on the south side not far away are so steep that they could not be climbed by all the branded alpenstocks that Switzerland ever produced. Looking to the east the gorge is very wild and grand, covered with pine-trees and steep crags, and no dwelling in sight; while to the west, in which direction Espedals Vand lies, it is more level and open, and slopes gradually downwards again, Dalbakken itself being the highest point in the track.

CHAPTER V

THE FIRST CAMP.

July 15. – We slept well, and at eight o'clock the Skipper, always first to wake, got up, and looking out of the window saw thence the four bad men who had taken the rooms before us and hung their socks out of the window, just starting on their journey, and looking as if they did so with an easy conscience.

Some men can carry with a light heart and gay demeanour a weight of crime that would wreck the happiness of less hardened rufflans.

Then he turned his gaze in the opposite direction, and oh, joy! our luggage and boats were in sight, and arrived directly afterwards. The man in charge said he had travelled all night with them without sleeping, and, to judge from his appearance, we imagined that his statement was correct. He had been sitting on the Skipper's bag for thirty-eight miles, and from the state of its interior we calculated his weight to be about twenty-two stone. He was very ill-tempered after his mere trifle of a journey and vigil, and asked for more money on hearing that he had three-quarters of a mile further to go. This was very sad, and we thought showed an unchristian spirit; but we sternly urged him forward, and all ended happily on our arrival at Espedals, when we paid him his money and a shilling extra.

It only took us a quarter of an hour to get to the lake, and after unpacking there and dismissing the men we put the canoes into the water, and then put water into the canoes until they sank; while we sat on the shore watching the trout rising all over the rippled surface of the lake, occasionally eyeing our sunken canoes in an impatient, longing sort of way, but never attempting to start on our great voyage.

These tactics to an inexperienced 'voyageur' might look like the acts of an ordinary lunatic; but it should be explained that the long exposure to the sun which the canoes had undergone had caused them to leak badly, and they required soaking to swell up the joints, before they could be intrusted with our valuable property and persons. Besides this we were hungry, and thought it a good opportuni-

The Start on Espedals Lake.

ty for lunch, and had to make some previously arranged alterations in the baggage with a view to lightening it. As long as the land journey lasted, strength was the chief object to aim at, but now lightness was of more importance. About one o'clock, when we had got all our things aboard and were just starting, a strong head-wind arose. This was always our luck. We decided to make only a short voyage. The waves were fairly big, but the canoes weathered them bravely, though they were very low in the water, and we had to keep the pumps going (*i.e.*, mop them out with our sponges) during the whole voyage.

We landed not more than a mile and a half from the end of the lake, and found a very nice campingground about ten yards from the shore on the south bank, with what the poets call 'a babbling brook' close to it; pitched the tent, and had a simple dinner of bacon, eggs, and jam, the last dinner during our trip at which trout did not find a place. Then we sallied forth in the canoes to fish. Esau was the last to leave the shore, and as he paddled off he noticed the Skipper's rod in the familiar Norwegian shape of a bow, and found him struggling with two on at the same time, both of which he landed, and found to be over 1 lb. each. 'First blood claimed and allowed,' to quote the terse language of the prize ring. Not a bad beginning, but we only got a few more about the same weight. They came very short, but were remarkably game fish when hooked, and in first-rate condition. We turned in about eleven, when it began to rain a little, and slept with

Our Camp on Espedals.

our heads under the blankets, the mosquitoes being in countless multitudes.

July 16. – It was a lovely morning, and the lake looked its best, but it is not strikingly beautiful compared with many that we have seen. It has high rugged hills on both sides, and pine woods down to the water's edge, and some small islands dotted about the upper end of it; but the lake is rather shallow, the pine trees rather stunted, and there are a good many wooden huts and sæters on the hill-sides, which, although they appear to be mostly uninhabited, detract from the wildness of the scenery.

The natives have one or two boats on the lake, and do some fishing on their own account. To-day we saw a man engaged in the atrocious employment of fishing with an 'otter.'

The Skipper's first Cast.

Any natives who see our camp when rowing past come to shore to inspect us and our belongings. They all adopt the same course of procedure. They land, and stare, and say nothing; then they pull up their boat and make it safe, and advancing close to the tent stare, and say nothing either to each other or us. Then Esau says confidentially, as if it was a new and brilliant idea (he has done exactly the same thing some scores of times), 'We'd better be civil to these fellows; perhaps they could bring us some eggs, and they look pretty friendly.' The natives are all the time staring and saying nothing. Then Esau remarks in Norwegian, 'It is fine weather to-day; have you any eggs?' To this the chief native replies at great length in his, own barbarous jargon, and Esau not having understood a single syllable answers, 'Ja! ja! (yes), but have you any eggs?' Then aside to the Skipper, 'Wonder what the deuce the fool was talking about?' Soon the natives perceive that their words are wasted, and relapse into the silent staring condition again, and after a time and a half, or two times, they depart as they came. Sometimes they return again with eggs in a basket, when we pay them well and give them some fish; at other times they look upon us as dangerous lunatics, and avoid us like the plague.

Esau learnt this habit of asking for eggs when we were on a fishing expedition near the south coast of Norway. On one occasion there we arrived at a small village, with an enormous quantity of trout that we had caught in the adjoining fjord; and found a small crowd of about fourteen or fifteen seafaring men, idly lounging round an open space between the cottages. He first went round and presented each of those men with two trout solemnly, without a word, as though it were a religious ceremony. Then he began at the first man again and said, 'Have you eggs?' and receiving a reply in the negative, he went on to the next, and to each one of the group asking the same weird question.

The men, who had been chatting busily amongst themselves up to the moment of our arrival, became silent; they did not laugh, but only looked at one another; and one of them shyly felt in his pocket to see if there were any eggs there whose existence he might have chanced to forget.

Presently, as we could get no eggs, we moved off sorrowfully but not discouraged; and the men remained looking after us silent and uncertain. Thus the interview ended and we regained our boat.

The beach here was capital for bathing, and we enjoyed a delightful tub this morning, the more pleasant indeed because at Dalbakken we slept in our clothes, and only had a soap-dish to wash in next morning. Immediately after bathing we lit a fire, and the cook commenced operations; the office of cook being held alternately by each of us for one day. The man from Dalbakken brought us some milk, so we indulged in coffee. When we have only 'tin milk' we drink tea; for though tin milk will do fairly with tea, we think it wretched with coffee. After breakfast we each took our canoe, and went fishing wherever the spirit moved us, taking lunch with us. On a day of this sort, if the fish are rising, we have a great time, and if they won't rise we lie on the bank in the sun and smoke, or sketch, or kill mosquitoes, and have a great time in that case also, so that the hours pass in a blissful round of enjoyment, and all is peace. Having each one his own ship we are quite independent, only taking care to return to camp about six o'clock to get dinner ready. After that there is nearly always a rise, and we fish till about eleven, when we generally turn in, though it is by no means dark by that time; and on a few occasions, when the fish were rising very well, we have fished on all through the night and into the next day, losing count of the almanack, and conducting life on the principles of going to bed when tired, and eating when hungry, so that, like the Snark, we might be said to

'Frequently breakfast at five o'clock tea,
And dine on the following day.'

There was very little wind to-day, and these fish being very shy, and apt to come short, it was almost impossible to get them without a ripple until evening, when large white moths began to show on the water, and the trout became bolder; consequently we did not make great bags, though the fish caught were very good ones.

At night there was one of the most lovely sunsets ever seen. The sun went down right at the other end of the lake, so that we had an uninterrupted view, with all the glorious colours of the sky reflected in the water; and we agreed that the effects about half past ten this evening formed as good a symphony in purple and orange as a man could expect to find out of the Grosvenor Gallery.

July 17. – The morning began with a dead calm, but this soon gave place to such a wind down the lake that we were induced to strike the camp, pack the canoes, and proceed on our voyage into the unknown.

We started soon after eleven, lunched near Megrunden,[1] and saw there two black-throated divers on the lake, which Esau pursued for some time, but of course never got near them. Some of the dives they made to avoid his advancing canoe seemed to be about half a mile in length. Just below

1 The various places mentioned on the voyage are not villages, as one might imagine from the dot that marks them on the Ordnance map, but generally only a single one-roomed log hut, and for the most part not inhabited or habitable.

Black-throated Diver.

Böle we caught several fish, but kept paddling on with our favourable wind, casting every now and then in likely places, and soon came to a rapid with a rough bridge thrown across its upper end. The rapid was very shallow, so that we did not dare to attempt to run it with loaded boats, and had to make a portage. Even then we got a few bumps in running it, but arrived at the bottom all right. Now the scene changed; we were in a smaller and narrower part of the valley; buildings had entirely disappeared; there was nothing to be seen but gloomy pine forests and black-looking mountains; the weather also was quickly changing, and evidently intending to be wet and stormy; so we pushed on rapidly, one coasting on each side of the lake till we reached its further extremity, where Esau was nearly swamped crossing the waves, as the wind began to blow harder every minute. Soon the rain was upon us, while we looked for a campingground but found none, as the shores were everywhere very swampy for a quarter of a mile inland. At length we came to a second rapid, where the natives have thrown a clumsy weir across for some unknown purpose, and here we found a fairly dry spot, made our portage in heavy rain and wind, with a great deal of groaning, misery, and brandy and water; pitched the tent, and after struggling for about half an hour, got a dyspeptic fire to fizzle, and so cooked some fish and eggs, and then had tea in the tent. After this we were a little more comfortable, as it was very nice and dry inside; but it was midnight before we had finished all our portage, got the canoes down into the next lake, and made everything snug for the night, so that we were quite exhausted, as our day had commenced at seven A.M. The mosquitoes were more numerous here than at any place we have yet seen.

Sunday, July 18. – It rained all night, but, as Tweedledum said of his umbrella, 'not under here,' and a ditch we made last night kept our floor quite dry. Lighting a fire for breakfast was a toilsome business, but at last we found some wood dry enough to burn. It continued raining in a nice keep-at-it-all-day-if-you-like kind of manner, so we resided in the tent and read, and indulged in whisky and water for lunch to counteract any ill effects of the reading – for some of it was poetry.

Our tent was about three-quarters of a mile from the end of Bred Sjö, and after lunch we both went in one canoe to reconnoitre the next rapid, which is a long one down to Olstappen Vand. We found that it is quite impracticable for canoes; the river simply running violently down a steep place till it perishes in the lake; about a mile of rapid with hardly enough decently behaved water in the whole of it to hold a dozen trout. But there *were* a dozen, for we caught them, one wherever there was a little turnhole. How we were to get down that river was concealed in the unfathomable depths of the mysterious Future.

CHAPTER VI

MISERY.

July 19. – It rained all night again and all day. This was dreadful, and not at all like Norway.

We have always made a rule that we may fish on Sunday, but not shoot. Some people draw an even finer distinction, and say it is allowable to shoot with a rifle, but not with a gun; this we have always thought too subtle. Now yesterday was Sunday, and Esau having observed two divers on the lake while the Skipper was out fishing, went and secreted himself with a gun where he expected them to come over, hoping that they would be alarmed by the other canoe on its return. This soon happened, and they flew within forty yards of him. Both barrels were discharged, and Esau returned to camp, muttering something about 'birds of that kind having immortal bodies if they hadn't immortal souls.' The result of Sabbath-breaking was no doubt this miserable weather.

The camp to-day presented a most cheerless prospect. The canoes were drawn up on land and turned bottom upwards; the kitchen stowed away under a soaked sack; a very third-rate camp fire smouldering before the tent, surrounded by old eggshells, backbones of fish, bacon-rind, and some apology for firewood; our two rods standing up against the gloomy sky with the wind whistling through their lines, and all the scenery blotted out with rain and mist, and scudding, never-ending clouds that drifted down the valley, and gave very occasional glimpses of extremely wet mountains. The cook, clad in a macintosh with a spade in his hand, watching a pot which was trying to boil on the spluttering fire, his trousers tucked into his

View of Bredsjö by Night.

socks, and his boots shining with wet, would have given any one a pretty good idea of the meaning of the expression 'played out.'

The mosquitoes were bad here, and we spent much of our leisure time making war against them. Esau's favourite way of 'clearing the road' was to bring in a smoking log of pitch pine, close up the ventilation, and fill the tent with smoke. It forced us to quit, but not the mosquitoes, as they appeared to fall into a deep and tranquil sleep, from which they awoke refreshed and ready to renew the attack just a few minutes before the tent again became habitable for human beings. Prowling round the tent and squashing them with our fingers was perhaps the best plan, but we were obliged to sleep with a rug over our heads and covered up at every point, to avoid their intrusion at night.

July 20. – Still rain, and nothing but rain it stopped for an hour or two last night, and the lake looked uncommonly pretty among its dark surroundings, but the downpour soon began again.

In our desperation yesterday afternoon we arranged with a native, whom the Skipper discovered, to bring a horse and sleigh to-day to meet us at the next rapid, and help us down with our baggage to Olstappen. Therefore we got up early and were down at the rapid about ten o'clock, where we found our man waiting. The rain at this period was the worst variety we have yet seen, and it has tried all kinds during the last four days. We packed everything on the sleigh, covered it with our groundsheets, and then put the wheels on our canoes, and followed down the track.

There is a saw-mill halfway down the river which is simply perfect. It is perched on piles over the middle of the stream, where it dashes through a rift in a huge black cliff, and the water goes tearing past down a long shoot made of logs, and plunges down at the end churned into a mass of white foam, with noise and spray that quite bewilder one.

We got down to Olstappen at last, not without a good deal of hard work, and paid our man 4s. 6d.

On our way we met a Norwegian tourist, who was on a walking tour with his sister, and had left her rained up, so to speak, in a Sæter, and was strolling about in the forest to wile away the time: he spoke a very little English, and we had a long talk with him; as he had a fellow-feeling for us, and was quite ready to curse the rain with us or any one else.

The Norwegians, men and women, seem to go a good deal on walking tours, and probably know infinitely more of their fatherland than does the average Briton of this island, the superiority of which he seldom fails to impress on the long-suffering foreigner.

At midday we launched our canoes on Olstappen, which is a fine wide lake, and not so rainy as Bredsjö, being several hundred feet lower. We paddled across to the mouth of the Vinstra River, a rather perilous undertaking, for where the wind met the river there was a nasty sea on, and we shipped some water, but got safe to land. We could not find a decent camp till we had walked a quarter of a mile from the lake up the river. There we found a nice sheltered place, pretty, and close to the river, made our portage, and pitched the tent, and with tea our drooping spirits began to revive (who is proof against a hot meal of trout and bacon, buttered eggs, and tea ?), even though our clothes and equipments were all wet through, and we had a damp change of raiment, sleeping rugs, and boots. But now the wind had changed, and we looked forward to the morrow as the wearied traveller always *does* look forward to the morrow.

There were many sandpipers at the mouth of this river; we caught one young one, and had serious thoughts of taking its innocent life for our tea, but better feelings prevailed, and we released it as an offering for fine weather, and caught four trout instead.

July 21. – Hurrah! the rain stopped during the night, and this morning actually the sun shone out now and then. We heaped up a huge fire and dried all our belongings, and then had nearly a whole day before us free for fishing.

A voyaging day is a big business. We calculate that it takes us two and a half hours to pack up from an old camp, breakfast, and get aboard ship; but to pitch the camp in a new place takes much longer. First you have to find a suitable place, often a matter of great difficulty in a country like this, where level spaces a yard square are very rare; dig a trench; pitch the tent, and arrange everything in it; collect firewood, and make a place for the fire; see that the boats and everything about the tent are safe from harm should the stormy winds begin to blow; and then cook dinner. All this cannot be done under three hours of hard work; so that if in addition you propose getting over a considerable amount of ground, it is sure to be a long and toilsome day. But the following day you wake up with a glorious feeling of duty performed and pleasure to look forward to.

The Skipper, with a hankering after cleanliness, washed a lot of clothes, and himself, having left the rain to perform the latter operation for the last two or three days; but Esau, not being troubled with any such absurd remnants of civilisation, went up the river reconnoitring in his natural condition. He came back to dinner in a perfectly rapturous state, having caught a remarkably nice bag of fish, got a beautiful view of the Jotunfjeld Mountains, and found a waterfall, which he said was the best in Norway, and therefore in the world. The Skipper had tried the lake in the afternoon without success, so after dinner we both went out and soon discovered the reason. Seven boats full of natives were out with a huge flue net, which they shot in a circle, and then beat the water enclosed till all the wretched fish were in the net. We saw them get thirty in one haul, and besides this there was a boat 'ottering;' and although we captured a few fish, it was obvious that with all this netting it would be impossible for the lake to be good.

CHAPTER VII.

HAPPINESS.

July 22. – This was a really fine day, such as we consider proper to Norway; no uncertain half-and-halfness, but a day when an untiring sun shone down from an immaculate sky; and everything looked lovely. Our tent was on a nice bit of turf close to the Vinstra River, which is about as broad as the Thames at Eton, but with probably twice the volume of water, and certainly three times its rapidity; it rushed past our door at such a pace that no boat could stem it; and as far as we could see up the reach it came down in an equally swift torrent, so that all day and all night there was a swilling, rushing sound very pleasant to hear, and creating a sensation of coolness in warm weather. Esau considered it just the *beau idéal* of a trout stream, for any fish hooked in it gave a lot of trouble before he was safe in the bag. It ran into the lake about a quarter of a mile from our tent, forming a good-sized delta at its mouth. At the further side of the delta there was some fishermen's huts (from which emanated the seven boatloads of natives whom we saw yesterday netting), and thence a track leads up the banks of the river to a lake called Slangen, two miles away.

The inhabitants of these huts came in a boat this

morning to see our camp while we were at break-fast inside the tent. They poked their heads in, grinning and staring, and saying nothing. Then we did the honours, showed them our most interesting possessions – American axes, fly books, knives, rods, &c., with all of which they were greatly impressed; then one picked up a bar of yellow soap that was lying on a box, and they all 'wondered much at that;' then we talked to them for a brief space, chiefly out of 'Bennett's Phrase Book', and considered the interview at an end, but they *would* not go, and remained silently staring at all our movements. So at last we ignored their presence altogether, which we have found the most effectual way of getting rid of a Norwegian peasant, and they gradually departed one by one till only one was left. To this man we gave a cup of our now cold coffee, which was not at all good, especially when compared with the delicious coffee which is always forthcoming even in the meanest Norwegian hut. He drank this, for they consider it a breach of etiquette to refuse proffered food; and immediately left, as if he remembered an engagement, having first thanked us in a rather constrained manner.

We were glad when our callers were gone, for we had found them 'difficult,' as the French say; but we took advantage of their arrival to make arrangements with one of them to bring three ponies and sleighs to the other side of the delta to-morrow morning, when we hope to renew our journey.

After this we both went up the river on opposite sides; for the Skipper had become inflamed by a wish to see the waterfall which Esau discovered yesterday.

One of the great advantages of Norway consists in being able to leave your tent and all other belongings quite to themselves, even when you know that there are several people about, and shrewdly suspect that the place where you have made your camp is a hay meadow belonging to one of them. We had a dim idea that such was the case here, not because there was any grass, but because there were very few stones, and a Norwegian mows down everything for hay except the stones. The Skipper came back with a very pretty bag of fish; he had been up to the fall, and thought it quite deserved all Esau's commendation; and his opinion is worth more because he has seen many of the great American falls and other stock sights of the world. It is not marked on the Ordnance map; there is no path to it, or near it, but, you come on it suddenly by following the river up through the pine forest, and on turning a corner see the whole body of the Vinstra shooting over a cliff in one mad leap of perhaps a little more than a hundred feet. Of course the height and volume of water are insignificant compared with many falls, but the beauty of its situation can scarcely be excelled; and to us its greatest charm is its solitude and freedom from paths, tourists, and all the other unpleasant attributes of show places.

Esau following up the north bank of the river was not so successful fishing, and after crossing the Slangen River (which joins the Vinstra about a mile above our camp) he struck across the forest to see his beloved fall again, and try to sketch it. He came back in a bad temper, saying that he thought Ruysdael and Turner could make something of it – the former to do the water, and the latter the spray, mist, rainbows, and roar – and he wanted to write home and get them to come out on purpose; and when the Skipper suggested that they had given up painting, he said it was a great pity, for he had not time now to do it himself.

There is a corduroy bridge over the Slangen River close to its junction with the Vinstra, and over this bridge we shall go to-morrow: we had intended to cruise up the Slangen and fish Slangen Lake, but we found that it would be impossible to continue our journey from the further end of it if we did so, and therefore decided to omit that part of the programme, though we are sorry to leave out Slangen, as it is a beautiful lake.

We have probably been repaid for the miseries of the last week by the beauty of our waterfall, the volume of which has doubtless been much increased by the exceptional rain of the last few days.

Early to bed –

July 23. – And early to rise. We breakfasted soon after seven, and then packed everything, and crossed the mouth of the Vinstra in two Norse boats, assisted by two or three men who had come to help our horses and sleighs on the journey. We had terrible difficulty in getting the canoes placed in what we considered a safe position on the sleighs, but it was done at last, and the motley caravan started about 10.30.

First the noble owners; then a man who had got nothing on earth to do with the affair, then two women laughing and yelling like lunatics, then a sleigh drawn by a large pony, and carrying two boxes, can, guns, and canoe; next some boys urging the large pony to herculean exertions; then the organiser of the transport department, who was apparently a professional fool, by the inordinate laughter which his every action caused; then some more women, and a smaller pony and sleigh, with the other canoe and all the rest of the luggage excepting one bag; lastly, another man leading an extremely small pony and sleigh with absolutely nothing on it, the man carrying the remaining bag for fear of tiring the pony. This mob of loafers had arrived in boats from Svatsum, which is a small village five miles distant at the north end of Olstappen. But they only accompanied us for a quarter of a mile, when they all departed except the three men, who remained to manage the ponies.

The pace was not very great, about a mile an hour, for these little ponies insisted on stopping to rest every hundred yards when the path was good, and every twenty when it was bad.

We followed the river till we crossed the Slangen bridge; after that the path began to rise and get rapidly worse. We strolled along very leisurely, sitting down from time to time to rest and admire the view. The scenery was occasionally very beautiful, with the Jotun Mountains gleaming white in the background; and the forest itself was an endless delight, with its hoary moss-covered pine-trees, and many-coloured carpet of berry-bearing plants, and the delicious odours with which a Norwegian forest in summer always abounds. In a fir-tree here Esau came upon a family of cole titmice, and another of creepers, all very busy swinging themselves about, and creeping up and down the tree in search of dinner. They appeared to take a certain amount of interest in his proceedings, but showed no fear, and after watching them a long time he put the point of his rod up to one of the titmice, which actually pecked it rather angrily, but seeing that it made no impression took no further notice, but returned to its occupation of collecting food. In the next tree was a little spotted woodpecker which they call a 'Gertrude bird.' The story is so prettily told in 'Forest Life in Norway and Sweden,' that it shall be inserted here.

'This woodpecker – or an ancestor of hers – was once a woman, and one day she was kneading bread in her trough, under the eaves of her house, when our Lord passed by leaning on St. Peter. She did not know it was our Lord and His apostle, for they looked like two poor men who were travelling past her cottage door. "Give us of your dough for the love of God," said the Lord. "We have come far across the fjeld, and have fasted long."

'Gertrude pinched off a small piece for them, but on rolling it in the trough to get it into shape, it grew, and grew, and filled up the trough completely. "No," said she, "that is more than you want;" so she pinched off a smaller piece and rolled it out as before, but the smaller piece filled up the trough just as the other had done, and Gertrude put it aside too, and pinched a smaller bit still. But the miracle was just the same, the smaller bit filled up the trough as full as the largest-sized kneading that she had ever put into it.

'Gertrude's heart was hardened still more; she put that aside too, resolving as soon as the strangers left her to divide all her dough into little bits and to roll it out into great loaves. "I cannot give you any to-day," said she. "Go on your journey; the Lord prosper you, but you must not stop at my house."

'Then the Lord Christ was angry, and her eyes were opened, and she saw whom she had forbidden to come into the house, and she fell down on her knees. But the Lord said, "I gave you plenty, but that hardened your heart, so plenty was not a blessing to you. I will try you now with the blessing of poverty; you shall from henceforth seek your food day by day, and always between the wood and the bark" (alluding to the custom of mixing the inner rind of the birch with their rye-meal in times of scarcity). "But forasmuch as I see your penitence is sincere, this shall not be for ever; as soon as your back is entirely clothed with mourning this shall cease, for by that time you will have learnt to use your gifts rightly."

'Gertrude flew from the presence of the Lord, for she was already a bird, but her feathers were even now blackened from her mourning, and from that time forward she and her descendants have all the year round sought their food between the wood and the bark; but the feathers of their back and wings get more mottled with black as they grow older, and when the white is quite covered the Lord takes them for His own again.

'No Norwegian will ever hurt a Gertrude bird, for she is always under the Lord's protection, though He is punishing her for the time.'

Whether this is the true reason or not, the fact remains that the bird is never harmed by any one, and is as tame as possible.

We continued climbing slowly up the hill till about one o'clock, when we came out above the forest on an open plateau covered with rocks, grass, and low scrub: this was the Fjeld. At Finböle Sæter we stopped to refresh on milk. The road – which had gradually dwindled from a decent path to a sleigh track, then a footpath, a cow-path, and a goat-path, just sufficient to swear by, or at – now lost itself altogether. The men had been complaining that it was a 'dole vei' (bad road) soon after the start, now they said it was 'schlamm' – a very expressive word; and Esau agreed with them, and said it was 'damm schlamm,' which does not sound like proper Norsk; but it was such heartrending work to see our beloved canoes bumping and jolting along, every moment in imminent danger of getting staved in, that to indulge in a few such Norwegian idioms was only human; and we decided to walk on and spare ourselves the agony of the sight; so, taking the bearings of 'Fly Sæter' – which was our destination for the evening – we rambled on across the fjeld – a splendid walk, with some of the most beautiful mountains in Norway all round us.

We got on very well with the assistance of an Ordnance map and compass, till we came to the river Hinögle, after passing Hinögelid Sæter. The bridge here was not in the place marked on the map, so that after crossing it we had some trouble in finding Fly Sæter, and might perhaps have perished miserably like the Babes in the Wood, had we not opportunely met a mediæval fisherman in a red night-cap, looking like one of the demons in 'Rip van Winkle,' who was going thither and conducted us. We arrived at seven o'clock, and appeased our hunger with the usual meal of trout and coffee, and such cream!

The sæter was a long low house, with three little rooms and only two windows. Its legitimate tenants were a very nice man and his equally nice wife and three children; but there were some occasional visitors here to-night in the shape of ourselves, our three men, the mediæval angler, and another traveller, twelve altogether to be apportioned among four beds; and to make matters worse, the rooms were continually invaded by sheep, pigs, and goats, of which there were a large stock.

The Norwegians are so uniformly kind to all animals, that their tameness is really troublesome; they insist on going where they like, and following one about begging for food like dogs, causing the Skipper to exclaim, –

'Ite domum saturæ, venit Hesperus, ite capellæ;' which he translated –

'Out of the house in the evening! Get out, ye goats of the sæter!'

Sunset at Fly Sæter.

We slept in the cheese-room very comfortably, one on the floor, the other on a good hay bed, and were warm for the first time for several nights, as we have not had sufficient blankets in the tent. Where the other ten people slept we did not inquire, but hoped they were happy. Our men and sleighs did not arrive till 10 P.M., at which time a most glorious sunset was going on, so that we could not attend to them at once. The sky, at first blue and yellow, gradually deepened into purple and orange, and finally the most brilliant red and almost black clouds, the hills all the time glowing with exquisite tints. After it was concluded we turned to the men, and were much delighted to find that nothing was smashed so far; the men had been very careful, and took eleven hours to perform a journey of ten miles.

CHAPTER VIII

FLY SÆTER.

July 24. – The morning was again beautifully fine, and the coffee at the sæter was passing delicious, even for this country, where coffee is always good. No doubt the chief reason of this is that it is never roasted and ground till just when it is wanted, not only at the hotels, but at the smallest sæters. The grinding of coffee and the frying of trout are grateful sounds to the wearied traveller, and if the walk across the fjeld has failed to give him an appetite, he has still the chance of obtaining one from the fragrant aroma of the roasting berry.

This sæter is in a most beautiful situation, perched on a little flat bit of ground on the mountain side, and looking down on a wide-stretching sea of grey undulating hills, with lakes lying among them dotted about near and far, and all the lower ground covered with the everlasting pine forest. To the south can be seen the river Hinögle, which runs out of the Heimdal Lakes, threading its way with gleams of white through the dark green and grey of the forest and fjeld. To the north far below in the valley is Aakre Vand, a beautiful irregularly shaped lake dotted with fir-clad islands; while beyond, high up, there can be just distinguished Aakre Sæter, and frowning over it the dark mass of Aakre Kampen, a mountain of considerable height. Aakre Vand is a lake that we had intended to fish after Slangen Vand, but as there seemed to be no possibility of getting our property from one to the other we gave up the notion. According to all accounts it is a good lake for fish, and its shores are untainted by the habitations of man.

We started about 9.30, having paid 5*s*. 6*d*. for the board and lodging of ourselves and our numerous retinue, including the price of a sack-full of hay for our beds, as this was the last place at which we expected we could get any.

After watching for a short time our valuables jolting, plunging, and splashing over the uneven ground, covered with rocks, junipers, and occasional logs and brooks, the wear and tear on our heartstrings became too severe, and we decided to walk on to Sikkildals Sæter, about four miles, and leave the baggage to its fate under its guidance of our three charioteers. It took us till eleven o'clock to get within half a mile of the sæter, and there we sat down and watched the track intently for two hours: then two hours more – and we began to lose patience; then another hour – and we began to lose hope also. Something must have happened; either a canoe was smashed, or washed away crossing a stream, or one of the sleighs was upset and broken, or they were bogged, or the man carrying the bag had fainted, or his pony become unmanageable and dashed through a shop window; or, most dreadful thought, the men had got at our whisky and become hopelessly drunk.

Another hour passed, and our small remaining stock of good temper went: we were very hungry, and all our food was on the sleighs, and the mosquitoes seemed to be even more hungry than we were. Hope deferred, with nothing but mosquitoes to distract one's thoughts, maketh the heart very sick indeed: and these were most annoyingly large mosquitoes; the finest brand that we have yet inspected, and with more strength of character than the ordinary kind. We were so much annoyed with the world in general, and each other, that we were obliged to separate, and Esau retired for a short time to attempt a sketch. He came back very angry, because just at the critical moment a mosquito had knocked his hat off, and he had had a desperate and perspiring conflict with it under a tropical sun; but eventually the brute was vanquished and its head cut off, which he said he would have stuffed, to hang up in his ancestral halls. He certainly bore on his face the marks of the struggle, so that there seemed to be no reason to doubt the story.

Desperate Conflict between Esau and the Mosquito.

Our state of despondency waxed worse and worse; we had not the slightest confidence in our head-driver; he was undoubtedly the Svatsum village fool, for he talked all day, and the other men went into roars of laughter at whatever he said, though the Skipper said he couldn't see anything funny in most of his remarks; but possibly the Skipper was jealous because this man made better Norsk jokes than his own. Besides this, the fact that neither of us understood the language detracted from the merits of the jests.

Years rolled away, and at six o'clock something came slowly into sight. 'Out with the glass!' (the spy-glass). 'Yes, by George! it is the men and sleighs at last. Out with the other glass!' and we finish the 'wee drappie' that we were saving to the last extremity. They soon arrived at Sikkildal Sæter with us, and we found that nothing had gone wrong, but the men had been *very* careful, and so had taken nine hours to make a journey of four miles. The track certainly would be a disgrace to a Metropolitan Vestry, and they managed well to arrive with everything uninjured. We consider the village fool to be a most painstaking and praiseworthy idiot.

At Sikkildal Sæter we got some food and called at a small house close to it, where a Mr. B., a Norwegian barrister, was staying for the summer. He is the owner of the Sikkildal Lakes, and we wanted permission to camp on his land and fish in his lakes. He understood English as well as all the upper classes in Norway do; and was very civil, giving us the permission most willingly.

On the Track near Sikkildals Lake.

We have heard from a good many people that the wealthier Norwegians do not like the English, and will not do anything to oblige them; but in all our wanderings we have met with nothing but the greatest kindness and hospitality from all classes. Several people have gone out of their way to voluntarily offer fishing and shooting, and in no instance has the slightest incivility been shown. Certainly Norway will compare with England very much to advantage in this respect, though of course we do not mean to say that similar conduct would be possible in England.

At about seven in the evening we got all our cargo shipped again and started up the lower Sikkildals Lake – having first paid our charioteers £3 for the trip from Olstappen, three men, horses and sleighs, sixteen miles over the rockiest, brookiest, and juniperiest country in this world; and offered them whisky and water all round, including two men from the sæter who came to our assistance when the smallest pony, not being accustomed to the deceitfulness and treacherous wiles of this life, got up to its neck in a bog close to the lake, and the man with the bag followed it. However, they were extricated with no damage done, as our provisions were all securely soldered up in tins. Curious to relate, our three men did not like whisky, but just sipped for 'manners,' and only the two old men from the sæter would drink it; but these two old men liked it very much, and drank all they could get – that is to say, their own glasses full, and the other fellows' glasses full, and just a drop after that, and then just a taste to top up with. Then we shook hands all round, and feeling in charity with all men, sailed joyously away up the lake.

It was a real Norwegian night, with the warmth and light of the departed sun still lingering on the mountain tops, and a midnight twilight glowing in the valleys. We had a beautiful full moon to help us on our way, so we went right to the upper end of the first lake, and found a camping-ground half-way between the two lakes, which are about a hundred yards apart. The portage took us some time, but we were full of energy from the cool night air, so refreshing after the long hot summer day. We dug out a nice level place for the tent, and got everything settled and ourselves in bed about midnight.

CHAPTER IX

SIKKILDAL.

Sunday, July 25. – We arose soon after seven; not because it is our nature to get up at that time, still less because we think it our duty to do so; but because the sun made the tent so intolerably hot that there was no pleasure to be derived from staying in bed any longer. Naturally after this we were very cross, which the Skipper says all really pious people are on Sunday morning; and he abused Esau shamefully, because the latter wanted the eggs buttered and the Skipper wanted them fried. Esau laid down the axiom that 'no gentleman ever eats fried eggs,' in a peculiarly offensive manner, and proceeded further to make ill-natured remarks with reference to violet ink; and the Skipper retorted with the observation, 'Wish you'd brought that anchovy paste.' Esau: 'Why?' Skipper: 'Because it's just the stuff to grease your boots with in a place like this; smells strongish, and keeps the mosquitoes at a distance.' Altogether we made ourselves as disagreeable as possible to each other – just as we do in our happy homes on the Sabbath morn in England. Fortunately Sunday only comes once a week.

Breakfast over, the Skipper devoted himself to the occupation of greasing his boots and shaving, which he seems to do at the same time, so that one brush may be used for both the soap and the grease; while Esau did some washing.

We had some trouble in getting good firewood, for Sikkildals Vand is more than three thousand feet above sea level, and consequently we were above the region of pine forests, and had only the stunted birch and juniper from which to obtain our supply. We divide the altitudes rather differently from the system adopted by other great explorers. The lowest belt is that of pine forests and strawberries, then comes the zone of stunted birches, above that only juniper and bitter willow are found; and the highest belt of vegetation contains only rocks, reindeer-flowers, and moss, and then eternal snow.

Now birch-trees do not make good firewood, for when they die they appear to get water-logged, and never burn well. The juniper is the most invaluable of all trees, for it will burn quite green; but at Sikkildals Vand it is very scarce, and so it took us quite a long time to collect enough dry wood to last our stay out, but it was done at last. We carried one canoe across the spit of land between the two lakes, and in it the Skipper went forth to get fish for the larder, while Esau took the other canoe down the lower lake to get some milk from Sikkildals Sæter.

The scenery here is very fine. The lakes are narrow, and highish mountains rise on each side: those on the south side had snow upon them, though this would disappear before the end of the summer, as we are not yet in the regions of perpetual snow; on the north side there is a very remarkable mountain called Sikkildals Horn, with a perfectly impracticable front of overhanging rock, very high and rugged. There was a constant rumbling and booming proceeding from it, as rocks from time to time broke off and came crashing down; but our tent – though seemingly under this cliff – was well out of their reach. At the further end of the upper lake we could see an apparently impassable mountain ridge. Beyond this, about four miles further according to the maps, was Besse Sæter, a farm, or ranch, only one day's journey from our final resting-place. How we were to cross that mountain with our canoes and baggage was a matter only to be determined by prophets and other beings of a higher order of intelligence than ours. Our friend Mr. B. thought it was almost impossible; the Skipper boldly asserted that it *was* impossible, and requested to be allowed to die here; while Esau, with the sanguine joyousness begotten of total ignorance, said of course it could be managed. We determined to move to the end of the lake the next day, and try the pass on the one following – barring earthquakes.

Esau had a most interesting voyage. His fishing was not very successful at first, and he paddled steadily on towards the Sæter, overtaking a boat quite full of girls, dressed in the very picturesque native costume which the people in these primitive regions still adhere to, especially on Sundays. The girls about here are rather pretty than otherwise, and these were a particularly good selection, and of course all in their cleanest and smartest clothes for Sunday. They *would* stop to watch him fishing, till

Sæter Girls in a Boat on Sikkildals Lake.

he got quite shy, and gave up throwing till they rowed on.

Soon he came to a brood of pochards under the leadership of the old duck, and spent half an hour trying to capture one by rapid paddling, in which endeavour he was nearly but not quite successful. There were a good many teal and pochards on the lower lake, and plenty of sandpipers on the shores of the upper one.

At last he reached the Sæter, and found there all the girls of the boat, and at least another boat-load and five or six strangers – quite a crowd: possibly they had been having a church service, but probably not, as they all seemed in the best of tempers, and were most amiable.

He got the milk, and coming back tried a few casts, and found that the fish were rising properly;

the result was nineteen good trout in about an hour
and a half. We had not been catching many fish
lately; so after his return to camp we concluded that
this was the hour and we were the men to revel in
a fiendish glut of capture. So there was a regular
stampede in that camp, and after dinner we *all* went
out armed to the teeth with rods and fly-books, and
clothed in landing nets and Freke bags, with our
teeth firmly set and a bloodthirsty look in our eyes,
intending to struggle with the great trout in his native element or perish in the attempt. ...

About ten o'clock that night there might have
been seen toiling wearily back to camp under a
cloudy sky and with a chilly blast a-blowing, two
forlorn youths, 'sans' fish, 'sans' hope, but still
armed to the teeth with the weapons of the chase.

However, we had now tried both lakes, and got
some knowledge of their capabilities. The upper
one is, we think, the better of the two, but more
difficult to catch fish in. The Skipper got some in it
to-day, and they were larger fish than those of the
lower lake, and a different sort, more like the silvery trout of the Jotunfjeld, whereas the others are the
ordinary brown or yellow trout.

This afternoon Mr. B. and his wife with a friend
came up in a boat to see our camp, at which they
seemed much pleased. We took them short cruises
in the canoes, showed them our various arrangements, and endeavoured to be agreeable.

The friend was the manager of the government
stud for this district, and spoke English fairly. He
told us that the government provides a certain num-

ber of good stallions, which are turned out on the fjeld and run with the peasants' mares, and that they take great trouble to provide the best that can be got, so as to improve the breed. He considered that there are very decidedly good results.

July 26. – A beautiful fishing morning, just beginning to blow up for rain. The Skipper fished his way down to the Sæter for more provisions, and had first-rate sport, catching twenty-two beautiful fish, mostly over a pound. He had such an exciting time of it that lunch was forgotten till three o'clock, a fact which spoke volumes for the excellence of the sport, for we generally acquire a very keen appetite every three or four hours so long as the sun is performing his daily duty (of standing still while we circulate feebly round ourselves). He came back to the tent, presenting rather a distended appearance, having stuffed most of his pockets full of potatoes, and a packet of salt in his hat; and while with his right hand he folded to his bosom a bottle of cream and another of milk, in his left he grasped a rod, a landing net, and paddle, and the rest of him was hung with fish. The Skipper objects to making two journeys where only one is necessary.

Esau thinks that 'flesh-meat' is a necessary of life, so he took his gun up the upper lake, and returned with the noble spoil of five sandpipers which he had shot out of the canoe by creeping along the edge of the lake, a most entertaining pastime.

There is an old ruined fisherman's hut at our end of the lake, and this bad apparently been taken as a habitation by a family of stoats, which Esau espied at their gambols on his return. Cartridges are precious here, but the instinct of destruction of a stoat was too much for him, and having chirped till two of them stood close together and a third just behind, he fired into the crowd and mortally injured the lot. Poor little things! It is rather a shame to kill them, for there is so little game that they cannot do much harm, probably feeding chiefly on mice and lemmings, which are very numerous; and they always look uncommonly pretty playing about the rocks. No more graceful animal exists than a stoat.

After dinner had been cooked and despatched we went forth to fish again, and had some good sport; but presently lowering clouds settled down over the surface of the deep, mosquitoes gathered round us in swarms, and a few spots of rain drove us home to the snug retreat of the tent, where, hidden away under the warmth of our bedding, we smoked in thoughtful silence, and gloated over the day's doings and our larder stocked with fishes.

July 27. – The day commenced with showers, and as there are no inhabitants here to whom we can give the surplus fish, we did not like to catch any more – for it is against our principles to waste food wilfully, woeful want being too near and probable a state to be trifled with – consequently we determined to move on, but first to bake some bread.

This, in a temporary camp, is done by putting the kneaded dough into a tin pot made on purpose without solder; this pot is then placed in a hole in the ground in which we have previously kept a good fire for about half an hour; before putting the pot in, all the embers and ashes are cleared out, and then raked back on to the top of the tin and all round it, and a small fire is kept going on the top. If well managed this bakes excellent bread in about twenty minutes, but of course it requires considerable experience and care to turn out really satisfactory bread. When we get to our permanent camp we shall make a proper oven.

To-day, when we had baked successfully, packed up our things, and were taking advantage of a break between the showers to start, we were hailed from the bank, and saw there old Peter Tronhúus, the tenant of Besse Sæter (whither we are going) and father of Jens Tronhúus, our former hunter, who is now getting what we require in the shape of food, ponies, and men, and whom we expect to meet at Besse Sæter. Peter had a great deal to tell us about all our affairs, which seem to be prospering under Jens' auspices. He talks English very badly, so the interview lasted some time, and then we pushed off and paddled straight away to the extreme end of the lake, where we found an inferior place to pitch the tent, very damp and unwholesome in appearance, sadly in need of sanitary inspection, but no doubt good enough for one night. We fished with fly and minnow all the way, but took nothing, there being a good deal of thunder round about; but Esau shot some more sandpipers.

Our tent is pitched at the commencement of an extremely vague track, which we believe to go over our mountain pass to Sjödals Vand (pronounced 'Shoodals'), and to-morrow we hope to follow its wanderings if two men and horses – with whom we have made an arrangement to transport us – turn up. These two men and horses are the sole inhabitants of this very thinly populated district, so that we are at their mercy, and if they do not come we must inevitably die of starvation after we have eaten all our provisions and candles.

Late in the evening Herr B. and a scientific friend who had just come to stay with him, came down the mountain to our tent. They had been for a short walking tour to Lake Gjendin – our future goal – where it seems that a tourist's hut of a superior sort has lately been built, and at this hut several kinds of food are kept, such as tinned meats and beer. B. and his friend have therefore been there shopping. The news of this hut is rather unpleasant to us, for Gjendin was chosen chiefly for its wildness and remoteness from civilisation, and now we are haunted with the idea that there may be tourists, and consequently no fish or reindeer. On the other hand, it has been erected so short a time that it can hardly have affected the country round about yet, and it will certainly be convenient for us from a commissariat point of view.

We were just beginning supper when they arrived, but they would not stop, for which we were secretly glad, as there was only enough soup for two; so we had a whisky 'skaal' (health-drinking) instead, and they went on their way full of beans and benevolence, as Mr. Jorrocks hath it.

We 'whisky' every one who turns up at camp, and as a rule they like it. We are not much of drunkards ourselves, so we can afford to give it to other people.

CHAPTER X

BESSE SÆTER.

July 28. – Our two men arrived while we were at breakfast this morning, and brought two sleighs in the boat with them; these they deposited on the shore, and then one of them departed into some secret haunt of his own in search of a horse. The last we saw of him was a wee dot struggling up over the mountain crest; and we began to feel what a hopeless sort of task was before us.

When we had finished our breakfast there were certain remnants of food, and these we offered to the other man, because he seemed to want something to do. We left him in the tent with a frying-pan containing two trout fried in butter, and a tin pot nearly full of soup. Some time afterwards we looked in, and saw him eating greedily off his knife-blade, and after a further interval we noticed that he had finished; then we examined the culinary utensils out of which he bad been feeding, and found he had left the trout untouched, but the butter they were fried in he had utterly consumed off the blade of his knife, and also all the soup through the same medium. But there was not more than a gallon and a half of the latter, so we did not grudge it.

Apparently he was like a giant refreshed after his meal, and seizing one canoe he carried it up to the top of the mountain, and then came back for the other and did the same with it; after this he returned again and borrowed our axe, saying he wanted to make the path better for the sleigh. He disappeared among the stunted birches, and we heard him chopping and slowly getting further up the track for about an hour. We naturally supposed that he was clearing away trees that obstructed the path,

Old Siva Carrying a Canoe up the Sikkildals Pass.

but when we came to traverse that path ourselves, soon afterwards, we discovered that he had only been filling up holes in the road by felling trees across it. Now a road that can be improved by this process is in a very bad state, and this one was decidedly improved.

Just before we started an English tourist came down the mountain and arranged with Siva (one of our men) to go down the lake in his boat. He was the first of our fellow-countrymen whom we have seen since Lillehammer, and proved to be the only one we met all through our trip in the mountains.

After some time we perceived three dots wending their way down the path again, and presently they arrived, proving to be our other man and two extremely shaggy ponies; and after the complicated Norwegian harness had been put on we began the ascent. The path was as bad as bad could be for a short distance, but when the level was reached it became much better than we had had hitherto; it was only the first climb up from the lake that presented any difficulty. The canoes could only have been transported as they were, on a man's back.

It continued showery, but we had a very pleasant walk, and launched our canoes on Sjödals Vand at about three o'clock. A short paddle across the lake not more than three-quarters of a mile, and we were at Besse Sæter.

Sjödals Vand is a long straggling lake, very much exposed to the wind, and not in any way beautiful except for its wildness, as its shores are almost treeless and rather flat. Its most remarkable characteristic is the colour of its water, which is a light greenish blue, like a starling's egg, and stands out in striking contrast against the yellow shore and dark mountain heights which surround it.

Besse Sæter is only three miles from Gjendin Vand – the haven where we would be; and the snow-capped mountains, which have been gradually getting nearer all the way from Olstappen, are now magnificently towering above us on three sides.

The Sæter is a hut, built, as they all are, entirely of wood, and only inhabited during the summer months. The hut in which we are living is not strictly speaking a sæter at all, but has been built for the convenience of travellers, and the Tronhúus family are intrusted with the duty of taking care of those who come hither while wandering about this, the wildest and grandest part of Norway. The real sæter is a larger building about a quarter of a mile from this hut, and higher up the mountain. And further away still there is yet another building, or collection of buildings, also called Besse Sæter.

Our hut has three rooms, two of which – a bedroom and eating-room – are occupied at present solely by us: in the other room dwell two girls, apparently guests of the Tronhúus. Peter Tronúus himself and his numerous family live in a one-roomed hut just opposite this. At present the family appears to consist of two men, five women, and two children, relationship to each other unknown.

Peter and his son Jens – who was with us on a former expedition – are both away at present; the latter engaged in procuring various articles for us, such as potatoes, men, ponies, and dogs, about which we wrote to him from England, and he is expected back to-morrow.

In spite of the crowd of people living here, everything is beautifully clean and tidy, and our eating-room looks very nice, with its floor always covered with fresh juniper sprays, and a cheerful fire burning in that most charming of fireplaces, the primitive Norwegian corner-hearth, which is being rapidly superseded everywhere by horrid tall, black, iron stoves, that look like coffins set up on end, and smell like flat-irons and rosin when they are lighted.

We shall have to make this place our home until Jens turns up; and we are not at all sorry to do so, for they take the greatest trouble to make us comfortable, and the trout, fladbrod, and coffee, are simply perfection. Besides, we are only a short day's journey from Memurudalen, where we intend to camp, and there is nothing to be gained by getting there before August 1, the opening day of the reindeer season.

Greenshank.

After supper we sallied out, the Skipper with rod, Esau with gun, to see what we could catch. Esau landed on the marsh at the head of the lake, to try and circumvent some duck he had descried; in this be failed, but shot a greenshank, of which there were several flying about.

The Skipper fished the river without success. Sjödals Vand is a fine lake, but not much good for fishing, because of the great amount of netting that is carried on in the summer by the dwellers in the Sæter; nevertheless there are good fish in it, as we have seen many of two and three pounds' weight, that they have caught in the nets.

July 29. – A friend of ours began the opening chapter of his virgin novel with the words 'It was a thoroughly cussèd morning towards the latter end of July.' The same applied exactly to this morning: but the arrival of Jens encouraged us; and Esau walked outside to look at the sky; where, thrusting his hands in his pockets and lodging an eye-glass in his eye, he focussed the heavens generally, with a cruel, inquisitive stare; and shaking his head knowingly, indulged in a prophecy concerning the weather – 'that the wind now being in the west, there would be continuous sunshine for three weeks at least.' Then he walked in again, and we all shivered over the fire.

Jens arrived at breakfast-time, and after greetings had been exchanged, reported all his achievements on our behalf. He had secured for us a stalker, one Öla; a hewer of wood and drawer of water, by name Ivar (his last office seems likely to be a sinecure, but we can work him double at the first-mentioned employment), a horse, and a sack of potatoes; all of which will arrive at Memurudalen in time for August 1. We hoped for a dog for Ryper, but he had not been able to get one.

Esau is always bemoaning the law which prohibits him bringing dogs from England; it is suspected that he has a large collection of useless animals there, that he wishes to import into Norway and sell to the guileless and unreflecting native. Unassisted by any of the canine tribe, however, we have now accumulated what we call 'a good larder of bird-meat;' for certain wild fowl were observed to-day to secrete themselves in the marsh at the head of the lake, whither we followed them with all our dread artillery, and we now have a lot of teal, greenshanks, sandpipers, and a ring dotterel stowed away and engaged in preparing themselves by decomposition for our consumption. Some of these birds are almost unknown to the table of the ordinary Briton; but if he will consider that our daily food depends entirely on what we shoot or catch, we hope, as the wri-

Ring Dotterel.

ters of hooks say, 'the kind reader will excuse' the sandpipers and dotterel.

We were wet through on the marsh, and not at all sorry to return to a comfortable fire in a warm room, instead of the streaming sides of a cold and cheerless tent. Shooting as we did above our knees in water, the rain did not make any appreciable difference in our great wetness. After the point of saturation is past, we have discovered that the human frame is as impervious to moisture (external) as a macintosh.

This summer so far has been remarkably wet and cold for Norway, but we have now the inexpressible consolation of knowing that they are in worse case at home; for we have received our first batch of letters and papers from England, which have been a fortnight *en route*.

July 30. – Prophets are without honour in these parts; they are also without truth, honesty, or any good quality or proper feeling. This day is worse than usual, and the good people here have been going about with blanched cheeks, whispering with bated breath of a great flood which occurred in the time of one Noah. We spent all the morning trying to teach the cows, goats, and poultry to walk two and two in case of any emergency arising, and the Skipper – who was engaged in building what he called a Nark – was repeatedly coming into the Sæter to ask how many yards there were in a cubit. However, at lunch-time the land was still visible, so we sallied forth into the marsh again, and secured some more teal; and then Esau went off in his canoe after some scaup ducks on the lake; and brought home two, after following them – according to his after-dinner account of the struggle – for about six hours, while they swam, and flew, and dived; and

Scaup.

he paddled, and swore, and shot. They appear to have roamed over the whole extent of this vast lake, seeking safety from his unerring barrels. And he now points to a little hill, far below the distant horizon, beneath which he affirms that he brought the last victim to bay and slew him. He was absent on the expedition an hour and a quarter; a canoe will go about five miles an hour; and the lake is seven miles long. But we did not come out here to do arithmetic.

We settled not to go to Gjendin ourselves to-day, as the weather was so very unfavourable, but we packed and despatched some of our luggage this evening, andpurpose following it to-morrow.

Before doing this we had a long interview with Jens Tronhúus, with the main object of settling all accounts. Now a long interview between three men who cannot speak two words of each other's languages is a somewhat intricate business, and would be decidedly amusing to beholders. How we got through it is beyond the wit of man, but nevertheless the fact remains that everything is beautifully arranged; we thoroughly understand each other; both sides are satisfied; and we concluded everything without the aid of that potent mediator, Whisky, the Great and Good.

Besse Sæter grows upon one: the people are all so simple and kind, and cook our food so well, that we shall be quite sorry to leave, even though trout and reindeer are in prospect.

CHAPTER XI

GJENDIN.

July 31. – The morning appeared rather fine, so we packed the rest of our baggage, and climbed the track which leads over the shoulder of the mountain between Sjödals Vand and Gjendin (pronounced 'Yendin'). It is rather steep, but nothing approaching the villainy of the tracks near Sikkildals Sæter, so the transit did not take long, and we got to Gjendesheim about twelve o'clock.

Gjendesheim is a very good two-storeyed wooden building, with a large dining-room, and about eight tiny cupboards of bedrooms; it has been erected just where the Sjoa River runs out at the eastern extremity of the lake, for the benefit of travellers, who can get food and lodging of a sort there, and generally boats to take them up the lake. Ragnild – the woman who presides over it – is very nice, kind, and attentive, and talks English well. Her latter qualification hardly gets fair play, as not many English people come here; and indeed the Norwegians who visit the lake are not very numerous. From the book we can only see two English names before us this year; and yet Gjendin is perhaps the most beautiful, certainly the wildest and grandest, lake in Norway, and is well worth a visit from any tourist who has time at his disposal.

It is eleven miles long; very deep; very blue; and on all sides rising sheer out of the water for from 1000 to 4000 feet are vast black mountains with snow-clad summits; for it lies in the very heart of the highest mountains in Norway. It may not unfairly be likened to an unfrequented and awfully desolate Lake of Lucerne.

Our First View of Gjendin Lake.

At 3200 feet altitude it is of course above the fir-trees, and only in a few sunny nooks along its sides can even stunted birches, juniper, and willow earn a precarious living. It is at these places alone that there is any exit from the lake; for along the greater part of its length there is no level place large enough to pitch a tent; no vegetation except berries and moss; and no possibility of scaling the frowning

cliffs by which it is surrounded. But there is a great
fascination in such a scene; and although its first
appearance is almost repellent, every moment of
gazing seems to increase its beauty and awe-inspi-
ring grandeur.

At lunch here a great event happened; we had
Salon öl (bottled beer), and immediately bought the
whole remaining stock, consisting of six bottles.
These we degraded by packing with the inferior
baggage in the canoes, and commenced the final
stage of our journey, or voyage – whichever is the
right term.

About two miles from Gjendesheim, on the
south shore, we came to a waterfall which runs out
of a small lake lying a short distance away up in the
valley. At the mouth of this fall was a small neat hut
in which a Christiania professor had just taken up
his abode for a few days' stalking; we stopped a few
minutes to talk to him, and then paddled on, trying
a few casts now and then until we came to
Memurudalen – our intended camp.

It is about half-way up the lake on the north
shore, and is a very pretty little valley, profusely
supplied with edible berries, surrounded by thick
birch covert, and with more grass than we ever
expected to find at this altitude; but it is by far the
most favourably situated bit of the Gjendin shores,
as it is sheltered from the cold winds and gets the
sun all day.

We found a remarkably nice level bit of grass,
screened by a rocky bank, and with what the Skipper
called 'a brattling brooklet' in front, about two hund-

red yards from the lake. There we pitched the tent and made everything comfortable, but of course we shall not decide whether to stay here or not until we have tested its capabilities as reindeer ground.

Beyond the purling streamlet, and about thirty yards from our front door, the Memurua River goes tearing down, the colour of dirty soap-suds from the mud which is ground into it by the mighty Memuru Glacier, whence it springs. This glacier is about three miles from us up the valley, but not in sight from our tent; in fact, the hills are so steep that we are quite shut in, and can see very little except the snow-fjelds and peaks just opposite to us across the lake. These peaks spring from the highest plateau in Norway, which has an altitude of about 6000 feet, and both the plateau and peaks are almost inaccessible to the hunter, as it is a day's work to climb them, and any one doing so would probably have to pass the night on the top. This is annoying, for it is a capital place for deer.

An ancient hunter, some years ago, spent a long time in conveying with incredible exertions to the top of the central peak, materials out of which he constructed a windmill; then he descended and never went near the place again, and his windmill scared all the deer away from that table-land, so that they frequented places where a man could get to them; and the cunning hunter was rewarded by many 'stor bocks' (big bucks). But now the windmill has been destroyed by time and weather, and we fear that the deer again roam there unmolested and unscared.

Sunday, August 1.–It is our custom to rise on this day singing, 'Come, rouse ye, then, my merry, merry men, for it is our opening day,' but on this occasion it would not have been appropriate. We were not at all merry, because it was Sunday, and raining; we were frozen in the night, our men and potatoes have not come, and altogether we could see nothing to be merry about, especially as, the opening day having fallen on a Sunday, we did not feel justified in going out to pursue.

So we devoted ourselves to the pleasures of the table. Last night we had dotterel and sandpipers for dinner, this morning greenshanks, which are very good birds indeed. There was also a large brew of a meritorious composition known as Skoggaggany soup; the name is a little difficult to pronounce, but the soup does not taste anything like it; it is merely the Norwegian for a scaup duck. In England people have been known to call scaups unfit for food, but here, under the perfectly awful appetites that we have developed, the Skoggaggany soup has very little chance.

After trying unsuccessfully to catch fish, we walked up the valley after lunch to look for a hut which is marked on the Ordnance map, and to see if there were any better camping-ground than the place we chose yesterday. We saw some beautiful reindeer ground, but could not find the hut or a camp.

On our return we perceived two men loafing about the tent, who we naturally concluded were thieves and murderers, and the Skipper hurried on to do battle with them to the death for the possession of our greatest treasure, the Salon öl. But on his arrival the robbers did not fly, but stood and stared with their hands in their pockets; so he lifted his hat and said, 'Öla?' (for of course he might have been a Dook in disguise); and one of them replied, 'Ja;' and cordiality being thus established, produced the sack of potatoes and the cook, like a conjuring trick, from somewhere behind him, out of his hat or coat tails.

Then we went into all kinds of details with him about his and Ivar's wages, which he did not understand, and he replied at great length in Norsk, which we did not understand, and so the interview concluded to the gratification of all concerned. Öla is a big good-looking man, rather too much of a gentleman, we fear: but Ivar is without doubt a perfect ass, and will never be able to do anything in the way of cookery, except perhaps boil a potato, and even in that enterprise we consider it would be six to four on the potato.

Two of our Retainers: Ivar and his Pony.

CHAPTER XII

THE CAMP.

August 2. – The Skipper won the toss (he always does, chiefly because the device on Norwegian coins is 'sorter indifferent like,' and when Esau has called heads or tails, he looks at it carefully, and gravely declares it to be the opposite), and was away eight hours wandering about the mountains without seeing a living creature except two buzzards, and hardly any 'spoor.' He returned to camp very tired and rather cross, to find a delicious meal nearly ready cooked by Esau, for the man whom we ironically call the cook has gone to fetch his horse, for which we are to pay 1*s*. 2*d*. a day as long as we have it. The cook's wages are to be 2*s*. 4*d*. a day, and those of the stalker 3*s*. 6*d*. We consider the latter cheap at that rate. He is a very tall man; very big, very heavy, and very bearded; and we hire the whole of him for the trifling sum above stated.

Besides cooking the dinner, Esau had been employed in rigging up the waggon-sheet as a continuation of the sleeping tent by planting an upright pole securely in the ground in front of the door, and connecting its top with the old tent by a birch tree ridgepole: it thus makes a very convenient place for all our large stores, and gives us much more room in the tent. We had expected the men to sleep in it, but they prefer living in a wretched little stone dog-kennel, which looks as if fleas would swarm in it, and has been built by drovers, or some other dirty people, for their lodging when they chance to come here: it is about 200 yards from our tent, and, as the men prefer it, it is very convenient for us.

The ground that the Skipper tried to-day seemed a first-rate reindeer fjeld; this means an uneven tract of mountain country, too high for vegetation, except occasional reindeer flowers and patches of gentian, but not high enough to be entirely covered with perpetual snow: this fjeld − where it is not snow − is made of rocks large and small, from the size of a haystack to that of road metal, some of them firm, but mostly loose, jagged, and sharp; the winter snow and frost leave them in this condition by continually splitting and re-splitting them: they are dark grey in colour, and at a distance look almost black.

What the reindeer can find attractive in such a place, possibly some one can tell; we cannot. There is apparently nothing for any beasts of the field to eat up there; but if you do happen to find deer before they see you, they are certain to be feeding, and Esau thinks they are eating the rocks; but the Skipper says it cannot be so, and inclines more to the theory that they feed on their 'young,' like tame rabbits, or possibly on their own blood, like the pelican of the wilderness. As for the reindeer flower, which is supposed to be their staff of life, it averages about half a stalk to the square acre, but possibly it is possessed of many highly nutritious qualities, and a little of it goes a long way. Anyhow they thrive on their food, whatever it may be; they are always very fat, and uncommonly good to eat when you chance to slay one.

After dinner we tried all this portion of the lake for fish without success, and coming back received the awful intelligence from Öla that there are no fish in any parts of Gjendin except the extreme ends, and the waterfall where Professor N. is living. This is a dreadful blow to us, for we always count upon fishing as our main employment, and fish as our staple food: and if we cannot get any here we shall have to leave. At present we have some which we brought with us from Sjödals, but when they are exhausted there will be a mutiny in this camp unless sport of some kind presents itself.

August 3. – A curious accident happened to-day; there was no rain. We have in vain tried to account for this phenomenon, and can only fall back on the somewhat unsatisfactory theory that it is all used up. Esau went after deer on the Rus Vand side, and came back very tired to dinner without having seen any, but reported fresh tracks; he was full of the glorious view that the fine day had given him. He had been close above the Memuru Glacier, which is a very large one, and stretching beyond it as far as the eye can reach is a sea of snow mountains, most of them peakshaped, but some domes or irregular precipices with immense glaciers lying between them, and here and there the greenish-blue waters of a lake distantly gleaming in the sunlight.

It is curious to note how the north and east sides of every peak are torn and ragged, with huge masses of rock riven from them by the action of the weather, while on the south and west they are comparatively regular.

The Skipper spent the day in camp, completing the erection of the outside tent. Our abode is now sumptuous in the extreme, as the new wing holds all the lumber which formerly blocked up our bedroom. There was some discussion as to whether we should call it the 'Criterion Annexe,' until we remembered that there are always policemen about that celebrated building, and this decided us not to do so.

August 4. – The Skipper went on to Bes Hö stalking. This is a high mountain 7400 feet above sea level. It is close to us, between Gjendin and Rus Vand, and is one of the dome-shaped species.

The Norwegians call their mountains either 'Tind,' which means a cone, or 'Hö,' a round top; 'Piggen,' a peak rather more jagged than a Tind; 'Horn,' apparently one steep side and one more gradual; and 'Kampen,' apparently a rough hill with nothing striking about its shape. Most of the mountains round here are Tinden, the finest being Memurutind, Skagastolstind, and Glitretind, the last over 8000 feet, only surpassed in height by Galdopiggen, which, though in sight of us, is beyond our reach.

From Bes Hö the Skipper got a good view between the storms of Gjendin lying encircled by its enormous steep black banks of snow-capped mountains, the whole of its eleven miles of length being visible at once. Its colour is a creamy greenish blue, caused by the snow-water which comes straight into the lake by scores of torrents, which collect it from the various glaciers. The Skipper, who is always bubbling over with poetic similes, said it looked like a cupful of very blue milk in a crease of brown paper; but, beautiful as this idea is, who can take any pleasure in scenery without a little, ever so little, sport to flavour it withal? Certainly not the Skipper; so he came back from his long tramp disgusted with life, and longing to find that Esau had

The Skipper Returns to Camp disgusted with Life.

114

played the fool in his absence, so that he might be able to pick a quarrel with him. Unfortunately Esau was provokingly amiable and had been performing acts of virtue, such as making soup, improving the tent, and swearing at the cook the whole day, so that the seething volcano of the Skipper's temper had to content itself without an eruption.

We did manage to get up an approach to a row about the Memuru Glacier, which the Skipper had visited to-day; he described its beauty and the extraordinary blue of the ice, where the large crevasses near its lower end gave glimpses of its real formation – for of course it is covered thickly with snow except just where it begins to break up. Then he went on to say how curious it was to think that this huge mass, covering square miles of ground, is always moving onwards, and that no more powerful agent exists for altering the arrangement of the earth's crust than that cold placid field of ice. Esau said it did *not* move. He watched it for half an hour yesterday and it never stirred, and he even pushed it with his stick without the smallest effect.

It is impossible to argue with a man of that kind.

Tyndall and Geikie being disposed of, we had a discussion in the tent over the map, with the result that we determined to leave the camp for four days in charge of Ivar; and we and Öla would go to Gjendesheim, and live there, and drink beer, and catch fish until the 8th, when we calculated that John ought to arrive; and we hope by that time some reindeer will have sought safety from other guns by flying to the sheltering embrace of our fjeld.

We always do our baking just before bedtime, when the men have gone to their hutch, and in a permanent camp it soon gets reduced to a certainty. We prefer milk to water for mixing with the flour, as it makes the bread crisper and shorter, and it does not matter how sour the milk is. This is most providential, as we have generally plenty of sour milk. We send twice a week to Besse Sæter, distant about eight miles, and the long journey does not agree with the milk, so that it is generally turned before it arrives here.

Another important article of food is soup, of which we have several varieties. When made of scaup duck, it is — as already mentioned — called Skoggaggany soup; but our present brew is 'gipsy soup,' which is made from potatoes, fishes chopped into small lumps, a square of 'Kopf's compressed vegetables' — a most invaluable article — and all the bones from the birds that we happen to be using. We never empty the pot, but keep adding water and bones as fast as we consume it, and it simmers by the fire all day. But when times are very bad, and we have no meat, and are living on fish, our soup is then called 'prairie soup,' and is composed of every scrap that we can collect — fish-bones; bacon; potatoes; milk; dandelion, and sorrel; bread, and biscuits: and whenever it develops any unusual flavour, we look suspiciously round to see if that boot-lace or candle-end is missing, or if any of the tent-pegs have been newly whittled. It is always very good, and we call it 'prairie' because of the dandelion, which is a prairie flower.

There is yet one more kind, known as 'Argonaut soup,' the recipe of which was introduced from America by the Skipper; but our resources have never yet been so low that we could not make something better than this.

Recipe for Argonaut Soup.

Take a pail of water and wash it clean. Then boil it till it is brown on both sides. Pour in one bean. When the bean begins to worry, prepare it to simmer. If the soup will not simmer it is too rich, and you must pour in more water. Dry the water with a towel before you put it in. The drier the water, the sooner it will brown. Serve hot.

CHAPTER XIII

GJENDESHEIM.

August 5. – Such a lovely morning at last that we were quite tempted to stay, but nobly stuck to our resolve, heaped everything we possessed except rods, guns, and a change of raiment, into the inner tent, and covered them with a ground-sheet; then packed the selected weapons into the canoes, and sailed from these inhospitable shores.

Not far from camp we saw some fish rising under a cliff, and though it was a dead calm, and the sun as bright as sun could be, we stopped to try for them.

Esau soon tired of casting, and mentioning that 'if he could not catch those fish no one could,' paddled off to make a formal call on the Professor, and ask if he had got any deer.

The Skipper persevered, and was rewarded with two fish weighing about three pounds, and the most perfect fish for shape and condition that we have ever seen. This was an important event for us, for it entirely demolished Öla's theory of the non-existence of fish here, and gave us new hope for the future, especially as the weather has been so bad all the time until now, that we should hardly have caught any even if they swarmed.

The Skipper is devoted to the sport of 'throwing

for a rise,' which he thinks the perfection of fishing. It can hardly be pursued with success anywhere but in Norway, for only there do fish seem to rise gree-

Throwing for a Rise.

dily after a constant succession of fine, hot, sunny days, with never a drop of rain or cat's-paw of wind.

The great charm to him is the extreme delicacy required. You *must* put on your thinnest cast, your smallest fly, and throw your lightest; and unless you throw a very long line you have not a chance for the beggar. Then, if he comes at you, you can see him through the calm clear water, and watch the whole performance. You get a rather better chance where two fish are rising close together, as there is some jealousy and competition between them, and each of them is likely to rush at your fly without

sufficient meditation, lest the other one may get it
first.

The Skipper has studied fish from a moral point
of view, and says that they are very much like men:
and he invariably turns his knowledge of their habits
to good account. Throwing for a rise – in a lake like
this, where the fish run large – on a calm bright day,
is decidedly his forte; his motto in fishing being 'far
and fine'. Whereas Esau shines more in a rapid
stream than elsewhere.

The latter had a great time with the Professor,
who he said was a capital fellow, and gave him
whisky, which they drank 'to better sport;' and they
both agreed that there were no reindeer to be found
in the district at present, and the Professor said he
was going further north if matters did not mend
speedily.

After the fishing and visiting were concluded, we
hoisted sails of primitive construction, formed of a
rug and a landing-net, which, with a fair wind, soon
brought us to Gjendesheim.

We think this wind is the chief cause of our misfortune. When we were in these parts before, the
wind was always against us whenever we journeyed; and in that year we had first-rate sport, both in
shooting and fishing. But this time the wind has
always been with us, and we pay for the luxury by
getting no shooting and not much fishing. 'No
mahtterr – a time will come.'

After food the Skipper with Öla went over to
Leirungen – a small lake about three-quarters of a
mile distant. Öla carried his canoe, and did not like

the job. It gives us considerable satisfaction to make Öla do any work, he is so abominably lazy.

It seemed that the tide of luck was already changing, as both he and Esau – who was throwing a fly on the river nearer home – brought in a few nice fish.

Just before bedtime there arrived at the rest-house three Norwegian tourists of the sterner sex, and a young lady the daughter of one of them. The father was a barrister, and the other two were the Lord Chief Justice of what they imagine to be Common Pleas, and a very thin, dried-up student of theology. They all talked English, and the young lady seemed anxious to practise the language.

August 6. – After a gay breakfast Esau went his way to fish, while the Skipper – ever devoted to the fair sex – offered Miss Louise a cruise in his canoe.

The sun shone brightly as they moved over the quiet waters, and the fish were too lazy to rise, but lay idly thoughtful at the bottom of the lake. The Skipper was very polite to his charming companion, as she sat in a state of blissful comfort amongst the rugs which he had placed for her in the bows of the boat; and no sound was heard but the gentle plash of the paddle in the water, and in the distance the Sæter girl calling home the grazing cows.

But presently a cloud gathered over the mountain tops, and thunder was heard rolling among the distant hills; a gentle breeze stirred the surface of the water, and every lazy fish woke up to seek his food. The Skipper longed to go and fetch his rod. He hinted at this, and at last became impatient; but, by Jove!

The Skipper takes Miss Louise for a Cruise at Gjendesheim.

Miss Louise would not go. There she sat and prattled on, charming, pleased with herself, and utterly unmindful of the rising fish and the fretting Skipper. Time kept passing on, till at length her father brought relief by appearing on the shore to call her in to dinner; but then the Skipper had to get his food too, and when he had bolted the humble but indigestible crust and cheese, and rushed out again to seize his rod, he found it too late, as the lake was now dark with clouds, and the fish had left off rising.

Soon after lunch it began to rain like a waterfall, and Esau arrived with a lot of fish – spoils from the Leirungen Ocean, and the result of Spartan indifference to the attractions of woman. There is a shining moral in this tale.

He also brought a romance about a rainbow, which had been so close to him that the two ends met at his feet. The rain hereabouts is very thick.

The evening proved too wet to fish, and this indefatigable young lady captured Esau, and after exhausting all the ordinary topics of conversation, began to show him every kind of puzzle that the mind of man ever conceived, puzzles with coins and puzzles with string; and she puzzled him with matches, and paper, and corks, till the poor young man became perfectly dazzled, and only longed for bedtime to put an end to his misery. Then she asked him riddles, first English and then French. The Skipper, apparently deeply interested in a book at the further end of the room, overheard Esau's answer to the first French riddle; it was 'Je le donne en haut.'

Presently, when they went up to bed, the Skipper said, 'I didn't quite follow your answer to that first riddle of hers. You said, "je le denne en haut."' 'Oh! ah!' answered Esau. That's idiomatic French, and means a good deal that you don't understand; I always use it to gals, especially when they're pretty.' The Skipper coughed, and turned into his bedroom without saying 'good night.'

We have always been told that the Norwegian aristocracy particularly dislike the English sportsman in Norway. We think, therefore, that our fair friend cannot have been of very noble lineage. But she was very nice and rather pretty.

She left early next morning, and Esau said he was glad she was gone, as the Skipper was getting entangled with her.

CHAPTER XIV.

JOHN.

August 7. – We began another day by catching a beautiful bag of fish, and about midday were just starting to shoot our way over to Besse Sæter, when a man came in sight stumbling down the mountain track towards the rest-house. He was red and sunburnt, with a beard of about three days' growth. He was coatless, collarless, and apparently exhausted. On his nearer approach we saw he was an Englishman, and presently when a few yards from us we recognised – John! Not the smart young beau we have always seen him in London; no longer the devotee to society and his club, but an almost unrecognisable John, so sunburnt and hot and hungry. Formal greetings were exchanged: 'Dr. Livingstone, I presume?' 'Mr. Stanley, I believe?' and we rushed into each other's embrace.

Then we besought him to refresh himself on fladbrod, milk, and coffee; which he did, largely. After this he became calm enough to give us a brief summary of his adventures since he left England.

He had done the journey from Christiania in very quick time, and had left all his luggage twenty miles behind at Hind Sæter, which is the nearest place to us to which wheeled vehicles can get. From thence he had started at five o'clock this morning. How he found the way is a marvel, but by great good fortune he met a man when he was about three miles out of the track, who put him right; otherwise he would probably never have arrived anywhere.

He has brought additional stores for the camp, as arranged before we left England, and we had left a note in Christiania asking him to call at the shop in Vaage, and try to get a small stove for the tent, or at any rate find out the price of one. Vaage is our nearest village, about fifty miles distant.

When John arrived there, seeing the shop as he drove past, he descended from his cariole and entered. The shop was full of people buying all the necessaries of life; for in these villages there is only one shop, which is a general store for everything. John was a little confused at his first experience of a Norwegian shop, but at last pulled himself together, and seeing a stove standing in the middle of the room, intended for heating the place, he walked up to it, and stroking it gently with his hand, looked round at the people generally and remarked, 'Hvor meget' (How much)? Dead silence not unmingled with awe followed this observation; for those simple rustics thought there was a maniac among them. This perplexed John, and as everybody was staring at him, and he began to find himself in a remarkably tight place, he concluded to make another remark, so asked in Norsk, 'Have you any whisky?' The storekeeper having no license looked horrified, and said 'Nei.' So John pursued his advantage by inquiring, 'Have you any aquavit?' 'Nei' was again the answer, and an ominous whisper of 'landsmand' (the policeman) was plainly audible. John thought he had asked enough about stoves to quiet his conscience, and guessed it was time to quit that shop. So rapidly regaining his cariole, he vanished before any of the crowd had made up their minds what to do.

We kept to our plan of going to Besse Sæter, starting as soon as John had finished his lunch, and got several teal and a greenshank on the way. On one little bit of water we spied three teal near the bank, and having both together made a most skilful stalk, got them all.

Arriving at Besse Sæter we found one of the two rooms occupied by two Swedish ladies, who were travelling about by themselves for the sake of their health. One of them spoke English well, and told us they had been up several of the high mountains round, and intended to wander about all the summer.

We three had to be content with the other room, and two beds; odd man out for the whole one. Those who only had half a bed reported it rather a crowd in the morning.

Sunday, August 8. – Our object in coming to Besse Sæter was to break the journey to a place called Rus Vand, where a Norwegian owns a lake and hut: it is distant about two hours' walk from Besse Sæter, and we had a letter of introduction to Mr. Thomas, the owner, which we were anxious to deliver, so as to obtain leave to fish in the lake, the western end of which comes to within walking distance of our camp in Memurudalen; and the fishing is remarkably good.

Therefore this morning we started to clamber up the steep mountain side that has to be crossed between Besse Sæter and Rus Vand, and skirting the shores of Bes Vand – which lies on a small plateau at the summit – we soon found ourselves scrambling down over the loose stones, and through the willow scrub that covers the uneven slopes approaching the east end of the lake.

From our side of the river – when we reached its banks, while a boat was crossing to fetch us – we saw several men, and a couple of English-looking setters, a pointer, and a target fixed up about 200 yards from the huts, so that the place presented a very sporting appearance.

Mr. Thomas received us very kindly, and at once gave us permission to fish in his lake. Both he and his wife spoke English perfectly, as did another lady staying with them, and as most emphatically did *not* another sportsman also living there.

These two ladies and two gentlemen were all living in a little two-roomed hut, each room being about nine feet square, and the doorway about five feet high and two wide; the gentlemen's bedroom being also the kitchen. How the ladies managed to turn themselves out in such faultless apparel was a mystery, but it was done, for we saw it.

It is a very plucky thing for ladies to come up here and live for a month, even now when there is a wheel-road (of a sort) to within fifteen miles, but

The Huts at Rusvasoset.

the same thing was done by English ladies ten years ago, when there was no road nearer than forty miles. Are their names not written in the chronicles which adorn the walls of the hut, and carved on the profile fishes which decorate the floor?

In the other hut – which is little more than a boathouse – there are living Jens Tronhúus, our old stalker; 'Siva,' the man who carried our canoes up the mountain at Sikkildal, and another native, also the dogs; besides bottles and churns, grindstones, pack-saddles, saws, axes, and all the other heterogeneous articles which accumulate in a place of this kind. It looked full.

We found the party just sitting down to breakfast after a rather unsettled night, as they had been roused about half-past two in the morning by some one hammering at the door, and found it was a young Norwegian, named, let us say, Coutts, who was making a walking tour, and was more or less lost. They succoured him with coffee and other refreshments, and sent him on his way with Jens to guide him. Coutts's intention was to struggle on to Besse Sæter, but we had seen nothing of him there.

We stayed some time at the huts, talking and looking at all the memorable objects that were there under our *régime* (as we had occupied these huts and had the fishing to ourselves two, years previously). There was Esau's celebrated 'biggest trout whatever was seen,' carved on the floor; the Skipper's favourite cast, and the ice safe that we cunningly devised and constructed in the lower hut. The Thomas's are in even worse case than we, for like us they have seen no deer, and they have so many more mouths to feed. However, they have any quantity of fish, for Rusvasoset is as good a place as the Sjoa at Gjendesheim, which is saying a great deal.

About one we commenced the homeward journey. Two of Jens' sisters had come with us, nominally to see their brother, but really – John asserted – for the purpose of flirting with *him*. He was extremely polite to one of them – though of course he could not speak to her – and would insist on carrying her shawl and other impediments; and he confided to us afterwards that 'women were generally a good deal taken by that sort of mute homage.' She was a dear little girl, and we called her the 'Sæter darlen;' which we believe to be the only Norwegian pun we ever attempted.[1]

The walk home to Gjendesheim is a long one, and although it was Sunday Esau insisted on making a *détour* over the marsh with his gun, as he said he had lost his knife there yesterday and wanted to look for it. He arrived late at Gjendesheim with a satisfied air on his face; without his trusty steel, but with his pockets thrust full of too trustful teal, that had adventured themselves within his reach.

At Gjendesheim we found the young Norwegian who had roused up the Thomas's at Rus Vand, and perceived that he was not without some peculiarities of character. Although the weather was as wet and cold as weather could be, he was attired in a suit of white duck clothes like an English mechanic; even his hat was of white duck, and Esau declared afterwards that his boots were made of the same material; that he had a cigar-case and cigars of it, and ordered white ducks for his dinner. The appearance of his head caused us to be very anxious about any little articles of value that we had about us, for it looked as if it had been shaved all over about two days previously to our making his acquaintance. He looked very strong, tough, and active, and no doubt was so, for he had just performed a most extraordinary walking feat. He is going over all the Jotun Mountains by himself, and yester-

---

1 John said this pun might be elucidated with advantage to the British public, as he did not believe any one could possibly see it. Who cares? Down it goes, and we can assure any one who likes to wrestle with it that it is something very good indeed.

day morning he started from a place an unknown number of miles away at 6 A.M. He walked all day and all night, till it got dark, at which time he was somewhere near Glitretind, in a country he had never seen, with only a vague notion of where he wanted to get to and a pocket compass to do it with. The country about there is perfectly awful to walk over even by day; but he kept at it through the dark, following a torrent up till he crossed the watershed, and following another torrent down till he got to Rus Vand, and staggered into the hut there at 2.30 A.M. almost fainting, for he had had nothing to eat all day: true, he might have got flad-brod at the sæters during the day, but he said he did not care for fladbrod: certainly, he had plenty of chocolate in his knapsack, but he was tired of cho-colate. At Rus Vand he got some coffee, as Thomas told us; and then he walked over the mountain with Jens to Besse Sæter, intending to sleep there: but we were snoring at our ease in all the beds of Besse Sæter, and he hated sleeping on floors, so he walked on again to Gjendesheim, arriving there at half-past five this morning.

Then he produced his knapsack, which he said weighed twenty-five lbs.: it seemed to be chiefly fil-led with packets of most delicious chocolate, some of which he gave us.

We thought him a first-rate fellow, but certainly a little peculiar. He has been all over the world, and is great at natural history, having stuffed many birds in foreign countries for the museum at Christiania.

The Skipper had the next room to his, and told

us that at bedtime he washed himself all over, cleaned his teeth, and brushed his hair: he then stayed in bed till eleven o'clock next morning, when he rose and went through the whole performance again. Now we did not mind him washing or brushing his teeth; we even respect him for doing it; but brushing his hair was a simple insult to common sense, and a wicked waste of time; for not a bristle on his head – whether hair, moustache, or beard – was more than an eighth of an inch long, and all of it was much stiffer than any hair-brush yet made. It was suggested that perhaps he was only combing his hairbrush with his head; and with this explanation we had to rest content.

We luxuriated on meat to-night, for they have actually caught and killed a sheep.

We fish with considerable success now at every odd moment of the day, as the canoes are moored to the shore, not six yards from the house; and it takes no time to get into them and push out into the deep lake, or hover about the brink of the long rapids where the lake begins to be a river.

CHAPTER XV

BACK TO CAMP.

August 9. – The morning was again very wet, but we are men of great decision and firmness; what our friends call 'obstinate' if they are civil, and 'pigheaded' when they want to be disagreeable, as friends usually do.

Therefore we started for the camp after lunch: that is to say, the Skipper and Esau started, as John remained to await the arrival of his baggage, for which Ivar had been despatched. At present his wardrobe is not very extensive, and he will perhaps be more comfortably fixed after the arrival of his valise. He has one coat, one flannel shirt without collar, one pair of trousers, socks, and boots, one pipe, one cap; one fishing rod, line, and fly-book; one watch-chain, and a newspaper of July 23.

About two miles from Gjendesheim on the north side of the lake there is an apparently perpendicular cliff, half a mile long, and over 1000 feet high: this is called the Beseggen, and at the top of it lies Bes Vand, so close to the edge of the cliff that it seems impossible to believe that the lake is 1000 feet above Gjendin, with nothing but a narrow strip of rock to hold it within its bounds, and yet the books say it is so, and we always believe anything we find in a book. The cliff looks perfectly unscaleable, but we believe it has been descended twice by an Englishman who used to live here, and once by a Norwegian youth.

Bes Vand is so high that fish will not live in it; the professional liars of these parts say it freezes solid every winter, and kills any that have been put into it. It is a little difficult to believe this statement, as it is a large and deep lake; but John says that a man who will believe a guide-book can believe anything; so we all do our best to swallow it (the statement, not the lake; we have hardly enough whisky to make the latter palatable).

Gjendin is liable like all mountain lakes to be suddenly visited by squalls, so that we generally like to paddle pretty near the side, but on this voyage it was not safe to do so; for under the influence of the rain, which was coming down as if it had never done so before, stones and boulders were rattling and crashing down the sides of the lake, and plunging into it, in a most alarming manner; and as far as we could see, the steep black rocks were thickly streaked with white lines, denoting torrents rushing down in places where ordinarily none were to be seen.

Just as we were passing the Beseggen, a dull boom like that of a distant cannon was heard, and looking up we could see far above our heads a huge spout of muddy water shoot out from the cliff, carrying with it masses of stone and *débris* of all sorts; evidently some bank had given way under the increased pressure of this enormous rainfall. We thought for one brief moment that it might be Bes Vand let loose on us, for even in fine weather it can always be seen leaking through fissures in the rock, so narrow is the division between the two lakes, but we did not stop to ascertain where it came from.

It soon became necessary to land and empty the canoes, by reason of the heavy rain, the bottom boards being completely under water, though we had only been afloat for half an hour.

Just before we got to Memurudalen the sun came out; Esau had a chase after a black-throated diver that came up from a dive quite close to his canoe, and then we both fell to fishing and got several good fish. This is just our luck: we had left camp for the last few days on purpose to get fish for food; we had caught many and salted them, and brought back 40 lbs. weight with us in a large tin can, and then, behold! we caught fresh fish in a place where we were assured by Öla that there were none, not even salted ones.

We found the camp looking uncommonly pretty and comfortable, and all our things perfectly dry and nice. The sun shone, and blue sky appeared, so that hope, contentment, and joy reigned supreme, for we knew that it could not rain any more now for at least a month, from the way it stopped quite with a jerk as the supply ceased.

John spent his day at Gjendesheim in eating, drinking, and fishing, especially the two former amusements. Truly that is a glorious country where a man can over-eat himself three times a day, and never have indigestion!!

August 10. – Esau stalked with the usual result, 'Ingen dyr, ingen fresk spör, ingen gammle spör,' as the Norsk jäger would remark; which means 'no deer, no fresh tracks, no old tracks;' and he returned to camp to find the Skipper had erected a flagstaff on the little mound beside our tent, and from this staff now floats proudly 'the flag that braved a thousand years, &c.,' which we brought with us for this purpose: a smaller one always adorns the ridge of the tent. We do not know exactly the use of this flag; we say it is hoisted to annoy the Norwegians, but this reason will not bear criticism, for that is the last thing we should think of doing, and it certainly never seems to have that effect on any one who has yet seen it. But we think that no gentleman's residence is complete without a red ensign, therefore on high days and holidays that rag will flaunt itself in the breeze; and every day will now be a holiday, for the fine weather has begun at last.

The Skipper had made all sorts of improvements in our domestic arrangements, and after tea we completed the alterations in the bedroom which were necessary before John arrived. This he did in a boat with Ivar about nine o'clock, pretty well tired with his row against a head wind. He was received with much kindness by the barbarous islanders, but it took us until late at night to get everything comfortably and conveniently placed under canvas; for John made no slight addition to our already ponderous stores, in the shape of two more boxes containing tea, coffee, candles, sugar, jam, and at last Esau's long-desired anchovy paste.

We placed the three beds side by side in the inner tent, John being in the middle for the sake of greater warmth, for the nights are very cold. Among the things that we obtained through Jens were two sheepskin rugs, invaluable for protection against cold. Till we got them we were more or less wretched every night, but since they came our sleep bas been perfectly luxurious. John has only two ordinary Scotch rugs, and feels the cold a good deal, so we, from our impervious sheepskins, give him any coats, shirts, or trousers that we do not want.

CHAPTER XVI

TROUT.

August 11. — Last night at sunset we 'could not see a cloud, because no cloud was in the sky;' the distant mountains looked as black as coal, and the heavens were yellow-ochre colour; whereupon Öla committed himself to the statement that the fine weather would now be a permanent institution. Consequently our life has once more resumed its proper phase of perpetual picnic, and we roam about without coats or waistcoats or any other garments that seem superfluous unto us; and to John all garments except a landing-net and boots appear to be unnecessary incumbrances. Reversing the natural order of things, we put on all our available clothes when we go to bed, and peel for the day when we get up.

It is difficult to believe that only two days ago we were shivering with cold, wrapped in gloom and indiarubber clothing, and wet through all day, when now the horizon is dancing with heat, the lake is perfectly calm, with the high snow mountains mirrored in its blue depths, and we are delighting in every little bit of shade, having pawned our macintoshes and thrown the tickets into the glacier torrent.

That same stream has been a source of great annoyance to John during the night. He wants to have it turned off, because its roaring kept him

John Returns from Fishing in Summer Costume.

awake, and he was going first thing after breakfast to see the turncock about it; but, of course, it is hopeless. The municipal arrangements here are much the same as in London, and that official cannot be found when wanted; so he will have to content himself with damming it.

The hot sun has brought out flies in great profusion; the fish are rising freely, and man goeth forth

John and Esau: 'How's that for High?'

to his labour rejoicing, and cometh home with a heavy bag and a light fly-book, for the fish here seem to be all good-sized; and as we have to use the finest tackle and smallest flies, the odds are rather in favour of the finny prey.

We all went fishing, and made a very pretty catch among us, the Skipper securing the greatest weight, and Esau the largest fish, weight 3 1/2 lbs. The Skipper also made some interesting notes on the moral and physical characteristics of these Gjendin trout. He said there seemed to be three methods of feeding in vogue among them. Some were moving in a large circle about two hundred yards in diameter, and rising at very short intervals as they went – these never came within ten yards of the shore. Then there were some that were travelling along about a yard from the shore, and these seemed to be rising even more frequently than the others, as there were more flies close to the rocks than out in mid-ocean; and there were a few cunning old beggars that had got a comfortable hole under a rock which they did not like to leave, and only rose at longer intervals, as especially tasty morsels floated by.

All the fish, to whichever class of risers they might belong, often took the moving artificial fly in preference to real dead ones that were lying on the surface of the water close by: from which we opine that they resemble us to the extent of liking fresh food better than stale; for our flies had no attractive tinsel to commend them to the notice of an epicurean trout, being the best imitations we can manage of the predominant fly, which is a small dark-coloured winged ant, with a little reddish orange about the long black body.

These flies have but a brief and disastrous existence. They only flew for the first time this morning, most of them had died by noon – for the lake was strewn with their corpses – and the survivors were all worried and consumed by fish before nightfall. Luckily there are plenty more where they came from, and the process can be repeated on new flies tomorrow.

It is very interesting to catch a fish off these rocks on a perfectly calm day like this; for in the clear water you can see the whole of the struggle, from the moment the fish rises till he is lying panting and exhausted in the net. How beautiful a big fish looks when he first comes ashore! How brightly he shines in the sunlight, and how sleek is his portly person!

Even if you cannot see your fish rise and take the fly, you can soon tell by his behaviour whereabouts the needle will come if you succeed in getting him on to the weighing hook. A large fish very seldom rises with any dash or swagger, but just a smothered ripple; perhaps a glimpse of his nose as he sucks in the fly; and he moves as if he were a nobody: then when he feels the hook, there is none of that dash and wriggle that you find in a small fish, but generally a rush like a rocket towards the middle of the lake, making you tremble for the safety of your reel line, and after that a stately diving and calm, dignified resistance for five or ten minutes till he has to give in. Sometimes, though not so often, the rocket business will be repeated more than once and a fish that does this deserves to escape, and often gets his deserts. There is something very fine about the proud bearing of a big trout in difficulties; for here in the lake he has not the same chance as his relations in the running water at Gjendesheim.

The largest fish seemed to be those feeding in a circle, and it was one of these that Esau caught, which he said was the father of all fish. He lost another much larger – no doubt the grandfather of all fish. He said it weighed five pounds. It is an extraordinary piscatorial fact that the largest fish always do get away.

In the afternoon Esau commenced excavating the long-promised oven from the face of the little hill against which our tent is pitched. It stands about a hundred yards from our hall door, and is constructed chiefly of large stones and mud – clay not being obtainable – with a flue cut in the hill-side: a single stone acts as the floor of the oven, under which the wood-furnace is kindled, and a sod of turf, from time to time renewed, does duty as a door.

Dinner at seven.

John wishes that the menu should be occasionally inserted for the benefit of gastronomic readers.

Vins.	*Potage.*	*Légumes.*
Tea.	Prairie.	Potatoes,
Beer.		Fried and Boiled.

Poisson.
Fried Trout.

Entrées.
Sardines.

Gibier.
Teal. Greenshank.

Entremets.
Compôte of Rice and Wimberries.
Jam. Marmalade.
Whisky.

After this Esau finished the oven, and accomplished a bake of bread therein, which proved so successful that on returning from fishing at about ten at night, we all turned our attention to the production of the staff of life, nor desisted from our labours till eleven o'clock, by which time there was a goodly show of rolls and loaves spread out, and we went to bed feeling that we had spent a glorious day.

CHAPTER XVII

REINDEER.

August 12. – We wonder whether our friends in Scotland and Yorkshire have such a day as this: if they have, it is rough on the grouse.

There is not a breath the bottle-green wave to curl, and the sun shines as if Odin had redeemed his other eye.

The Skipper and Öla went forth to pursue, and walked over an enormous distance into the previously unknown region of Memurutungen. Up on the mountains life on a day of this kind is bliss; there is more air there than in the valley, and it is delightful to be far away from the busy world – consisting of your two pals and Ivar – below; surrounded by the snowy peaks and sky, with not a living thing save perhaps an eagle in sight.

In the middle of the day they came on fresh deer tracks, at which of course their flagging interest revived; and presently they descried, on a snow fjeld about a mile away, two deer 'scooting' over the opposite mountain side. These they followed and made a long *détour* to get the right side of the breath of wind that occasionally made itself felt up there, for the reindeer has probably the most acute scent of all the deer tribe. In the midst of this *détour* they suddenly came in sight of two other bucks, about 300 yards away, much finer animals than the first two; in fact, they had the best heads the Skipper ever saw. But luck was against him; they were wrong for the wind, and a puff came just at the moment, which carried the unwelcome intelligence to those deer that their hated enemy was upon them, and they departed round a corner at a rapid

The two 'Meget Stor Bocks' (very big Bucks) on Memurutungen.

trot, and were no more seen. Then Öla looked at the Skipper with a sorrowful shake of the head, and said, 'Meget store bocks!' (very big bucks), and the Skipper replied, with a still more portentous shake, 'Meget, meget.' So they were left with their mouths wide open, muttering, 'Meget, meget store bocks.' And after following the tracks some time without seeing anything more of the deer, they gave up the chase and returned to camp, getting home in a very exhausted state about 6.30.

During dinner old Peter Tronhúus arrived in

camp with a packet of letters and papers, and a fore-quarter of venison from Rus Vand. Mr. Thomas had been like ourselves reindeer-less until yesterday, when he found a large herd, and was lucky enough to get two out of them.

Peter also told us that two friends of Thomas's who had been staying with him were walking over the mountain to see our camp, and would then go to Gjendesheim with him in the boat in which he had come.

Presently these two men arrived extremely hot, and looking as if they would like beer; so we appeased them with one of our few remaining bottles, and after showing them all the sights of the camp, took them out on the lake in the canoes. One of them spoke a little English, the other only French and Norwegian. The latter asked the Skipper, in the Gallic tongue, 'if we had entrapped many fish?' and 'if we had not fear to venture on the lake in such small boats?' and informed him that 'there were many savage ducks about this year.' The other one, regardless of his own life and safety, and also of Esau's – in whose canoe he was sitting – *would* keep throwing up his arms and exclaiming, 'It gives us moch playsure to make a travel in the Canadian cáno.'' But we think they were proud and thankful when the experiment was over, and they were safe in Peter's boat. These strangers displayed unwonted courage, for the ordinary native has a wholesome dread of our frail craft. The hardy Norseman's house of yore was doubtless on the foaming wave, but that was before the days of Canadian canoes.

147

At dinner John informed the company that his bath in the lake yesterday was the third of a series, the first of which took place in Montenegro, the second in Algiers, and now this in Norway. He calls this a humble tribute to the geniality of the English summer, and thinks that he may be termed 'a polyglot ablutionist.' Some of the sojourners in this camp say it may be so, but it does not speak highly for John's love of water when undiluted with whisky.

Subsequently we found that the bath which he swaggered about only occurred because he fell off a rock into the lake, and so dabbled about afterwards while his clothes were drying, which does not take long in this weather. This also accounts for the condition in which he returned to camp, 'sans bags, sans shirt, sans everything,' – barring his boots.

Late at night Esau, who was up last, put his head into the tent to remark that there was a first-rate comet on view, but he was received with such execrations from the other two lazy people in bed that he thought it prudent to say no more about it, and not to look at it any more himself.

August 13. – We spent the morning making a meat safe. This meat safe consists of a hole in the ground, neatly flagged with flat stones, and walled with the same, and furnished at the top with a wooden frame, into which fits a lid with hooks underneath it for birds. The whole is covered with a piece of muslin to keep off the villainous bluebottles. The muslin was brought to make into mosquito nets inside the tent, but in this happy spot the 'skeeter' is unknown, the sand-fly very rare, and the great greeneyed Möge – which bites a lump out of your leg and then flies to the nearest tree to eat it – is conspicuous by its absence.

We have always been very careful not to prepare in any way for game before it is killed, but this usually successful plan has been a failure this year, so now we are desperate, and have made a safe which will hold a reindeer, and probably with a little more bad luck shall even go out stalking with ropes in our pockets ready to tie up the animal when killed. We caught Öla a week ago carving a piece of stick into the double-ended thing that butchers put between the legs of sheep to keep them apart (name unknown), but we promptly seized it, and made it into the handle of a frying-pan. But who can escape his destiny? We hoped that we had averted misfortune, but the deed was done, and no doubt it was owing to this that the Skipper failed to get a shot at the 'store bocks.'

When John and Esau had finished the safe and succeeded in catching enough nice fish for the requirements of the camp, they were seized with the desire of making a good bath. We have no first-rate bathingplace near the camp, as the glacier-river has made the lake too shallow round its mouth, and it is some distance to where the shore becomes bold and rocky.

They selected a nice little stream on the hill just above the tent, and toiled like navvies there for about four hours under a blazing sun, excavating and paving with flat stones, making a most palatial bath in the bed of the stream; when behold, just as it was completed, to use the graphic language of one of the constructors, 'May I be dodderned, and dog-goned, and dingblamed by Pike, if the blooming stream didn't cease to run!' It did. Just supply about a pint of water before it quite stopped, into which Esau's watch flew as he flung on his coat with some slight, and perhaps excusable, show of temper. A pint of water is not enough for a man to bathe in, but it is quite sufficient to saturate a watch, especially if a stone obligingly smashes the glass and makes a hole in its face, obliterating the vii. viii. and ix. at the time of its immersion. However, he dug the mud out of the works, filled them with Rangoon oil, and is under the impression that that watch can be made to go again, and that a new face and glass and silver case will make it look all right. He is of a sanguine disposition.

They returned to camp saying that it would be all right as soon as the first rain came, but they reckoned without their host; the stream came from a little snowdrift on the mountain, and next time that Esau went up there he found that the heat of the last few days had melted it all away; hence its sudden stop. It never ran again. Perchance some future traveller will find the bath ages hence, and rejoice in its luxurious arrangements. In anticipation of this John wrote the following beautiful lines on the most prominent rock:–

'Stranger, pause and shed a tear:
There used to be a streamlet here;
But seeing Esau strip to lave
His sordid body 'neath its wave,

All filled with shame and blushing red,
The streamlet left its gravel bed;
Its only wish from him to flee,
It ran away and went to sea.'

The Skipper returned rather late with some very good fish from our old lake Rus Vand, and dinner was consequently at the extremely fashionable hour of 8.30.

MENU.

Poisson.

Truite à la Norvège.

Gibier.

Teal en matelote de Bacon.
Pommes de terre sautéd in a frying-pan.

Potage.

Skoggaggany.

Potage is frequently eaten last, for it keeps hot longer than the other dishes, and as we always feed in the open air in fine weather, they cool more quickly than in civilisation.

About nine o'clock a splendid display of northern lights was produced for our benefit, and we stayed up till twelve o'clock baking bread and gazing at the ever-changing beauties of this glorious sight. In the course of conversation it transpired that the same thing happened last night in a milder form, and it was this that Esau had announced as a comet. To-night he was immensely delighted with the show, because he says it will bring good luck; quoting

'Aurora bright, dear harbinger of dawn.' He said this was Shakespeare, and if Shakespeare called Aurora a 'deer harbinger,' that ought to be enough for us. The other two agreed, but did not believe

Hot Soup and Northern Lights.

Shakespeare ever wrote that, or anything like it. 'What play was it in?' 'Play!' said Esau, with the utmost contempt, 'you awful duffers, it's in the sonnets; I dare say you never read all of them.' This was unanswerable, for of course no one ever did read all the sonnets. But in revenge John composed some poetry about Esau, after the manner of Walt Whitman, he said.

If Walt Whitman ever wrote anything like this, he ought to be made to read it. We give a few lines: –

'Twas he who culled the bluest berry sweet,
And with his jodelling made the heights reply
To airs that oft have graced the music hall:
Anon when work or sport was put aside,
The fragrant omelette he would deftly roll;
No better man to fry the curling trout,
None with more appetite to make it scarce.
When tired nature seeks repose in bed,
To lie when others rise and calmly rest,
He most surpassed the seven Sleepers' selves.
This is the sort of rubbish men can write
Who to inanity devote their minds;
But not save great experience will suffice
To do the trick; no amateur can hope
To vie with those who've studied it from youth.'

And so on for pages.

On examining the diaries which we all keep, the following remarks on the aurora were found:–

No. 1. – By the Skipper.

'The heavens were illuminated by most brilliant northern lights, which flickered in a great arch over the starry sky.'

No. 2. – By Esau.

'A most glorious display of northern lights, huge bands of light across the sky; waving, flickering, and disappearing, then suddenly shining out again more brilliantly than before, while all the time straight streamers of light were shooting upwards from the horizon.'

No. 3. – By John.

'The glow of a remarkably fine aurora borealis, whose silvery shimmering shafts flickered incessantly all over the heavens in the most fantastic shapes.'

It will be observed that we all agree in the flickering, consequently you may bet it *did* flicker. But for this fortunate fact it would be hard to recognise the three descriptions as identical, and yet this is the way history is written.

CHAPTER XVIII

SUCCESS AT LAST.

August 14. – This was a most eventful day in our quiet life, and one fraught with episode. For the first time there was a breeze, so the Skipper went out fishing, and John to practise canoeing in a wind, which is an art requiring considerable dexterity in these Canadian canoes. They are beautiful sea boats, and beat the 'Rob Roy' hollow for any purposes where room for baggage is required. In our two, which are only small, we have transported between 800 and 900 lbs.; but their worst feature is decidedly exhibited in a wind, for the broad flat bottom and absence of keel cause them to drift very fast, and make it difficult to keep them straight. It can only be done by paddling from amidships instead of from the stern.

Esau went out stalking, full of hope from the aurora and the favourable wind.

The Skipper was lucky and caught some very good fish, and then returning to camp constructed a most lovely wimberry tart. He had just finished the enclosure of the same in the oven, and was proceeding to remove the flour and ashes and other *débris* from his hands, while John reclined at his ease under an awning with our latest 'Field' – three weeks old – when they heard a hail overhead, and behold a swarm of visitors from Rus Vand! Mr. and Mrs. Thomas, Miss A—, and their friend F—, who is the most celebrated deerstalker in the country. He is reported to never miss a shot, and occasionally shoots flying ryper with a rifle.

They tumultuously demanded lunch, and the Skipper with John had a pretty busy time of it for about twenty minutes, and the wimberry tart had to be left to its fate in the sultry climate of the oven. Our larder just now is not well supplied with anything except fish; so that the utmost exertions could only produce a meal which to people who have had reindeer for several days must have seemed poor indeed. Fried trout, Skoggaggany soup, tea, beer, bread, biscuits, and marmalade, was the bill of fare, for there was no time to do anything in the 'gibier' line, birds taking some time to pluck and clean. However, to our guests there were some points of this meal decidedly worthy of attention, viz., the beer, marmalade, and bread: they have none of these at Rus Vand, as their attempts at bread have hitherto been failures, while ours has been very first-rate ever since the oven was built, and was much appreciated.

We have been informed that the proper thing in these days, when writing a book, is to recommend some condiment or patent medicine to the notice of the confiding public. As there is no chance of our meeting any Arab sheiks in Memurudalen, we have to fall back on this episode of the bread, and seize the opportunity to sing to the world the praises of

'Yeatman's Yeast Powder,' by far the best that we have tried, and invaluable on an expedition of this kind for bread, pastry, and pancakes. Now let old Yeatman send his hundred guineas, care of Esau, and we will see that they are devoted to a proper use.

To return to our guests. We made an awning on what we call the lawn – size six feet by fourteen feet – out of two rugs and some birch poles, and lunched under that, as the sun was cruelly hot. There was a good deal of the ordinary picnic about the meal, as we have only four plates, cups, knives, &c., and had to eat fish out of the frying-pan, and drink beer out of a jam pot, and a condensed-milk tin with the top cut off and the sharp edge turned down. But all these drawbacks were met in the true picnic spirit, which 'de minimis non curat' so long as there is something to eat. Our two last bottles of beer were sacrificed, and it went to our hearts to have to pour away our beloved Skoggaggany soup when the cups were wanted for tea, for our visitors did not 'go for' the soup with the same alacrity that distinguishes us. Possibly it occurred to them that the middle of a blazing hot August day was not the most suitable time for highly seasoned, substantial, nearly boiling liquid to be poured down their throats.

Mr. and Mrs. Thomas and Miss A— all spoke English well, but their friend young F— could neither speak it nor understand it: however, he wished to be genial and polite, and replied 'Oh yase, tank you,' whenever any remark was made to him. In consequence of this amiable trait, John, who thought he could talk our language as well as the others, supplied him with beer, whisky and water, tea, soup, and marmalade all at the same time, to each of which articles when offered he had replied 'Oh yase, tank you.' This made a sad run on our limited supply of crockery.

Lunch ended, the Skipper volunteered as usual to take the party one by one for a cruise in his canoe. This with the ordinary English lady would be a matter of considerable risk, but all Norwegians – ladies as well as men – are accustomed to boats, and very nearly all of them can swim. But the trip was quite dangerous enough, for both the ladies insisted on kneeling in the right position and paddling themselves, and there was a good sea on, with a distant threatening storm. While Mrs. Thomas was pursuing her adventurous career, her husband danced on the bank after the manner of a hen with ducklings, crying, 'Come back! come back! you go too far out!' but we grieve to record that she did not care a little bit, and was so delighted with the canoe that the Skipper had some difficulty in persuading her to return. May she live long to paddle that canoe, for it now belongs to her.

About four o'clock the call came to an end, and our friends departed over the mountain to Rus Vand, at the west end of which they expected to meet their boat. Before going they made us promise to go and see them next Tuesday, and will send a boat to convey us down the lake.

Soon after six Esau came into camp in an offen-

Esau and Öla Return in Triumph.

sively jaunty manner, followed by Öla with the heads and skins, and what the lawyers call the appurts, to wit, the heart, kidneys, feet, and liver of two reindeer bucks. Then was there great rejoicing in that little colony, and dinner was served and disposed of with light hearts, even the neglected wimberry tart being a complete success, for owing to its gigantic size, its long baking in a cooling oven had not been too much for it, and it was finished to the last crumb of paste and spoonful of juice.

Our custom is, when a man returns with deer, that he shall lie on the sheepskin of indolence if so disposed, while the other fellows prepare dinner; and after the meal is finished and men are beginning to lean back and fill their pipes, he is expected to relate his adventures without interruption; after this he is never to refer to them, again unless specially requested. Now for Esau's story.

'We went on to Memurutungen and began to find fresh tracks and signs of deer almost direetly, so were on the tiptoe of expectation all the morning. About midday Öla found two deer on a small patch of snow, five or six miles from camp, in a very favourable place for approaching them, with the wind as right as it could be. We made a lovely stalk; but when after an hour's creeping we got to the spot, we were just in time to see them disappear, slowly feeding over the hill. We followed as fast as possible, and soon came in sight of them again, for as the deer always feed against the wind there is no danger of alarming them, by following on their tracks. A few minutes of breathless crawling like serpents, and we were within 100 yards, nearer than I ever got to reindeer before. One of them soon gave me a nice side shot, and when I fired he almost fell, but recovered himself, and they both ran down the hill towards a little glacier. I fired again at him and missed; and then ran as hard as I could towards the glacier, cramming in cartridges as I ran. They were both out of sight for a moment behind some rocks, and then the unwounded one came into view again, and I had a nice shot at him at about 150 yards, and was lucky enough to send a bullet just above his heart, which killed him instantly at the edge of the glacier.

I ran straight on, and following round the shoulder of the hill, saw the other one standing about 100 yards away, unable to go any further. I was in about the same state myself, so sat down, took as careful

an aim as I could, and fired a shot which finished
him. How he had ever got so far is a mystery, as the
first shot only missed his heart by about an inch.
The second went in touching the hole made by the
first, and killed him at once.

A Careful Finishing Shot.

'We gralloched them, and built the meat up with
stones to preserve it from ravens, and the great bug-
bear of hunters, the "jarraf," as they call it; filfras is
its English name. I think it is identical with the
North American wolverine or glutton.'

The lecturer concluded his observations amid
great applause.

Let it be understood that the running which is
done in pursuit of deer is a gymnastic performance
of the utmost difficulty, for these mountains are

almost entirely composed of loose stones with sharp, clean edges. These stones vary in size, but otherwise are all similar, and have no more tendency to stick together and lie quiet than the lumps in a basin of sugar. So that running over them means – for an extremely active man – a pace of perhaps four miles an hour; for a deer about six or seven. Consequently the deer always when disturbed try to get on to snow, for there they can go a great, but unascertained pace – apparently somewhere about eighty miles an hour.

We find that after all we were quite right to make the meat-safe before killing the deer, for we only made it to hold one, and now we have killed two, and so are quite properly behindhand with our arrangements, and shall be obliged to make another.

After dinner Esau went down to the lake and tried a few casts from the shore. He speedily hooked a fish, which he thought the biggest ever made, and never got a sight of it for twenty minutes. He thought this a grand top up for a truly successful day, but on landing it, it only weighed a pound, but was hooked in the tail, hence the struggle.

CHAPTER XIX

GJENDEBODEN.

Sunday, August 15. – Still the same beautiful weather. We spent the morning fishing and bathing. Esau distinguished himself by falling into the lake off a cliff, just as he had finished dressing after a bath; nearly swamping his canoe, full of fish, rugs, and other valuables. There was such a sun that he merely hung his things on the rocks and went on fishing without them until they were dry, which took a very short time. He always had savage tendencies, and would like to live without clothes, but we consider this is not dignified, and will not tend to promote discipline among our retainers. The Skipper got the best bag, as he generally does on a calm day.

After lunch we packed our rods, fowling-pieces, and change of raiment into the canoes, and started on a voyage of discovery up the lake, intending to spend the night at Gjendebod – a hut at the western end somewhat similar to Gjendesheim at the eastern, though not so large or so well built, for the upper end of the lake does not get as many visitors as the lower.

The expedition commenced with a disaster, owing, no doubt, to its being Sunday. As John and Esau in the larger canoe were crossing the glacier stream, something caused the boat to almost swamp, but fortunately right again with a good deal of water in it. Esau said it was John's clumsiness; John said it was Esau's recklessness in crossing at such a rapid place, and much recrimination ensued. They went to shore and emptied the water out, and then continued the voyage, nothing being wet except the rugs used to kneel on. Only the Skipper lingered on the voyage to fish; the other two paddling against a heavy head wind completed the journey of five miles in about an hour, and had dinner cooked and ready by the time the Skipper made his appearance with a beautiful basket of trout.

Our dinner was made from the shoulder of venison sent us by Mr. Thomas. It was utterly ruined in the cooking, for we are getting fastidious after our own luxurious meals, and think as poorly of Gjendebod cookery as a certain friend of ours did of English, when he complained that 'in all the houses of the rich and great which he had ever known, he had never seen a decent hot dinner served except when they had it cold for lunch.'

We found here a young Norwegian who spoke English well, and gave us some very interesting information, chiefly about the winter life in Norway; also a very intelligible account of the land system of the country, which we intend to send to Mr. Gladstone for use in his next Irish Land Bill. We think it peculiarly adapted for Ireland, because, though we all understood it perfectly at the time, we cannot agree about any of its main features on comparing notes afterwards.

Presently there arrived here Coutts – our Gjendesheim acquaintance who had made the extraordinary walk over the mountains. His hair had either not grown since we last saw him, or else he had sandpapered it off again. He had just achieved another remarkable feat. This was a climb to the top of 'Stor Skagastolstind,' a mountain which has only been ascended twice previously; first by an Englishman who spends most of his time in doing such things, and afterwards by a Norwegian, the last time being two years ago. Many others have tried and failed. The ordinary traveller will find the feat of pronouncing its name fluently in the course of conversation quite difficult enough; but it can be done by the exercise of an iron will, and if not attempted more than once in a day, no fatal effects need be apprehended. Once we met a very care-worn-looking man who told us he had been trying to make a pun on the name, but we felt no pity for so foolhardy a wretch.

The authorised procedure for those who accomplish the ascent, is to enclose their name and some coins in a bottle, and build a little cairn round the bottle, leaving their handkerchief with it, and bringing down the corresponding articles left by the last man. Coutts showed us the handkerchief and bottle which he found on the top, but the coins he must have spent in drinks on his way home, or else did not like to trust us with them, as he could not produce them. He had, of course, left his own handkerchief, and John, who is short of these useful though not indispensable articles, was seized with a

great longing to risk his life and go to the summit of
that mountain for Coutts's. At least he was very
keen about it immediately after the description of
the ascent and hiding of the treasure; but since he
became calmer we almost persuaded him not to go,
as he hates walking, especially uphill walking; it
takes two days to ascend the peak, one to get down
again; and the whole performance is slightly more
difficult and hazardous than the ascent of the
Matterhorn.

It will probably be unnecessary to remark that
Coutts did not for a moment condescend to follow
the path chosen by former climbers, but having
after considerable search found one at least twice as
dangerous, he chose that, as he had not time to look
for a worse one.

August 16. – After breakfast we found a drover,
who was living in a hut here, and impressed him to
come out with us after ryper – his function being
that of the dog. There are many of these drovers in
the mountains during the summer. They get cattle
– how, we do not know; whether they buy them,
or merely drive them on commission for the
owners; then they feed them on the common lands,
and drive them to some town at the end of the
summer. The huts that they live in are wretched
little places. There is one about two miles from our
camp, built of rough stones against a rock which
forms two of the sides, without any door or window, and only a hole to creep in at. No Englishman
would keep his dog in such a place, unless it were
dead; but we are told that a drover lived there for a

month this year before we came, and it is considered of sufficient importance to be marked on the
Ordnance map, otherwise we should never have
seen it.

Our drover, however, was rather a great man,
living in a hut with a real door and a window, and
a live woman inside to cook for him and iron his
shirt – at least, we imagined she must be doing this,
as he had not got one on.

Ryper shooting began by law yesterday, but our
Sabbatarian proclivities prevented us from going
forth to the chase. The true reason is that we super-
stitiously believe it will rain again if we shoot on
Sunday, though no one will confess that this is the
feeling by which we are possessed.

We crossed the lake in the canoes – the Skipper
and Esau to shoot, John and Herr Drover to beat.
There was a narrow belt of birch trees between the
lake and the willow belt in which we hoped to find
the birds, and before we got through this, our ears
were gladdened by the sound of two shots from
Esau, who had walked on to two old birds and got
them both; but alas! disappointment was in store for
us. We walked up hill and down dale, dry ground
and marshy, willow belt and birch belt, but never
saw another ryper for five hours, and then we put
up one old cock who fled away with a derisive crow
before we got within sixty yards of him. It is hopeless work hunting ryper without dogs. We found
plenty of places where they had fed or sat, or been
running on wet ground; but they hate flying unless
they are compelled, and on a day of this sort lie like

stones, though we have seen them after windy weather get up almost as wild as Yorkshire grouse. But we feel that we have done our duty in trying to shoot ryper, and so now can go back to our fishing and stalking with a quiet conscience.

And if we got no more ryper we found such a quantity of 'möltebær,' that there is every prospect of Esau being seriously ill for some days, which would be a distinct gain as far as the consumption of our stores goes. The 'möltebær' is a berry like a large yellow raspberry, very good indeed to eat, with a sort of honey flavour about it. The Norwegians think it better than the strawberry, though we hardly indorse this opinion. It is a beautiful scarlet before it is ripe, and a dirty pale yellow when ready to gather. It grows low down, and is difficult to find, as it conceals itself in low, swampy, and rather dark places.

When we returned from the pursuit of the disobliging ryper, there was a fair breeze down the lake, so we hoisted sails and were soon back at Memurudalen.

CHAPTER XX

A FORMAL CALL.

August 17. – This was the day appointed for our visit to the Thomas's at Rus Vand, but though we told Öla as usual to call us at 7.30, he never came until about half-past eight. His watch is a curiosity among bad watches; he sets it by one of ours every night, and it has always gained or lost several hours before morning: on one occasion it actually lost nearly, a fortnight while we slept. The Skipper says it 'ain't worth a smothered oath;' and this morning, as we specially wished to get up early – and did get up, owing to Öla's watch, more than usually late – he is getting lower in his valuation, and estimates it at a 'whispered d—.'

We have begged Öla to pawn it, or refrain from winding it up, but without effect, and Esau lent him his – which has never moved since its bath, and is fixed at 5.20. This was very successful for two days, as it made Öla call us about six o'clock, and we had lots of time to go to sleep again afterwards; but after that the discontented fellow came and asked for one that would go faster, and of course we have nothing that will compare with his own either at trotting or cantering.

First thing this morning the Skipper was seen

shaving his meagre chin with no little care, and reflecting himself with considerable interest in a slip of looking-glass that he keeps under his pillow. We all made elaborate toilets, but the Skipper was especially beautiful by reason of his necktie, and the least threadbare of his two coats, which he wore with what he considered a careless grace.

We started up the mountain at half-past ten, and arrived on the shores of Rus Vand very hot and tired in about two hours. There we saw a dim speck on the distant horizon which we imagined to be the boat coming to take us down the lake. So we began to fish till it should arrive; and it was a considerable time before we realised the fact that the speck we had seen was indeed the boat, but it was *going*, not coming, for the soulless wretch who had control of it had presumed to think, and his thoughts being of course the mere unreasoning impulses of a brutish and degraded mind, had caused him to suppose we were not coming. This was a terrible blow, but at last we bravely decided to walk on to the hut – about eight miles. During the next six pages of this book we walked and walked and walked, with hunger and thirst raging inside us, a broiling sun over our heads, and the most frightful language proceeding from our lips; tramping along cattle tracks, wading through mountain torrents, and stumbling over willows and rocks, till about half-past three in the afternoon, when turning the last corner we came on the two huts, and our olfactory nerves were greeted by the welcome scent of adjacent cooking food.

Thomas was most profuse in his maledictions of the idiot who had left the west end of the lake without waiting for us, and we had great difficulty in persuading him not to shed his blood there and then. Thus far the misery.

But now a change came o'er the scene. Behold the wearied travellers lying on the sward, in the cool shadow east by the hut; surrounded by iced whisky punch, brandy and water, rum and milk, and claret, and drinking them all at once under the entreaties of our hospitable entertainers. Anon a sumptuous feast was spread under the canopy of a tent pitched just above the roaring waters of the Russen River where it leaves the calm of the lake for the turmoil and trouble of a hurried descent to busier regions. That trout, reindeer, roast ryper, and the various smaller birds will be remembered by all of us as long as we live.

The Skipper confessed afterwards that all along that burning shadeless cattle track – with its atmosphere perfectly blue with execrations – he had thought that life was but a 'wale of tears' at the best of times; but when after dinner cigars and black coffee were produced, he began to believe we had had rather a pleasant walk after all.

We left the hospitable hut about six, in the boat, Thomas himself and Jens coming with us. Jens rowed, and we four fished all the way up the lake, so that the water was stiff with minnows and flies. John with a minnow caught one three-pound trout and some smaller ones, and the Skipper and Esau several good fish with the fly, but we had no time to really

try to catch fish, but kept rowing steadily on and getting what we could on the way. Thomas got out
half-way up the lake to fish from the bank, and John
at once trampled on a spare rod which had been
brought in the boat and reduced it to matchwood.
Then to witness John's polite protestations and apologies from the boat to Mr. Thomas on shore was
truly gratifying to us as spectators. When they were
concluded we rowed on to the end of the lake, climbed over the dreadful mountain – which was by no
means a pleasant task in the dark – and reached camp
at half-past ten – just twelve hours employed in
making a formal call. Think of that, ye gentlemen of
England who grumble at having to leave a card on
the people the other side of the square.

August 18. – We all stayed at home to-day, as the
weather – although still perfectly fine – was not
favourable for any sort of sport with which we are
acquainted except kite-flying; and the tent was constantly in such imminent danger of being blown
from its moorings, that we feared if we went away,
we should not be able to find it when we came
back. It was great fun during breakfast to watch Ivar
sailing after our goods and chattels whenever a sudden gust of wind sent them scudding over the
ground till brought to a standstill by a juniper or a
rock. Before starting in pursuit he always opened his
mouth to its utmost width – which is enormous –
and then extending his arms and legs till he looked
like a demoniac windmill, he swooped down on the
quarry, never failing to secure the fly-away article,
dish-cloth, or towel, or whatever it might be.

The Skipper was the only one who attempted fishing, and he had but poor sport, and soon returned to camp to assist in the operations there going on. The most important of these was the construction of a new game cellar in the ground near the old one. Esau was 'bossing' this thing, while Öla worked. Esau, being very lazy himself, takes a fiendish delight in getting any work out of Öla; and now his portion of the job seemed to be standing with an axe in his hand revolving things in his great mind while Öla undertook the labour. The Skipper and John devoted themselves to baking, and produced an enormous quantity of bread and biscuits; and when these were finished the united strength of the company engaged itself on a meat pie.

The division of labour in this enterprise is always managed thus. Esau is butcher – an employment in which he revels, and at which he is decidedly an adept. He cuts up reindeer in convenient slices for placing in the pie-dish; adding thereto slices of bacon, and two or three hard-boiled eggs, with some liver, heart, and birds if we have any to spare. Meanwhile the Skipper concocts the dough for the crust from flour, butter, and boiling water; and after rolling the same on the top of one of the boxes with an empty beer-bottle, neatly lines the smaller of the two low tins with it; fills it with the various ingredients and plenty of pepper, salt, and some water, and then covers it with a thin disc of paste perforated with holes, and adorned with fantastic images of reindeer and birds. Now the pie is ready for the oven – which all this time John has been stoking indefatigably with arm-loads of wood; and when he announces that the oven is fit the pie is borne in solemn procession to it, and safely enclosed by the sod which acts as the oven door, and conceals it from our gaze for a time, which varies according to the size of the pie and heat of the oven.

We have some difficulties to contend with in the top of our oven, for the sods which fill in the holes thereof are liable to crumble with the intense heat

The Colony at Breakfast in Memurudalen.

and fall down in fine dust on our food gently stewing in its cosy nest. The only way to obviate this is to water the top of the oven every morning as if it were a spring garden, and then the clods never get dry enough to play their evil little games. The Skipper compares the baking of a pie to burial by cremation (if that is not a bull). Certainly it always comes out etherealised; a thing of beauty and a joy for at least two days. Esau called this pie after its resurrection 'a harmony in yellow and brown quite too too utter and distinctly precious;' and John added, 'Begorra, me jewel, it is that same, bedad.

We shall now be free to do what seems good in our eyes for several days without the trouble of baking: altogether our stock of provisions is enormous. This is always the way in camp life; first a week of existence on the verge of starvation, and then a time of milk and honey and tables overflowing with plenty.

August 19. – Some of the bread that John makes is rather heavy. Yesterday we were constrained to point this fact out to him. He pretended not to be able to see it, and in support of his theory ate at supper a quantity of the rolls that we had condemned. The consequence was that about two o'clock A.M. we were roused from our peaceful slumbers by John jumping spasmodically out of bed and rushing to the tent door, uttering at the same time most ghastly yells. At the door he appeared to be awake, so we said, sitting up in bed with our hair on end,–

'*Now* then, John. What's the row?' To which he answered very quietly,–

'Why, my line's caught on that rock over there. I wish you would stop the boat a minute.'

Then he went gently to bed again and continued his unbroken slumbers.

A sleeping man is selfishly regardless of the disquiet he brings on his fellow-creatures, and John, although he must have dreamt all sorts of funny things, did not dream that he was disturbing our night's rest.

The other night when we were returning from our visit to Rus Vand, John casually seated himself on a rock at the extreme top of the mountain. It was quite dark except for a subdued glow of light caused by the setting moon behind the mountains on the other side of Gjendin Lake. Now the Skipper and Esau take a good deal of interest in moons, because they are considerably affected by the pallid luminary when at the full; consequently they were aware that she had already passed her highest point for that night, and would not show above the peaks until the following evening; but John did not know this, and so when we asked his reason for sitting down on a very sharp and cold stone 5000 feet above sea level, with the quicksilver right through the bottom of the thermometer, at a time when all honest folk were in bed, he replied, –

'You fellows go on; I'm going to wait here and see the moon rise.'

We never disturb a man when he feels poetical, lest it should break out in some more dangerous form; so we left him on his 'cold grey stone,' and made the best of our way to camp.

When we had about half finished our soup, he came struggling and wading in through the shrubs and swamps, and sat down to supper without making any remarks about the scenery, neither did he touch upon the subject of silver shafts, or shimmering sheen, or a network of frosted filigree chaining down the ripples. He was evidently disappointed about something, and we possessed too much delicacy of feeling to ask what was wrong, and so the matter dropped. But at breakfast this morning the Skipper happened to tell a story about a man he knew, who waited on the quay for some friends who had arrived in a steamer that day. This man had ordered a sumptuous banquet directly the steamer was signalled, then waited three hours expecting a boat to come off every minute, but at last perceived that a curious flag was flying on the steamer, and on inquiry found that she was quarantined for a fort-night. Then Esau could not resist the opportunity, and remarked, –

'Just like waiting for the moon to rise when she ain't due over the mountains for twenty-four hours,' and the harmony of the meeting at once ceased to exist.

The Skipper went after deer, but only had a very long walk without seeing any. We have now got the kitchen into a great state of perfection, so that with-in ten minutes of his return a recherché repast was on the table. This is rather a difficult thing to mana-ge, as we never know to within a couple of hours what time the hunters will return; but it can be done by having the chops, steaks, or birds ready in one frying-pan, the trout in the other, the potatoes partially cooked, and the tea or coffee made: the leaves or grounds of the latter we remove always after eight minutes' brewing, so that it does not alter by standing. The table of course is ready laid.

Once and only once there was a long delay, owing to a misfortune with the water that had been boiled for the tea; but the explosion of wrath from the famishing hunter on that occasion was so dreadful, that the utmost endeavours have since been successfully used to prevent its recurrence.

MENU. – August 19

Potage.

Mulligawny.

Poisson.

Truite à la Maître d'Hôtel.

Entrées.

Venison Pie.

Rôts.

Venison Pie.

Gibier.

Venison Pie.

Entremets.

Pancakes.

Our procedure with pancakes is for every man to fry and toss his own; the frying of the first side is easy enough, but the tossing requires skill, for we do not allow the mean practice of helping the delicacy over with a knife, indulged in by some weak-spirited cooks.

John's first became a mangled heap of batter under his repeated efforts, and was finally eaten by him in that condition; his second ascended towards the heavens most gracefully when he tossed, and was absent for some minutes, but unfortunately he failed to hold the pan in the right place on its return, and it fell on the ground, where it was immediately seized and devoured by Ivar. The third was a complete success, and so were the fourth, fifth, sixth, and seventh; the eighth stuck to the pan, and was a failure; and after that he got along all right to the thirty-fourth, when he had another partial failure, owing to over-confidence. This made him more careful, and all the rest were quite perfect. When we had finished we gave the rest of the batter to the men, who fried it all in one huge pancake, about two inches thick.

We notice that all the diaries agree for once; the following note occurs in all: –

'Pancakes for dinner to-day; the other two fellows over-ate themselves.'

We told John this morning of his adventure with the boat and fishing line during the night, so he ate all the new bread at lunch, thereby laying its restless spirit long before bedtime; no doubt he and his dinner will slumber more peacefully to-night.

It may be remembered that we brought a lot of fish slightly salted with us from Gjendesheim. Ever since our return here we have caught plenty of fish every day, and as we prefer fresh food to salt, the Gjendesheim fish which were placed in a little barrel have been neglected. Five or six days ago we noticed an unpleasant odour, and found that it proceeded from this barrel, the fish being in an advanced stage of decomposition, and the men told us they were making 'raki fiske,' a thing which they informed us in Norwegian is 'real jam.' We were very angry, and gave orders that the whole thing should at once be thrown into the glacier torrent. After this the affair faded from our minds, but yesterday we again noticed a suspicion of the same smell, and this morning it was so powerful that we began to invent theories to account for it.

John, who is a man of great scientific attainments, proved to his own complete satisfaction that it proceeded from the bodies of prehistoric reindeer which had been engulfed by an avalanche ages ago and entombed in the glacier until now, when at last their decaying corpses were being washed down the stream.

He said Huxley had often observed the same thing and told him about it.

Esau's theory was that the glacier itself was decomposing. 'Look what a long time it had been standing exposed to the air, and most likely in a damp place; everybody knew that snow water was not good to drink, witness the goitre of Switzerland; and why was it not good? Simply because it was putrid, and now that the hot sun was shining upon it, no wonder it smelt a little.'

He concluded his remarks by inquiring who Huxley might be, and was just setting off up the valley with a bottle of Condy's fluid to pour over the glacier, when the Skipper, who had wandered down to the Memurua River instead of arguing, suddenly rushed back with his fingers tightly holding his nose, and shaking his fist at Öla, said something that began with 'Dab,' and went on with other unknown words.

At last we gathered from his expressions that the barrel of 'raki fiske' had not been thrown into the torrent at all, but our villainous retainers had secreted it near the stream, intending to have a feast as soon as it should have become rotten enough to please their cultivated taste. Truly a Norwegian has the nastiest notions of food. Now the 'raki fiske,' barrel and all, is buried a yard deep, a long way from here, and life is again pleasant, but we have little doubt that Öla and Ivar will come back and root about and dig it up after we have left the country say a month hence: it ought to be in perfeet condition by that time.

CHAPTER XXI

FISHING.

August 20. – The first thing this morning we sent Öla to Gjendesheim with some venison for the people there, who have been very kind in sending milk, eggs, rice, onions, &c., to us. We have more meat than we shall be able to eat if the weather continues as fine and hot as it is at present.

We three walked over the mountain to spend the day at Rus Vand, taking our lunch with us. We got there about half-past ten, and the fish were then rising well, so we separated and commenced fishing, the Skipper and John taking the north side of the lake, Esau the south. After catching a few fish the rise stopped, as it always does on these lakes about midday.

There is no doubt that on a Norwegian lake the fisherman should above all things 'make haste while the fish rise.' It is all very well for the ancient sportsman to remark, 'Take your time, my young friend, there are as good fish in the sea as ever came out of it.' It is no doubt true enough; but at this time of year they will not rise to fly for more than about a couple of hours twice a day, and if you do not make the best of your opportunities then, where are you? Put yourself in the place of the fine old veteran three-pounder who has got into the habit of taking his meals at regular hours for fear of spoiling his digestion, and has selected the hours between 10 and 12 A.M. and 4.30 and 6.30 P.M., because he knows from long experience that these are the most likely times to find flies on the water. He has come in from roaming in deep waters to the shades of the

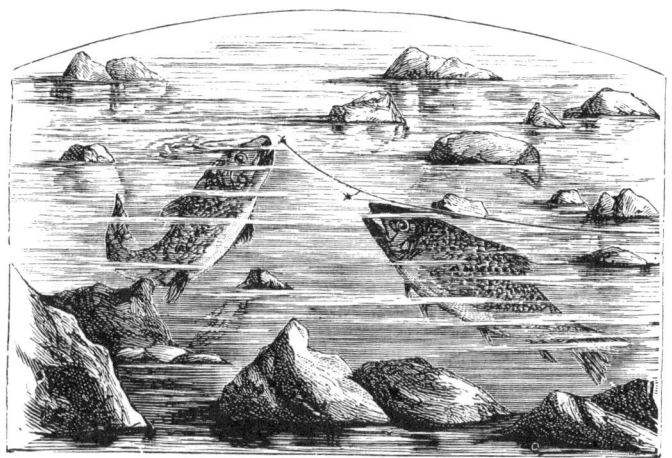

An Exciting Moment in Rus Lake Shallows.

rocky coast, and has a certain appetite to allay after his bath and morning stroll. There he waits, and thinks of old times, and of how fat and shiny his tummy became the last hot summer there was, when flies were plentiful, and he had not to resort to this abominable device of catching small trout and eating mice[1] to keep him in daily food, as he

1 We have found as many as three mice in the stomach of a Rus Vand trout.

nearly always has to do now that the summers are so wet, and he is no longer active enough to compete with his younger relations in the struggle for existence.

'What times those were, and how he wishes he were a year or two younger again, and not crippled with useless length; and, by George! now he comes to look at his reflection against that stone, he's getting quite yellow and bilious under the belly, and' — But he can't stop to moralise, there is a luscious March Brown of unusual solidity skating right over his pet rock, and he can't let it pass. So up he comes and gulps it down with a lazy flop of his tail that leaves quite a swirl on the lake surface. 'Why, the thing's got no flavour, and how I've hurt my jaw with it!' Poor old chap, his day is over, and after ten minutes' struggle he has left his favourite haunt to be occupied by another tenant, and is safe in the landing net, a good three-pound fish, but, like most of those who have reached this size, not quite in as good condition as he was at 2 1/2 lbs., and just a shade longer than he ought to be. Don't stop to gaze at him, put him in the bag with all speed – it is necessary to hurry up and fish on while the rise lasts.

But all this time the hours have been slipping away, and we have lunched, and smoked, and sketched till the rise began again soon after four; and though there was a strong cold west wind, the change seemed to encourage the fish to feed more greedily than usual, for trout are terrible Radicals, and rejoice in any alteration of the existing condition of things.

Our old experience of Rus Vand taught us that one side was sporting-looking and interesting, while the other was bleak and ugly; but Esau, who took the ugly side, had much the best of it to-day, as the place seemed alive with fish, and he kept catching them all the time, so that his little ten-foot rod was continually to be seen in the form of a hoop, from which position it reassumed the perpendicular in a way that reflects no little credit on Mr. Farlow.

When we met again at the end of the lake on our way home, we found that we had twenty fish, weighing just 44 lbs., of which Esau had caught fifteen weighing 32 1/2 lbs., the Skipper four of 9 lbs. weight, and John, who was very unlucky, only a single two-and-a-half-pounder. The smallest of the bag was a little over a pound, the largest three pounds, which was reached by more than one; and nearly all were caught in water so shallow that the dorsal fin of the fish was often visible in his mad rushes hither and thither; this made it extremely difficult to prevent the tail-fly being hung up on a rock whenever the fish was hooked on the dropper, and not a few were lost in this manner. All were caught on two patterns of fly, namely – No, philanthropy has limits, and no man can expect to be told patterns of flies. Go to Norway, and the time and trouble spent in acquiring that knowledge will be amply repaid by the pleasure that no one could fail to derive from a visit.

No doubt, with the usual discontentedness of man, we shall regret for ever that we did not all go to the ugly side of the lake, of which Esau was obli-

Esau's Best Day among the Trout.

ged to leave the best piece untouched as he came back, from sheer inability to carry any more fish over the rough ground. But the ways of fish are inscrutable: we hardly ever caught any number on that side before, and probably shall not do so again. It was just Esau's day. Kismet.

After weighing our catch, we cleaned them and cut off their heads to lighten them for the journey over Glopit, and even without this extra weight we were a good deal troubled and felt overburdened on the up-hill side, which is terribly steep and rough, only just practicable for a man on foot.

When we got back to camp we found that Öla had not returned from Gjendesheim, which caused us some sorrow, as Esau wanted to go out stalking on the morrow, and could not go alone. At least, he would be extremely unlikely to see any deer, for the reindeer being exactly the same colour as the mountains among which they live, it is almost impossible to see them before they see the enemy and depart hastily.

These native hunters are wonderful at the profession, and seem to know by instinct when they are in the vicinity of deer, as if they could feel their presence in the air. No doubt they really see indications that we should never observe, for they always begin to go cautiously, crouching and peering over rocks when deer are about, long before we amateurs are aware from the ordinary signs of footprints, nibbled reindeer flowers, or newly-moved stones, that there is likely to be any sport.

August 21. – It was cold and windy last night, so we turned into bed early and lay in luxurious comfort while John read out choice bits, all of which we know by heart, from the works of Mark Twain. We all think Mark Twain the best writer for camp life that has yet been discovered, and we have three or four of his books here. Besides these our library of light literature consists of Shakespeare, Longfellow, Dr. Johnson's Table-talk, and novels by Whyte-Melville, Walford, and Thackeray. But Mark and William get more work than all the rest.

It is quite dark now during the night, and we have made a wooden chandelier out of a curiously

On the Top of Glopit. Returning from Rus Lake.

bent piece of birch wood, which holds two candles and hangs down from the ridge-pole by a string. In the daytime it is hoisted up to the roof, but at night we let it down till it swings about two feet above our heads as we lie in bed. This contrivance is capital for reading, and also affords considerable diversion to the last man into bed. The candles are just too high to be reached with a puff easily from a recumbent position, and yet we persistently try to blow them out without moving. Just as sleep is creeping over two of the wearied sportsmen, the last man begins blowing and cussing at these candles every night regularly. The scene is generally this. Skipper and John just dropping off to sleep. Esau lies down, makes himself extremely comfortable, and then − puff, whoo, whew, puff, − gasp for breath, rest a moment. Pouf. Chandelier swings round under the impulse of the strong wind thus created. Esau makes a brilliant flying shot at one candle, as it circles swiftly past. Skipper: 'Thank goodness.' Pause. Esau: Poof, whoo, whoof. John: 'Dash it all, get up and put it out.' Esau: 'Get up yourself.' Skipper: 'Let me blow it out. Potif, puff, whoosh.' Chandelier swings madly round, drops grease on John's nose. John: 'Tare an 'ouns.' Throws tobacco pouch at it, more grease all over the place, tobacco pouch rebounds from tent into Esau's mouth. Recrimination for five minutes. Chandelier at last stationary. Everybody at once: 'Puff, boo, pouf, whew, — it, — it, pouf, — it, — the — thing, – pouf. Thank goodness;' and we all turn over with a sigh of relief, to repeat the performance the following night.

Öla not having turned up, there could be no stalking, so the beautiful morning was wasted. The Skipper got so angry about it that he said he would go in his canoe to find the absentee, and take at the same time a lot of our surplus fish for the people at Gjendesheim.

Leaving the tent on its grassy sunlit lawn he walked down to the edge of the great lake, and turning over the smaller of the two canoes, which were lying bottom uppermost, launched her and got in with rod and fishing bag, and pushed off into the deep. Opposite to the place where the canoes were drawn up, and apparently only a hundred yards distant though really more than a mile away, were the snow-capped mountain steeps that rise almost perpendicularly from two to three thousand feet out of the lake; and for these he made, gradually becoming a mere twinkling speck till he faded out of sight from the tent. The lake was as smooth as glass, only occasionally rippled as some monarch of the deep, excited for once in his life by some specially fascinating fly, condescended to make a rush for it instead of the gentle suck by which he usually took his food, and the Skipper paddled leisurely along within twenty yards of the rocks, with his rod bending over the stern, and trailing behind a couple of flies in the hope of catching a trout without the trouble of angling for him.

It is very pleasant to be alone once in a way in this overcrowded world. Not alone as it is possible to be in England, but absolutely alone, with no living thing near except the trout, the insects, and one's image in the water. Oh, blessed Norway! when we get back to the turmoils, troubles, and pleasures of a London season how we shall long for you! There is only one word to express this existence, and that is Freedom – freedom from care, freedom from resistance, and from the struggle for life. What a country! where civilised man can relapse as much as seems good to him into his natural state, and retrograde a hundred generations into his primeval condition.

But we forget that the Skipper is coasting up towards Gjendesheim in search of the miscreant Öla.

He procceded for a couple of hours, catching a few fish now and then, but presently, as midday approached, the sun became too hot to be pleasant, the fish would not move, and the Skipper began to get impatient and annoyed at not meeting Öla. After a while a black speck with two flashing arms appeared rounding a promontory; this was Öla in the boat. The Skipper was boiling with rage under the influence of various incentives as he approached. Öla, like most Norwegians, was calm, placid, and utterly unconscious of the flight of time and the shortness of life. The Skipper had been primed to exploding point by his two friends before starting, and as he had now paddled five miles from home without meeting the adversary, he was, to put it mildly, 'indignant.' So, when he found Öla smoking serenely, and sculling along as though his brief span were going to stretch through the unending cycles of eternity, he gave way to the most horrible outbreak of temper in English, which must have

lasted four or five minutes, and then telling the cai-
tiff in Norwegian to take the fish to Gjendesheim
and return to camp by five o'clock whatever the
weather might be, he turned and left that hardy
Norseman open-mouthed and bewildered, looking
as though he had seen the Strömkarl, or had had an
interview with his mother-in-law.

Then a great wind arose, and blew against the
Skipper all the way home, but he arrived in the
most beatific frame of mind in spite of it; the relief
of the storm of temper and bad language had been
so great to him, that he was filled with a blessed joy.
He said it was the most invigorating and refreshing
pastime he ever indulged in, for Öla could not
understand a word of it, and therefore no remorse
could follow the outburst, not a thoughtless expression or hasty word could go home to his heart and
there rankle, to recoil on some future occasion, but
the whole vial of pent-up wrath could be emptied
on its object without fear of retribution.

The explosion must have been something very
fine to enable the Skipper to make light of the
headwind, for a wind on Gjendin is not to be scof-
fed at in any boat, and least of all in a cockle-shell
of a canoe. The mountains are so high and steep
that the lake lies as it were in a trench, and any wind
always draws straight up or down the length, and
soon gets a big sea up. All the Norwegians we have
seen say it is the height of madness to go on Gjendin
at all in such boats, the sudden squalls are so dangerous; and neither of our men can be persuaded to go
a yard in them.

Esau and John, for want of better employment, after fishing a little, began to bake, and had laid out a goodly show of dainty confections, two dozen rolls, four wimberry tarts, a lot of biscuits, and a venison pie of the ordinary size (9 inches diameter). When the Skipper returned it was decided to make another, as we imagine the meat has a better chance of keeping when hoarded up in pies than when left in its raw state.

So we each took our usual share in the construction of a PIE, before which all other pies should be as nought.

It was made in our largest baking tin, 12 inches across, and contained nearly a hind quarter of venison, our last six eggs, a heart, a liver, and about 1 1/2 lb. of bacon. The crust was put on about nine o'clock, and after we had all gazed at it and unanimously agreed that it was the 'boss pie,' we bore it proudly but gingerly to the oven, heated by John seven times hotter than before, and now gaping to receive it; a great full moon rose up from behind the mountains and seemed to smile on our good work; the bright fire shed a red glow over the three figures bending o'er the simmering treasure, and a more peaceful, domestic group it would be impossible to conceive.

About eleven John and the Skipper turned in, but outside could be seen for some time the solitary form of Esau still crouching over the expiring embers of the oven, and tending with a mother's care the tempting food that he already tasted in imagination.

Baking by Night in Memurudalen.

Most of the berries of the country are now just at their best, and Memurudalen is a grand valley for all of them, except of course the strawberry and raspberry, which will not grow at this altitude. But we have 'klarkling' (the English crowberry) in great abundance; blau bær (wimberry), the finest and best ever seen, in quantities; also 'skin tukt,' another blue berry rather larger than a wimberry, and with a thicker skin and wonderful bloom on it; this we think does not grow in England. Then less numerous are a berry something between a raspberry and a red currant, but of better flavour than either of them; and the great and glorious 'mölte bær' (cloudberry); to say nothing of 'heste bær,' and 'tutti bær,' and several others of unknown names. The last one grows in England, but we have forgotten its name; they make jelly from it here, and prize it highly for its acid taste.

CHAPTER XXII.

MEMURUDALEN.

Sunday, August 22. – We woke up this morning with a bright sun shining through the canvas of the tent, and making it intolerably hot inside; and as we threw open the door of the inner compartment, the fragrant aroma of the 'boss pie' was wafted to us on the morning air.

We spent the morning in quiet Sunday fashion, chiefly in lying under the shade of an awning made with rugs which we call the 'sycamine tree,' and eating wimberries and cream. Besides this we perpetrated a great deal of high art; every one was seized with the desire of sketching the camp, and so we sat around on pinnacles like so many pelicans, libelling the unfortunate place from every position whence it could be seen.

It is looking very comfortable just now. The tent itself is pitched in an angle of a steep little cliff which effectually protects it from cold winds at one side and the back, and at the other side we have put up a thick fence of birch branches to temper the storm to the sleeping-tent. We find it very convenient to have the two compartments: the inner one is only used for sleeping in, and always immediately after reveillé is plunged in an apparently hopeless

196

confusion of rugs, sheepskins, mattresses, and boots, with here and there a book or a hat protruding (to use the Skipper's beautiful simile) like brickbats in a dust-heap. After breakfast all the bedding is dragged out to be aired on the rocks, and the tent generally tidied.

But the outer tent is always a picture of order and neatness, for here we keep our stores, boxes of flour and biscuits, cartridges, cooking utensils, tools, whisky, and potatoes. One of the boxes was made specially under Esau's directions to be used as a table: the top and bottom are both hinged, and so when the box is put on its front and these two lids opened it makes a very good large table; the lids are held up by a batten screwed underneath them, and for greater security we have added two legs. But at present the weather is so pleasant that we always feed outside, a few yards from the tent and nearer to the oven.

On the extreme left, as the penny showman says, you will observe one of the meat safes, the other one 'thou canst not see, because it's not in sight,' being close to the back of the tent. Also behind the tent may be faintly seen the mustard and cress garden, always covered with a sheet by day to save it from the heat of the sun, and with the same sheet by night, to guard it from the cold, so that the poor thing never gets any light, and does not flourish very exceedingly. None of the mustard seeds have as yet grown up as big as the one in the parable, but when one does we mean to make a lot of salad out of it, enough for all the camp.

The Camp in Memurudalen.

Above the middle of the outer tent are three things which look like lightning conductors, but are only our rods, which are always stuck in the ground there when not in use. At their foot under the rock is the egg larder, neatly constructed of stones and turf, with a wooden lid; and hanging from the cliff hard by is a very pretty and curious spider's nest made of paper, like a miniature wasp-nest, about two inches in diameter.

High up in the centre is 'the meteor flag of England' engaged in its customary occupation of 'yet terrific burning,' there being absolutely no Dutch Boers here. Underneath its shelter are many forked poles with cross-bars, all made from the birch with which the valley abounds just here, and on which clothing of some sort is always hanging out to dry; so that the place looks like a laundry-ground, and deceives even the ravens, which come down in swarms from the mountains in search of maids' noses to devour. In the midst of these poles may be seen the oven, with its flue reaching half-way up the hill, and its two openings, the lower one for fuel, the upper for food.

Right in front of the tent is the fireplace, a long trench in the ground, faced with stones of such a size and shape that they form apertures suitable for our numerous pans; and simmering by the fire is the perennial soup. Nearer to the front is the wood pile, and nearer still the board on which the cooking things are placed after washing up. In front again of this is the little stream which supplies us with water, now rapidly beginning to fail under the influence of the long drought: it may be noticed that the engineers have changed its course in several places for greater convenience in getting water, and to give more room on the camp side.

The foreground is a mass of juniper, wimberries, skintukt, crowberries, and rocks, and then comes about thirty yards from the tent the Memurua torrent, all thick and milky from the glacier, cold as Christmas, fishless, uninteresting, not drinkable, only useful as a refrigerator for milk, and only agreeable to look upon from a distance, but faithfully keeping up the unceasing roar that is customary among such torrents. This river makes the waters of the lake too cold to bathe in and too cheerless for fish to abide in near our camp, but it does not come into the picture, partly because it runs in a ravine, but more because it was right behind the artist.

The lake itself is to the extreme right, with unclimbable snow-capped rocky mountains forming the opposite coast.

To-day we dined at 4 P.M. in order to get an uninterrupted evening's fishing, but the experiment was not a success and will not be repeated, for it spoilt the dinner and we caught no fish. On returning to camp at night rather cold, very cross, and exceedingly hungry, we agreed that the best antidote for these dangerous symptoms would be hot soup, so John put the pot on the fire, while the Skipper and Esau were attending to the tent and domestic duties.

Soon the caldron was heated and brought into the tent, and the eager crowd drew near with cups and spoons, and one lifted the lid, while another plunged his cup into the steaming savoury mess. And then arose a great cry of horror and desolation, and the sleeping valley rang with the wail of men in despair, for John had put the wrong pot on the fire, and we had been presented with boiling dirty water in which the dinner-things had been washed up; while all the time the soup pot was quiet, un-touched, and cold in the corner of the tent where it is kept.

But three hungry men are not to be balked of a meal on which their hearts are set by any trifle like this, so we all commenced with a will to stoke that fire up and put that other pot on, and we got our soup and were snugly packed in bed long before the gentle August moon had sunk to rest behind the sheltering mountain tops.

The Skipper, by the way, is very much exaspera-ted with this same moon just now. He says she is a fraud, for this morning when we got up, there she was high in the heavens.

'What right,' he wants to know, 'has this moon – any moon, in fact – to be up there blinking away in the middle of the day when we have plenty of sun to light us? forward, dissipated thing! and then pro-bably after this week we shall have ever so many nights without any moon at all, and all the earth left in total darkness to take care of itself; while here we are to-day with an absurdly round moon at one end of this comparatively diminutive valley, and a most extravagantly blazing sun at the other.' The whole thing is ridiculous, he says, and it must be confessed that there is some justice in his complaint; though no doubt there could be a good deal said on the other side.

August 23. – While Esau went out after deer the other two crawled up the mountain and over to Rus Vand to fish, and had a good day. Two of the Skipper's fish were three pounds each, but, like most of the biggest fish, not in that beautiful condition which the smaller ones always show. The Skipper is sure that the old worn-out fish creep up to the stony shallows at the western end of the lake to die in a sunny spot, just as we men creep away in our old age to Bath, Cheltenham, Cannes, or Algiers, to breathe our last in a warm place, thereby taking one step in the direction of the proverbial future.

Esau arrived in camp about half-past seven quite exhausted, and followed by Öla, also dead beat, and again bearing the heads and skins of two deer, a buck and a doe. He was hailed with fervent joy and many congratulations: it is certainly great luck to fall in with deer on two stalking days in succession, for they are by no means numerous here this year. Dinner was served in a marvellously short time.

MENU. – August 23.

Poisson.
Truite à la Fried in Butter.

Entrées.
Kari of Reindeer Tongue.

Rôts.
The Boss Pie.

202

Gibier.

Ryper à la Spitchcock.

Entremets.

Jam. Wimberry tart. Marmalade.

Potage.

Could not eat any.

Then came Esau's romance.

'We walked up the Memurua to the great glacier, and then skirted its south side. We found many fresh tracks, and about two o'clock, when we were seven miles from home, Öla spied three deer chewing stones about three-quarters of a mile away. The wind was just in the right direction to allow us to approach them, and they were in capital ground for stalking, full of little hollows and slopes. But there was a serious drawback: on one side was a lake, on the other an impassable precipice; and before we could get into a place out of their sight we should be obliged to cross a narrow strip of ground in full view of them, though perhaps half a mile from them. We sat down and had our lunch, and waited an hour watching for them to lie down, and at last they did so; then we determined to risk the passage of the dangerous strip, and by crawling like serpents and aided by luck got across without the deer seeing us. Then we had to creep along the side of a scandalous precipice for the next half-mile, in no danger of being seen, but with our hearts constantly in our mouths, as, despite our care, some stone was dislodged and went clattering down the rocks, sounding to my strained ears as if it must disturb every living thing within a mile. Very slow and difficult was our progress, occasionally dangerous, but at last we arrived at a Spot 200 yards from the deer, which were still lying down, and pronounced by Öla to be a buck and two does.

'This was a very awkward place to shoot from, and I thought I could see my way to a better one much nearer, so tried it and found it was just pos-

Esau Stalking near Hinaakjærnhullet.

sible, and after about a quarter of an hour's worming, I arrived at a place only 100 yards from them. From this I could see both the does well, but only the head of the buck, and so had to lie there an hour waiting for him to get up. Both the does did so twice, offering beautiful shots, but he would not

move, and they lay down again. I dared not whistle to make him jump up, for fear the does might
possibly be in the way at the moment. So there I
lay, miserably uncomfortable, with cramp in every
muscle; and at last I tried to crawl to another stone
about five yards away, from which I thought I could
see to shoot at the buck. When I got to it and pee-
red cautiously over, I was horrified to see the deer
some distance away, and running as hard as they
could towards a small glacier which was close to
them.

'Of course I instantly lost my head, and jumping
up fired at the buck without much aim, and missed
him. Then I recovered my senses and made a careful shot at the last doe, knocking her over like a rabbit. The other two were just then out of sight in a
hollow, but they appeared directly going up the hill
on the snow at a great speed; and getting a broadside shot at the buck I broke his shoulder ; after this
he went slowly, but still kept on up the hill, and
when he was about three hundred yards away I
fired two more shots, one of which hit him in the
ribs, and the other cut one of his horns off. Then he
gave up trying to mount the hill, and turned down
towards the lake out of my sight. I ran as hard as I
could across the shoulder of the glacier, and saw
him standing down below me among the rocks
close to the water, and sitting down I fired another
shot which killed him.

'This is not a creditable performance in the
shooting line; but my solid bullets have a good deal
to do with the matter: either of the first two shots

would have stopped him at once if fired from an express with hollow-pointed bullets.

'The doe is a barren one with a beautiful skin, and very fat, and the buck is the best we have killed at present this year, a four-year-old, what Ola calls a "litt stor bock" (little big buck), which I suppose is the next best thing to the mythical "meget stor bock," whose footprints we are always seeing, but who carefully absenteth himself whensoever the jovial hunter goeth forth to pursue him.

'We saw a great deal of fresh spoor to-day, so that we may hope the deer are beginning to come to our part of the country: perhaps the poor things have been very much bullied in other places. Anyhow, they won't find any better country in Norway than where we went to-day; and the scenery there is glorious.'

Esau was so tired that he fell asleep once in the midst of his exciting narrative, and as dinner was very late we all turned in almost as soon as it was finished.

CHAPTER XXIII.

A PICNIC.

August 24. – There is a brood of ryper on the brow
of the mountain above our camp, which we always
put up when we walk over Glopit armed with rods,
but never when we take a gun. There were originally eight of them, but one has succumbed to a
merlin which hunts up there; and they are remarkably tame, so that when we put them up we throw
stones at them, and fully expect to kill them by that
means, but somehow they have escaped with their
lives until now. This conduct has become unbear-
able, and we have sworn 'this day that brood shall
die;' so the first thing after breakfast Esau and the
Skipper toiled up the mountain with pockets full of
cartridges and guns ready for the slaughter of the
innocents. It takes just three-quarters of an hour to
get to the top; and after reaching it we tramped over
some millions of acres in search of that brood, and
of course it never obtruded itself on the scene.
Finally the Skipper went home in disgust, remar-
king that 'he wished every ryper in Norway was at
the bottom of Gjendin;' while Esau said 'he would
stay up there a month or two and find those birds if
they were anywhere on our sheet of the Ordnance
map.'

The Skipper had hardly walked 200 yards towards camp before he trod on the old cock, who got up observing kek! kek! kekkekkek*kek*, kurrack: kur*rack*; kurrack, krackrackackekkkkk! in an extremely indignant tone of voice, and the rest of the family immediately followed him, astonishing the Skipper so much that he missed the lot; and though we marked them down quite near we could not persuade any of them to risk their lives in flight again.

The language used on this occasion scorched the herbage off so large a patch of ground, that John down below thought that Glopit had suddenly commenced a volcanic eruption.

There are two kinds of birds known as ryper in Norway – the fjeld or skarv ryper, which is, we think, identical with our ptarmigan; and the dal or skog ryper, which we believe to be the same bird as the willow grouse of North America. The former of these is not numerous anywhere, but a few are always seen by the reindeer hunter up on the highest parts of the mountains, among the snow and rocks. They do not attempt much concealment, but their grey bodies and white wings are so exactly the colour of their habitation that it is very difficult to see them, as they sit perfectly still on the stones. If you do happen to catch sight of one, in all probability after looking at him for a little you will suddenly be aware that there is a small family of others all about him, and will wonder how they escaped your notice at first. They are not very useful for sporting purposes, as they are never found in great numbers,

are too tame to give any trouble, and not particularly good to eat. The skog ryper is the bird which
takes the place of the British grouse for the sportsman in Norway: he lives at a lower altitude than the
skarv ryper, among the willows, wimberries, and
stunted birches. In plumage he is not unlike our
grouse, but not quite so red in shade, and with a
white wing. During the summer he feeds on wimberry leaves, heather, and occasional bits of willow,
and he is then almost if not quite equal to a grouse
in flavour, but in winter, when there is nothing but
willow to be had, the flesh becomes bitter and not
nice to eat: the poor birds are then snared in great
numbers, and may be seen hanging in English shops
as 'ptarmigan,' which with their then white plumage they much resemble. After a good breeding season these skog ryper are very numerous in any
favourable place in Norway, but they are so much
inclined to lie close, that without dogs it is impossible to do much with them. Gjendin is too steep
and desolate for them, but between the east end of
the lake and Sjödals Vand there is some first-rate
country, and also a little at the west end.

After lunch we all manned Esau's canoe, which is
the largest, because he is the smallest man; and set
off down the lake to Leirungsö, the place where the
professor's hut is built at the edge of the waterfall
which runs out of a small lake there (not the real
Leirung's Vand, which is further to the east).

The Skipper had noticed a remarkably fine bed of
mölte bær there, which we expected to be just
about ripe now, and so we had determined to pic-

nic (!) there, forsooth, as if our life were not one perpetual and perennial picnic.

Leirungsö is nearly four miles from our camp, and the professor's hut is an extremely comfortable and convenient little dwelling, in a most charming situation. Only one thing has been wanting, reindeer: he never found any, and left his hut a fortnight ago for a place further north, where we afterwards heard he had good sport.

After landing, the Skipper and Esau climbed up the valley to the little lake in search of something to shoot, while John remained to bathe and fish at the fall. There were lots of duck on the little lake, and in the rushy swamp at its upper end, and the Skipper put up a large brood of ryper, which we marked into a very small patch of willow scrub surrounded by bare ground. We walked through and through that patch, and threw so many stones into it that we fancy we must have killed and buried most of them, for we only persuaded four of them to fly again, three of which we secured. Our shooting was soon over, and then we gathered a lot of mölte bær, and returned to John, who was getting dinner ready; and after a regal repast of kidneys, reindeer pie, and mölte, paddled home by moonlight, arriving soon after nine.

We beguiled the journey home by songs and accompaniments by the following celebrated artists: Messrs. John, Skipper, and Esau. Among other songs was an original composition by John – air 'Bonnie Dundee' –

A Picnic

ODE TO THE LAST POT OF MARMALADE.

To the fishers of Gjendin the bold Skipper spoke:
'There is one two-pound pot that as yet is unbroke[1]
So rouse ve, my gallants, and after our tea
Let us "go for" our Keiller's[2] own Bonnie Dundee.'

(*Chorus.*) Come! up with the Smör![3] Come! out with the Brod,[4]
      We'll have one more Spise[5] that's fit for a god;
      Come, whip off the paper and let it gae free,
      And we'll wade into Keiller's own Bonnie Dundee.

You may talk of your mölte[6] with sugar and milk,
Your blueberry pasties, and jam of that ilk;
They are all very well in the wilds, don't you see?
But they can't hold a candle to Bonnie Dundee.
                  Chorus as before.

Oh! the pies they were good, and the oven baked true,
With its door of green sod, and its sinuous flue.
Oh! the curry was toothsome as curry can be,
But where is the equal of Bonnie Dundee?
              Chorus again, gentlemen.

There are ryper on Glopit[7] as fleet as the wind,
And the Stor[8] Bock roams on the Skagastolstind;
There are trout, teal, and woodcock, a sight for to see,
But what meal can be perfect
without our Dundee?
                Chorus, if you please.

Pandecãgos[9] are tasty, and omelettes are good;
Our eggs, though antique, not unsuited for food;
You can always be sure of at least one in three,
But blue mould cannot ruin our Bonnie Dundee.
               Chorus, only more so.

Take[10] my soup, though 'tis luscious, my öl,[11] though 'tis rare,
My whisky, though scanty, beyond all compare;
Take my baccy, take all that is dearest to me,
But leave me one spoonful of Bonnie Dundee.
                   Chorus ad lib.

211

Esau supplied an encore verse: –

It has made our lot brighter, and helped us to bear
Our troubles, the rain, mist, and cold northern air;
And the Gjende fly,[12] green fly,[13] bug,[14] skeeter,[15] and flea,
We should ne'er have *done Deeing* them but for Dundee.

Chorus (of big, big D's).

NOTES ON THE ABOVE COMPOSITION.

1 'Unbroke.' This is bold poetic imagery, meaning unopened. Break-ages were unknown during our expedition, and long experience justifies us in assuring the world that breaking the pot, though an effectual way of getting at the marmalade, is not a satisfactory method. It will be found much better to remove the bladder at the top. This may be depended on.

2 Need we explain that 'Keiller's own Bonnie Dundee' alludes to the marmalade made by that great and good man? No, a thousand times no!

3 'Smör,' Norwegian butter, pronounced Smoeurr – and it tastes like that, too.

4 'Brod,' bread. The word does not rhyme to god, being pronounced something like Broat, but it looks as if it rhymed.

5 'Spise,' a meal, pronounced Speessa.

6 'Mölte,' cloudberry, pronounced Moulta.

7 'Glopit,' the mountain between Gjendin and Rus Vand.

8 'Stor,' big, pronounced Stora before a consonant.

9 'Pandecágos,' pancakes.

10 'Take.' This word is only used by poetic license, and must not be construed literally. When we attempted to 'take' John's whisky on our return to camp, there was a good deal of ill-feeling engendered, and he said that no one but himself understood the subtleties of æsthetic metaphor.

11 'Öl,' the ale of the country, 'rare' both in quality and, alas! in quantity.

12 'Gjende fly,' a fly peculiar to this lake, of which more anon.

13 'Green fly,' a charming creature like a large grey blue-bottle with green eyes; it bites a portion of flesh sufficient for its wants, and then goes away to eat it.

14 'Bag.' Again poetic license. *Cimex lectularius* has not been encountered during our stay in Norway this time; nevertheless he is not un-

212

known in the country, as the sojourners in one of the Lillehammer hotels, not the Victoria, can testify.

15 'Skeeter.' The mosquito is a mournful and disgraceful fact; and so are the sand-fly, the stomoxys, and the flea. Memurudalen is more free from insects than any place we have tried.

August 25. – Still the same glorious weather, rather too glorious for our purling rivulet, which has now dwindled away to a mere thread of water, while even the larger stream on the hill behind the tent, which we use for bathing, is showing a marked decrease in volume.

The Skipper and Öla went out stalking directly after breakfast, and Esau climbed up on to Bes Hö to shoot ryper. John went over to Rus Vand to fish, and had a pleasant day. He managed somehow to drop his native 'tolle kniv' into the lake, and of course immediately discovered that that knife was the most precious thing he possessed, in fact, the only thing he cared about in this world; though until it fell into the lake, he had regarded it with very unenthusiastic feelings – feelings of tolle-ration, the Skipper said. So he undressed and dived for it for a long time, and at last was lucky enough to recover it.

It would have been a pleasing sight to a spectator, if any could have been present, to watch John playing at being a seal all by himself in Rus Vand, or standing on a rock poised on one leg like a heron, with his head sideways and keen eye piercing the cerulean wave. And it was good to see his proud bearing as he returned to camp with the 'tolle kniv' slung jauntily at his waist, and carrying over his shoulder the scaly spoil snatched from the vasty deep, as we used beautifully to word it in Latin verses – meaning the fish he had caught.

John Diving for his Knife in Rus Lake.

At 8 P.M. the Skipper had not returned, so we dined, and then sat round the fire wondering what could have happened to delay him; and as time went on and still he never came, we began to get very uneasy; there are so many dangers by which the reindeer hunter may be overtaken – avalanches, crevasses, fogs, snowdrifts, broken limbs, or getting lost. We could only hope that none of these had happened to the Skipper, and at eleven o'clock gave up any hopes of his return that night and turned in, there being then a very decided fog a short way up the Memurua valley.

CHAPTER XXIV

THE SKIPPER'S RETURN.

August 26. – At breakfast-time the drover who had accompanied us to shoot ryper at Gjendebod arrived here on his way towards lower and more genial regions for the winter. We always feel that we are killing more game than we really need, and here was an outlet for our superfluous meat, so we gave him half a deer, and he went homewards rejoicing greatly.

We had sent Ivar up to the drover's den in Memurudalen at daybreak to see if our missing ones had found their way to it and spent the night there, but he now came back without having found any traces of them. However, under the cheering influence of the morning sun we soon became resigned to their fate, and Esau so far regained his spirits that he crossed the glacier torrent with a gun, and penetrated the birchwood on the other side, to what he called 'shoot the home coverts.' He presently brought back a woodcock, which had got up about fourteen times before he killed it, and each time he had thought it was a fresh cock, so that he had had a regular sporting morning after it, 'seeing lots of cock get up, shooting at two, and killing one of them,' the wood being so thick that it was almost impossible to get even the snappiest of snap-shots at the agile bird.

Esau then busied himself with the construction of a rack to hold all our guns and spare rods, cleaning rod, &c., with a shelf near the bottom for books, and another one whereon each man might keep his little valuables, such as pipes and watch, fly-books and reels. This contrivance was chiefly formed of birch boughs of peculiar shape, and when finished and placed in its proper position at the further end of the tent just behind our pillows, it presented a truly noble appearance.

Lunch-time passed, and still the Skipper had not returned, so we decided that he must be defunct, and proceeded to write his epitaph, preparatory to organising a search expedition to bring in his remains.

Here is one touching little poem:

> He was rather tall and terribly thin,
> But remarkably roomy inside;
> We put up these stones to cover his bones
> Near the place where we think he died.

This is another:

IN MEMURUHAMEREN
(HILLS ROUND THE CAMP).

> Our Skipper has gone, our great head cook,
> On a tour that e'en Cook won't find
> In a fissure he's surely taken his hook,
> Nor left any trace behind.

With a rod or pole he would fish for perch,
  Now a rod, pole, or perch of ground
Is more than he needs, and in vain we search,
  For his body will ne'er be found.

Now his angling is finished, though once every fin
  Which came within reach he'd attach;
He was really so clever at reeling them in,
  And his terms were to fish, 'nett catsh.'

On a lake or pond, or even a moat,
  He beamed wherever he went;
How cheerfully he would tar his boat!
  How gaily would pitch his tent!

After ryper or deer he would walk all day,
  From the top of a hill to the bottom;
And we feel it unpleasantly sad to say
  That the dear old Reaper's got him.

But we think it is time that this verse were done,
  Which to mournfully write we've tried
In memory o' our darlin' one,
  Who in Memurudalen died.

While we were still lingering over these beautiful and appropriate sentiments, and deliberating as to whether they should be cut on a stone or only on wood, the corpse suddenly walked into the tent and announced that he wanted something to eat. We soon got over our natural disappointment at the waste of a good epitaph, and really welcomed him quite warmly, much more so when Öla appeared laden with the tit-bits of a reindeer buck. Then we set food before the Skipper, and after he had feasted he related unto us his story.

'I left camp yesterday morning determined to beard the savage untamed reindeer of the mountains in his lair, and soon came on very fresh tracks, which we followed for some time, and at each step seemed to get "hotter," as the children say, and the indications of deer being near got more and more encouraging. However, by one o'clock we had seen nothing, so sat down behind a little rocky eminence to have our "spise." Mine was a particularly good lunch, as I had spread some gravy from the "boss pie" on my slice of bread and butter, and this with the icy cold snowwater was very grateful after a four hours' walk uphill under a scorching sun.

'Öla also seemed to devour his food with considerable relish. So we had been sitting there some time, happily silent, as we cannot talk each other's tongue, and I was just preparing to move on, and putting my knife back in its sheath, when we heard a slight snort quite close to us.

'Öla immediately peeped cautiously over an adjacent stone; then he pushed my rifle into my hand and whispering the magic word "Reins," pointed to another stone a few yards away, whither he wished me to crawl. To unsling my cartridge-bag lest it should jingle, and creep to that stone, was what the novelists call the work of a moment: then I raised my head *va-a-ry* gingerly, and saw forty yards away a single four-year-old buck standing broadside to me with his head in the air, sniffing suspiciously, and his whole attitude denoting uncertainty and caution. This buck, as we found out afterwards from the spoor, had walked up to within ten yards of us as we sat at lunch; then he must have either heard me or smelt Öla, probably the latter, for Öla seldom washes his hands, never his blood-stained hunting coat; and when I encountered his gaze he had evidently just decided that this was not a good place for reindeer to be about in. This was an excellent frame of mind on his part, but he arrived at it a couple of seconds too late: my rifle was levelled, and the shot hit him just above the heart. At that dis-

The Skipper about to Astonish the Reindeer.

tance the express bullet smashed a portion of him about as big as a hat, so that he rolled over stone dead, and had no time for lingering glances or last words. Half an hour more, and he was skinned, gralloched, put in a hole and buried under a heap of stones, to remain there until we need his flesh and send the horse to bring him home. Then we built a little cairn to mark his resting-place for future use, and wandered on in search of the rest of his party.

'Very soon we came on the tracks of four other deer, one of them only a calf, but although we followed the spoor all the afternoon we never came up with them: probably they were near enough to hear my shot when I fired, and at once betook themselves to remote regions.

Öla Performing the Funeral Rites.

'It had got so late before we gave up the search, and we were such a long way from home, that we determined to go to Gjendebod, at the western end of the lake, hoping to get a boat there and return to Memurudalen by water. But on arriving there very tired, hot, and hungry, we found that the men had taken their boat down the lake, and would not return until to-day. This was a great blow, for it is quite impossible to walk along the shores of Gjendin, except, as John says, for a bird – and even it would have to fly all the way. Climbing up the mountain again was out of the question, as it is a seven hours' walk from Gjendebod to our camp, so there was nothing for it but sleeping there – a course which was very distasteful to me, as the food is bad, and I had no book with me, no tobacco, no hair-brush, and no fishing-rod.

'To-day I started for home directly after breakfast. We wished to combine a little stalking with the walk, for we had to pass through some first-rate deer country – all that part, Esau, where you got your first two bucks; but of course we had not much chance of doing anything, as the wind was with us all the way. As you know, deer almost always feed up wind, so by walking against it you are safe from their ears and noses, and also are likely to be warned of their presence by coming on their tracks first. But in walking down wind all this is reversed; you come upon the deer without any warning, and they are almost sure to smell or hear you long before you discover them. Consequently, as we expected, we saw nothing on our way here to-day.'

The Skipper's buck is a very good one, the best that has been killed at present, and there was much joy at his change of luck. But strictly speaking his bad luck has pursued him even in this instance, for if he had not been obliged to shoot when he did, in all probability the rest of the herd would have appeared on the scene, for their tracks showed that they were following the lead of this buck. Besides, there is not the same excitement in a chance shot like this as there is when you first find the deer, and then spend two or three hours in all kinds of uncomfortable modes of progression in order to approach them.

However, when we were in this country before, the Skipper had all the good luck, and Esau the bad, the former getting five deer and the latter only two, so that the present state of affairs may be looked upon as the working of retributive justice. When this view of the matter was suggested by Esau to the Skipper, he said, 'Retributive justice be blowed!'

We celebrated the joyful reunion of loving hearts by a skaal, and so to bed, perfectly happy after the events of the day.

August 27. – We sent the men off this morning with the horse to bring in some of the meat now lying in the mountains, while we went by canoe to Gjendesheim to stay for a couple of days, as we cannot go stalking again till the already slain deer are brought home; the fish in the lake are not rising well after this long spell of fine weather, and with the exception of Esau's 'home coverts' there is no shooting for a fowling-piece at Memurudalen.

Very few tourists find their way to Gjendin, but the season for them is over, and we expected to have the place to ourselves; but how fallible is human prescience! To our astonishment the sportsmen from Rus Vand had already occupied the greater part of the house, having abandoned their own hut for the same reasons which had led us to forsake our camp, and here they were, armed to the teeth with rods and guns.

This seemed unlucky, and although we were outwardly glad to see them, at heart we could not help feeling how inconsiderate it was of them to come and shoot the fjeld and fish the river just when we wanted to do all that ourselves. No doubt they harboured precisely the same feelings towards us.

However, we had dinner together, and introduced the 'boss pie,' now rapidly disappearing, to the notice of our Norwegian friends, and as the meal advanced a feeling of genial contentment crept over us, which seemed to influence all our senses; we began to talk over sport and compare our experiences in various countries and in pursuit of various animals: some of us were good listeners, others fond of talking, but all animated by a love for the same occupation, so that when at length one of the enemy handed round the best of cigars, even the Skipper became so mellow and pleasant that before going to bed we arranged for a joint shoot after ryper to-morrow; and said 'Good night,' feeling that it was quite fortunate that we had all come to Gjendesheim on the same day.

One of our new friends is a Russian, an engineer officer; he speaks not the English, but we were introduced to him as a man who had shot more bears in Europe than any one else living. He has killed forty-two, and looks as though he had been hugged by each one of them before it finally succumbed. Now he wants to kill a reindeer, and has been attempting the feat to-day; apparently he will be *hors de combat* for the rest of the week, as he can hardly move for stiffness: he has not been accustomed to the awful walking that stalking round Gjendin entails.

Esau is also rather dilapidated, for he landed at

Leirungsö on his way down the lake, and walked round the mountain to Gjendesheim, leaving John to bring on his canoe. On his way he was obliged to wade across the Leirungs River, a wide and rapid stream, and just in the roughest part he trod on a loose stone and fell, cutting his knee and making a bad dent in his gun-barrel. Of course he was wet through and a good deal hurt, but hardly enough to account for the frightful state of his temper, till it came out that though he had walked through miles of beautiful ground for ryper, snipe, and duck, he had never got a shot at anything.

CHAPTER XXV

THE GJENDE FLY.

August 28. – This was the hottest, most windless, and cloudless day that has yet been made. The Russian and F— went out with Esau and the Skipper to shoot ryper, accompanied by a pointer, which the Norwegians call a bird-hound. A brood was soon found and rose in front of Esau, who with his usual promptitude got a right and left; whereupon the Russian took off his hat, and bowing profoundly, advanced and solemnly shook hands with him, protesting that he had frequently seen marvellous shooting, but never, never aught like this; at least, that is what we imagined to be the translation of the neat little speech which he made in Russian.

A ryper is easier to kill, if possible, than the tamest young grouse which gets up under a dog's nose on the calmest 12th of August; and Esau thinks fame is like an eel on a night-line, easily caught, but very difficult to hold afterwards.

Satisfied by having witnessed this extraordinary specimen of our skill, the Russian gave up the chase, and returned to Gjendesheim completely exhausted by the heat; but the others went on till the afternoon, now finding a selfish old cock, whose fate no one regretted; now a young brood only just old enough to be shot: anon lying down to rest and eat berries, or bathing in the Leirungs Lake, but all the time extremely happy.

F— was so exceedingly polite that he would not shoot unless birds enough for all of us happened to get up at once, and one brood escaped without a shot being fired, in consequence of our unwonted emulation of his courtesy.

Near Leirungs we were fortunate enough to drive three large broods into the same bit of willow scrub, and had some very pretty shooting as the dog set them one by one; but there was hardly any scent, and the heat soon proved too much for our bird-hound, so we returned to Gjendesheim with a very considerable addition to the larder.

Then followed hours of inability to do anything except lie on our backs with lighted pipes in our mouths, far too exhausted to smoke them; and at last-dinner; and soon the cooler air brought relief and engendered a return of bloodthirstiness, which impelled the gang of sportsmen to sally forth and rake the river till it was quite rough with artificial flies.

This was a trying time, for by some means we have established a most dangerously flattering reputation as fishermen, and were bound to do all we knew to retain it. However, all turned out right; the Skipper went into the lake and got several beauties, and Esau did the same in the river, so that we came in with the best bags by a considerable margin, and could now afford to catch nothing for a whole day without being dethroned from our pedestal,

The river, Gjendinoset as it is called, just in front of the rest-house, is a wonderful piece of water; there are about 150 yards of rapid in which the fish lie, then comes a fall, and below that there are nothing at present but small fish, though the big ones will soon begin to drop down lower for spawning. Consequently we all fish in the first 150 yards, and to-day between 50 and 60 lbs. weight has been taken out, the same quantity yesterday, and probably for some days before; and the fishing will be even better a few days later, for the Gjende fly is beginning to hatch, and as long as he lasts the fish will rise well.

We have heard so much of this fly that we had been expecting something rather gorgeous, a monster dragon-fly, or at least a second-rate butterfly, or a decent imitation of a stag-beetle; and we have been looking up gaudy Scotch and Canadian salmon flies, which we hoped might be passable substitutes; but, alas for the vain hopes of foolish man! the Gjende fly has come, and he is only a wretched little black beast like a very small, unenterprising, common or garden house-fly of Great Britain. He cannot fly decently; he is apparently devoid of sense; he has no moral, physical, or intellectual attributes for which a human being can learn to respect or love him; but – he *can* CRAWL. If he alights on the water it never occurs to him to rise again, and he allows the trout, mad with the excitement of a fortnight's prospective gluttony, to scoop him down their capacious throats by companies. If he enters your mouth, which he does with a numerous retinue every time you open it, retreat from that untenable position is the very last thing he would think of; and with what may be a gleam of momentary intelligence he seems desirous of still further increasing his knowledge of the rest of your interior arrangements.

With characteristic obstinacy, unmindful of the teachings of logic, he invariably acts on the fallacious maxim that 'an ink-bottle cannot be so full that there is not room for just one more Gjende fly.' The whole of the river here at the end of the lake, and for thirty yards on each side, is now pervaded by this noisome creature; the water looks as if it were covered with a mixture of soot and tar, the rocks are black and slippery with him, and the atmosphere is charged with him, so that the landscape dimly seen through the cloud looks as if it were dancing.

Gjendesheim itself is unfortunately not quite beyond the zone which he infests, so that the windows look loathsome with crawling blackness; the table-cloth is strewn with the corpses of those who have imbibed the honeyed poison of the paraffin lamp and come to an untimely end, and the remains of the 'boss pie' would warrant a stranger in the belief that it had been composed of currants.

We think Pharaoh must have been a man of extra ordinary resolution, or else inane-mildness of character, otherwise he would have sacrificed Moses long before the fourth Plague was concluded.

Fortunately the Gjende fly has no insatiable craving for human flesh; the Skipper, indeed, asserted that one fastened on his hand and inflicted a wound that swelled enormously and remained swollen for several days, but the better opinion is that the creature that perpetrated this outrage must have been a viper, though we did not hint this to the Skipper, because he is firmly convinced that whisky is the only remedy for snake-bites, and that it must be taken in large quantities.

If any one stuck up a rod near the river, in two minutes it looked like a black fir pole with a bunch on the top; and John, who is a man of great entomological knowledge, spent some time in studying this phenomenon. He reported that the flies crawled up for fun, intending to jump off the top ring, but when they got up it was so much higher than they expected that they were all afraid to try, and those at the bottom and halfway up kept jeering at the top ones and calling them names, and jostling them so much that they could not crawl down again. He also said that the swarm in the air was so dense that he wrote his name in it with his finger, and it remained visible for nearly a minute.

Probably it is difficult for a man to speak the exact truth with his mouth full of (*f*)lies.

When it was too dark to fish we sat round the fire and heard a good deal about the various winter sports of Norway, capercailzie stalking, bear hunting, elk and reindeer shooting, and running on skier, the snowshoes of the country, which are very different from the well-known Canadian shoes, being made of wood, from six to twelve feet long, four inches wide in front, three behind, about an inch and a half thick where the foot rests, thinner at each end, and turned up and pointed in front. Every district has its own peculiar shape; about here the right shoe is made six feet long, the left one ten or eleven feet, it being more easy to turn if one is shorter than the other: some are made of pine, some of birch, and occasionally oak. The men of the Thellemarken are the most skilful runners, but it is now quite a fashionable amusement in Christiania during the winter, just as skating is in England.

Sunday, August 29. – Our Norwegian friends departed for the happy hunting-grounds of Rus Vand this morning, but before doing so they most kindly offered us the hut there any time after this week, at the end of which they are going south. We can hardly expect the present glorious weather, which has now lasted for three weeks, to go on for ever; and when the change comes, a tent will no longer be the abode of comfort and luxury that we at present find it, so that the offer of the hut is most opportune for us.

We parted with great regret from people who have been so kind and hospitable, and many were the expressions of good-will and protestations of eternal friendship, as we shall not see them again till we pass through Christiania on our return home.

That return home has caused the Skipper hours of anxious thought already: there is to be a wedding in England about the end of next month, at which, although it is not his own, his presence is urgently needed. He knows he ought to go, but hates to leave this blissful life just when the best stalking is beginning; consequently he devotes much time every day to the consideration of the subject, torn by doubts, tortured by terrible misgivings, and harassed by indecision.

To-day, after being more than usually disagreeable under the malign influence of his conscience, and seeking for inspiration, first in the room at Gjendesheim, walking up and down like Weston; then on the lake paddling like a penny boat; and finally roosting on a rock at the top of the fjeld with his arms folded like Napoleon, and a gruesome scowl on his face, or at least on those portions of it which were visible through the mask of Gjende flies, he at last concluded to commit his fate to the decision of an unbiassed coin, if such could be obtained from any confiding friend.

With great difficulty he persuaded Esau to lend him one öre, value of a shilling, which seems on reckoning to be about half a farthing; Esau observing as he gave it, 'It isn't that I'm stingy, old fellow, though of course I don't expect to see it again, but it will throw my accounts out so.' *N.B.* – Esau's notion of keeping accounts is to put his receipts into one pocket, *and his disbursements into another;* if he has a vague idea to within £20 or so of how the money has gone, it will be more than any one expects; that everything he possesses will be spent is a foregone conclusion.

But to resume. The öre coin has no distinct head or tail, so the Skipper named one side heads, and tossed. The thing fell on its edge, and rolled round the table, and about the room till it struck the wall, whereupon it fell over 'heads,' and decided that the Skipper must go to the wedding.

So he sat down and wrote a letter saying that they must not expect him, and that he should stay out here the whole time that was originally intended; for as soon as he had dated the letter it occurred to him that it would be childish to allow such a weighty matter to be decided by the whim of a half-farthing coin, which might very likely be interested in the affair in some way, and which, as he truly said, would possibly have turned up 'tails' if it had not happened to fall on its edge and been interfered with by an unauthorised wall.

Having thus acted according to his incrinations, and given his missive to Andreas to post when he leaves Gjendesheim next week, the Skipper became quite pleasant again, and went forth to his fishing 'ever and all so gaily O.'

The ponies of Norway are wonderfully docile and clever; these qualities were well shown to-day in a black one belonging to Jens which came to take F—'s baggage over the mountain to Rus Vand. This pony was brought down near the door of the rest-house, and left standing there without any fastening or any one to look after him. The things were not ready, so he waited about two hours, occasionally wiping off the Gjende flies with his tail when their weight became insupportable, but otherwise never moving. The busy world (consisting of Andreas and Ragnild) pursued their usual avocations around him, goats ran against him, and insects climbed over him, but there he stood placid and motionless as a wooden rocking-horse. At last the baggage was ready, and they brought it out and piled it on his back until we feared he would break, and then Jens turned his head in the direction of Rus Vand, and gave him a gentle push to start him; and he went slowly off up the mountain, choosing the best way for himself, for no one went with him; in fact Jens did not follow him for about half an hour, but no doubt he was found at the right place in the end. The whole performance reminded one of a clockwork toy, and John remarked as we stood and watched him out of sight over the pass, 'Now, that's what I call a well-trained pony.'

During our stay here we had the pleasure of forming the acquaintance of an elk-dog. This animal is taken out in a kind of harness to which a rope is fastened, the other end of the rope being attached to the hunter's belt; and his legitimate occupation is finding elk in a forest by scent, and denoting their presence by his behaviour before the hunter gets within range of the elk's eyes, ears, or nose. Mr. Thomas brought him up here hoping to find reindeer with him in the same manner, as he bad been unable to get a Finmarker[1] broken to reindeer; but the experiment has not been successful, for the dog has been so carefully trained to elk, that he exhibits a large and lofty contempt for so pusillanimous a creature as a reindeer, and will not confess that he has discovered the existence of such a thing at all.

---

[1] Finmarker is the kind of dog usually employed for finding reindeer the name being derived from the district of which it is a native.

But in addition to the fact that he finds no deer, he is a good deal of trouble from the fastidiousness of his appetite. It appears that he is accustomed to feed on dogs, and when he cannot get dogs he can rough it very well for a short time on boys or any other plain fare; but up here, where dogs are few and boys are extinct, he is having a very poor time of it. The last place where he had a really square meal was at Skjæggestad, on the journey up, where he was lucky enough to get a whole dog and some portions of boy; since then he has only had limbs snatched off adventurous observers, and altogether seems to be pining for want of proper nourishment. He is about the height of a colley, but with an enormous chest and limbs, a head something like an Esquimaux, a wiry reddish yellow coat, and a most unkindly expression of countenance. In the absence of sufficient flesh food he appears to be developing a liking for man-diet, so we did not remain long in his society, for which indeed we only craved after we had perceived through a chink in the door of his dwelling that he was moored to a beam by a kind of anchor chain. We have often heard that there is a certain amount of danger in the pursuit of the elk; if the hunter is always accompanied by a dog of this kind we can easily understand it. However, he was a very interesting animal, and if we had a National School at Memurudalen we should certainly have tried to buy him, as there is any amount of room for *débris* there. What a boon he would be in some of the thickly populated districts of England!

In the afternoon we paddled leisurely back to our

camp and found it looking prettier than ever, but, alas! our little stream had ceased to run. However, there is another one not more than forty yards away, so we shall not be much troubled by its loss.

August 30. – The sun still shines upon us from a cloudless sky, and early in the morning, before any breeze springs up, the lake makes a most beautiful picture, with its steep mountain sides and foaming torrents so perfectly reflected in the green unruffled water. But, lovely as it is, its beauty is rather wasted on us now, for it has been just the same for the last three weeks, with the outlines all hard and clearly defined, and none of the graduated effects of distance which we get from the hazy climate at home: in this clear atmosphere the peaks twenty miles away are as bright as those a mile or so beyond the lake. Probably this is the reason why we so seldom see pictures of Norwegian mountain scenery, and that the few which do appear are often condemned as hard, cold, and unsatisfactory.

The most prominent object in looking towards the lake from our camp is a curious pyramidal mound, about thirty feet high, close to the water's edge. It is so regular in shape that we have devoted many hours of cogitation and argument to the discovery of its history.

John (who is a man of considerable archæological fame) maintains that it is a funeral barrow in which some ancient Viking was buried, and he wants us to give up our cartridges for the purpose of constructing a mine and blasting him out: we have vainly represented to him that it cannot be a

Viking's tomb, because there is absolutely nothing to Vike up here.

The Skipper says it is a glacial moraine, 'any donkey can see that at a glance;' and Esau holds to the opinion that it is an artificial mound put up for ancient regiments of Gjendin yeomen and Memurudalen militia to practise archery at. Possibly none of these theories give the correct solution; but, whatever its origin, it makes a capital rifle butt for our occasional shooting. Esau was heard to irreverently remark, as he aimed at it with the Skipper's rifle, 'he guessed an express bullet would rouse old Jarl Hakon out of that,' but nothing particular followed.

To-day the Skipper composed an Irish stew as a *piéce de résistance*, which, when it came to table, was unanimously voted the best of all the excellent dishes on which we have feasted here. After dinner we made an enormous fire for the sole purpose of warmth, as the nights are now very cold, and during this fine weather after sunset a strong draught sets down our valley towards the lake. We have ascertained that a like draught blows down each of the other valleys running into Gjendin, making the lake a centre. That in ours begins gently directly the sun has set, and increases in strength until it amounts to a stiff breeze; and as it comes direct from the vast snow fjelds, it is a disagreeably chilly blast, which freezes that side of our bodies remote from the fire, and leads us to envy the happy condition of a leg of mutton attached to a roasting-jack. That, 'o nimium fortunatum!' enjoys equally in every part the genial warmth, while man has no mechanical arrangement by which his immortal soul can be rendered blissful through the medium of a temperate body.

In the morning a breeze begins to blow out of the lake into all the valleys; illustrating on a small scale the cause of land and sea breezes all over the world. The Skipper and John (who is a man of profound science) have elaborated a theory explaining the exact reason of this interesting phenomenon: but as their explanation is entirely opposed to the teachings of Dr. Brewer and the opinions of Professor Tyndall, and involves a rearrangement of existing notions concerning radiation and the movements of the heavenly bodies, we think it best to exclude it from these pages, as this is not a simply scientific work, and we have no desire to hurt the feelings of even the above-named misguided philosophers.

CHAPTER XXVI.

DISASTER.

August 31. – We have got quite tired of writing 'Another beautiful day,' and in future shall bring notebooks to Norway with these words ready-printed at the top of each page.

The Skipper paddled away to Gjendebod, to bring home the deerskin which he had left there to dry. He returned with a splendid bag of the best trout that ever came out of Gjendin, and that means the best in the world; but he was in a state of great indignation because he had been charged 5*s*. 6*d*. for beds, dinners, and breakfasts for himself and Öla when they stayed there a few nights ago. This is the result of living in a cheap country for two months; to the ordinary Englishman it would not appear an exorbitant hotel bill, especially when the hotel (!) is fifty miles from a town, and only open for two months in the year.

Just at bedtime Esau crawled into the tent saying that he had strained his back in lifting a stone; he was in such pain that he could hardly stand, and was white and shivering. We undressed him and put him to bed, and then produced the liniment from the 'medicine chest,' by which name we dignify the cigarbox which contains our little stock of drugs.

Then John spent an hour viciously rubbing remedies into his victim's back, as one rubs oil into a bat, so that Esau presently groaned out, 'Thanks, John, I think that will do, I feel a great deal better now;' and certainly he did seem to experience a kind of relief as soon as the rubbing stopped. After this we turned in.

September 1. – Esau spent a sleepless night, and this morning could not move. Thereupon John nobly closed with him for another half-hour's rubbing, which had a decided effect, and after giving him some breakfast we carried him out and made a comfortable bed for him under the Sycamine tree, and there left him with the library and all his belongings in easy reach.

At midday John returned from fishing to lunch with the invalid, and we wondered how all our friends in England were getting on with the partridges, and almost wished we were there for a few minutes, as we pictured to ourselves Eddie and Jack both talking sixteen to the dozen at lunch over beefsteak pie and beer (fancy beer, John!); old Blank, with two young dogs tied to him, perspiring over the downs; and the Major sitting with his cigar aboard the yacht at Cowes, and thinking how snug his birds were lying down Gorseham way, not to be disturbed till his return next month to shoot at them, while all the time the Furzely boys were walking them up, and making them as wild as hawks.

After lunch, John accomplished what has long been his great desire, the ascent of the sugar-loaf mountain across the Memurua; and after boiling a thermometer at the topmost peak, burying a pocket handkerchief (thoughtfully borrowed from Esau, who was too unwell to refuse him anything), and 'carving his name on the Newgate Stone with his Tollekniv fine tra la,' he returned in raptures about the view and overcome with sublime and poetical emotions, which did not subside until he had poured forth his soul to his two friends at dinner.

The Skipper stalked without success, though he found the tracks of a good herd that had only just passed over the ground. Though the day was so pleasant, he had not exactly enjoyed his walk, for he could not help being filled with gloomy forebodings about Esau; picturing to himself the difficulties that would arise in getting men to carry the invalid down to Christiania in a litter, with him yelling at every step. But behold, how untrustworthy a thing is imagination! when the Skipper arrived in camp, he was agreeably surprised to find the object of his solicitude sitting up and actually stirring the rice for the curry, so marvellous had been the effect of John's lubrication; assisted by the support to his back of a kind of splint composed of birch bark, a towel, and two straps.

September 2. – John ate new bread again for dinner yesterday, and the Skipper was aroused in the middle of the night by a claw reaching out from the adjoining bed, which clutched his pillow and rug and tried to drag them away; the whole of this being accompanied by blood–curdling groans and hideous yells. He became more peaceful after a short time, but the Skipper is now in mortal fear lest

John should again suffer from indigestion, and again stretch out that gruesome claw, and grabbing him by the hair, drag him forth from the tent, and with demoniac shrieks stamp the life out of his frail body, while he makes the quiet valley re-echo to his triumphant mocking laughter. This, the Skipper asserts, would be only one step beyond his conduct of last night.

The latest scientific observations have caused us to re-classify the different altitudes thus: – First, the country of high cultivation and wild strawberries; above that the zone of uncleared pine forests and most of the berries; then the belt of stunted birches and black game; higher still, that of cows and goats; and above that, the country where reindeer flourish and snow lies all the year round. This takes us to the summit of all things earthly, and in this zone there is hardly any vegetation. Beyond it is the region of eagles, but in the present incomplete state of human knowledge we have been content to explore this highest zone by letting our spirits soar aloft without our bodies.

Gjendin is just at the highest point of the stunted-birch belt, and when the wind gets into the N.W. the thermometer, without waiting to reflect, falls a great distance very hurriedly. John, having no sheep-skin, suffers a good deal from the cold at night; and the haughtiness of his spirit is so far broken that he now sleeps in two pairs of trousers, three shirts, and a coat, besides all his rugs. A few short weeks ago he turned from us with an air of aristocratic nausea when we were getting into bed clothed in a single shirt and pair of trousers, donning for his part a linen night-shirt, an effeminacy previously unheard of in camp life.

These things are changed now, and it is difficult to persuade him not to go to bed with his boots on; but it has to be prevented on account of the new bread.

The monotony of an uneventful day was only broken by the occasional rubbing of Esau's back, amidst the victim's agonised appeals for mercy, as he thinks it is rubbed away to the bone. However, the effect is magnificent, and he can now hobble about camp and be useful to a certain extent.

MENU. – September 2.

Vins.	Truite à l'Irlandaise.	*Légumes.*
Onion Sauce.	Salmi of Ryper.	Crumpets.
	Woodcock à l'Oven.	
	Compote of Rice and Wimberries.	

After dinner we dug a small hole in the floor of the outer tent, in which we placed a spadeful of red-hot embers from the fire. This is a capital device for obtaining warmth in a tent, as there is no smoke, and the embers keep glowing for a very long time; possibly it might be dangerous in a very close-fitting tent, but ours is airy, not to say hurricany.

Round this fire we sat and talked and smoked until bedtime, hoping against hope for a few more days of sunshine; but when we turned in, the wind was howling and moaning along the hill-side in a very ominous and unpleasant manner.

CHAPTER XXVII

A CHANGE.

September 3. – 'Forty below Nero' was the probable position of the thermometer during the night. Esau declares that his back is quite well, but it is suspected that he only does this in order to avoid the administration of further remedies by John.

However, we consider this such a successful cure that we here give our recipe for strained backs to an expectant world, not as a sordid advertisement, but from pure philanthropic motives.

'Take the patient and place him on a grassy spot in the sun, and lubricate with oil; rub this in for three hours with the hand; seize his wrist and feel the pulse (if you can find it), displaying at the same time a large gold watch; look profound; mutter inwardly. Now shift him gently to a shaded position; and having lighted a fire to the windward, prepare and cook thereon fourteen or fifteen pancakes, and administer while hot (as a mixture, not a lotion). Take care that the aroma of each cooking pancake is wafted in the direction of the patient. Carry this principle throughout all his nourishment. Explain to him that deer abound in the neighbouring mountains; show him quantities of fresh-caught fish and newly killed ryper; ensure a week of fine weather, and if this do not cure him he must be a *malade imaginaire.*'

Notwithstanding the improvement, of course Esau was not fit to go stalking, and this and other reasons suddenly induced us to leave Memurudalen to-day for good, and go to Gjendesheim on our way to Rus Vand. So we made a last gigantic pie, packed up, lunched, and then pulled down the tent, which had been standing so long now on the same spot, and embarked everything on board our two canoes and the Gjendesheim boat, which had been lent to us. Then the whole fleet sailed from these hospitable shores 'neath a stormy sky, with cold wind and rain, and the towering heights of Memurutungen all wrapped in angry clouds, frowning blackly above us.

It was quite sad to leave the snug little corner where we have spent such a happy, careless time, with all the comforts which we have added gradually to our temporary home; and the valley looked very desolate without the tent, the cheerful fire, and 'the meteor flag.'

Esau's last act was to fill two brass cartridge cases with water and hammer them firmly into each other; the air-tight boiler so formed he put into the fire under the oven, and after waiting a short time for the explosion, forgot all about it and went away without telling any one. Just then John arrived at the spot to see if there were any loose belongings lying about, and was horrified to observe the oven suddenly elevate itself into the air and disappear among the clouds with a loud report. His mind at once reverted to the happy life of a landlord in co. Limerick, but he soon realised the true state of affairs, and came down to the lake muttering something about 'tomdamfoolery,' a Norwegian word which expresses censure of the silly custom of practical joking.

This morning we found a merlin sitting just out-side the tent door; it had evidently been stuffing itself with scraps of offal from the camp until it was perfectly stupid and could scarcely fly. Esau wanted to knock it on the head at first, but more humane feelings came over him, so he fetched his rifle and shot it for an hour or so, till at length the bird, wea-ried by the constant noise, retired into the birch woods, and we saw it no more.

There are usually several ravens near the camp, which come down to 'carry off carrion,' but other-wise there are not many birds here: the most com-mon are buzzards and kestrels, which abound; two eagles, which are generally soaring above Memuru-tungen; a pair of ospreys occasionally flying about the lake; a rough-legged buzzard seen once, a few merlins, and a small short-tailed red hawk, with whom we are not acquainted; sometimes black-throated divers and scaups on the lake, and a few fieldfares and redwings in the birch woods. We have found many nests of the latter in the trees, and one of a fieldfare in a bank.

What rare times all the birds and beasts of prey will have for the next few days in Memurudalen! only to be equalled by the early days of the Australian gold fever. Nuggets of inestimable value in the shape of heads, tails, and other portions of reindeer, ryper, duck, and trout – intermingled with other delicacies, such as potato skins, jam and marmalade pots, and whisky bottles – will from time to time be unearthed amidst shrieks of triumph. 'Claims' will be run up to a fabulous price, and many a battle royal will be fought in that happy valley where we have spent a month of peace. As we depart in mournful silence, brooding over the days that are no more, we see in fancy the numerous bright eyes which from lairs and eyries are watching our every move, their owners all ready to swoop down on our *débris* as soon as we have passed out of sight.

The lake was very rough, and we were quite afraid of being swamped and losing our baggage from the magnitude of the big little waves; but luckily the boat took our heaviest things, or we should not have been able to venture; and so the canoes, lightly loaded and with all sail set, rode gallantly o'er the foaming billows, and we all got safe to Gjendesheim. The cheery fire in the room with its bare wooden walls and benches, made a picture which seemed the perfection of comfort after the chilly tent and the freezing N. W. wind.

> 'It is the black north-wester
>   That makes brave Englishmen
> Use very naughty words, and wish
>   Themselves at home again.'

One of the party is always telling us that he intends to inflict on the British public a narration of our experiences on this expedition, and although he has not yet begun to collect materials for the work, we have begun to invent titles for the book that is to be. One is 'England, Canada, and Norway,' being a description of Englishmen travelling in Norway with Canadian canoes; and we think this tide might induce schoolmasters to buy it, under the impression that it is a geographical treatise on those countries.

The Skipper proposed 'The Fool with the Fowlingpiece, or Fishing and Flyblows.' John's title was 'Mems. from Memurudalen, or Jottings from the Jotunfjeld;' and Esau suggested 'Glopit, top it, and mop it,' alluding, he said, to the state of John's forehead whenever he arrived at the summit of that mountain; but the explanation was received with such a chorus of 'Oh! $\{{\rm drop \atop stop}\}$ it!' from the others that he gave up the idea.

One notion is to make the book a collection of cooking recipes for camp life, and call it 'Grunts from a Gourmand in Gulbrandsdalen, or Paragraphs from the Pen of a Pig;' but we think we should promote a more active sale among respectable people if it were called 'Self-Improvement, or Lights thrown on Good Living.'

Another idea is that it might get a sale by appearing surreptitiously among the Christmas books for the young, and for that purpose we should use the names of our two henchmen Anglicised. 'Oola and Eva: a Tale for Girls,' could not fail to attract the favourable attention of parents and guardians.

Possibly it might create a greater sensation if it were introduced to the world as 'Julia and Pausanias: an Idyll.' It is very difficult to decide on a good name, but we are all agreed that the name once found, it will be perfectly easy to write the book afterwards.

September 4. – How soothing and pleasant it is, when we hear the storm and rain shrieking and beating outside, to reflect that there is a good solid roof over our heads, and that we shall not be roused in the night by the cry of 'All hands turn out to slack off guy-ropes!'

This morning the lake was so rough that we perceived that we had been very lucky to make our voyage yesterday; we certainly could not have attempted it to-day. The man from Gjendebod was here, and started for the other end of the lake with Andreas in the big boat about nine o'clock, but at two they came back dead beat and wet through, having been obliged to desist from their attempt before they had gone two miles, and they considered themselves lucky to have got back.

The appearance of the lake is wonderfully fine as the white-capped breakers come rolling in, flinging the sprayhigh up the face of the opposing cliffs, and dashing with an angry roar against the black rocks where they jut out into the deep part of the lake. The Skipper, affirming that he could smell the salt in the air, began to look out pollack-flies, while John put on a beautiful brand-new shooting-coat, and went down to the shore to pick up seaweed and dig on the sands: he came back saying that the tide was coming in, and he thought he had seen the smoke of a steamer in the offing.

Close to this end of the lake a little promontory runs out, which forms a breakwater, so that the sea just opposite the house is comparatively calm. In

Canoeing after Duck in a Storm.

this bay, directly after breakfast, we saw two scaups, and the Skipper and Esau manned a canoe to try for them, the former to paddle, the latter to shoot. Only one was shot at, and it managed to fly beyond the headland before falling dead, and we dare not go after it in our frail craft.

In the afternoon we took all the male inhabitants of this district, viz., Öla, Ivar, and Andreas, to act as spaniels and retrievers, and went into the fjeld above Gjendesheim for ryper. We had quite a sporting afternoon, as we managed to find a good many broods: the strong wind had made them so much wilder that they got up with reasonable haste and energy, instead of waiting to be kicked and then only running away.

We had great fun also in watching the behaviour of our men, especially their method of capturing a wounded bird. One which was hit in the head had dropped among some rocks, and Öla and Andreas went in pursuit; they crawled suspiciously about, peering over the stones as if they were stalking reindeer; then suddenly catching sight of the bird, which was crouching down as birds hit in the head sometimes do, they advanced cautiously upon it, each with an uplifted stick in his hand, and crept like assassins nearer and nearer to their victim. At last they stood within reach. Ola gave the word to strike, and strike they did, as if they were breaking stones, and the poor old ryper lay at the feet of its murderers a mangled bleeding corpse.

Andreas: Our Retriever.

Öla and Andreas Capturing a wounded Grouse.

We shot all the afternoon with almost unvarying luck, hardly ever losing a bird; now getting four barrels into a large brood, now picking up a solitary old cock that had selfishly separated himself from his family, and selected a particularly advantageous feeding-ground for his own exclusive benefit, and at intervals having a little recreation afforded by our men, especially the professional buffoon, Ivar.

In one marshy bit of ground a pair of short-eared owls were incautious enough to fly up in front of Esau, and were promptly added to the bag; they were in beautiful plumage, which was luckily not injured by the shot, so we were much pleased at getting them. Then we went towards the river into the ground frequented by ducks, and got a little shooting there, and finished the day by walking round the shoulder of the lower fjeld about the time that the ryper were coming there to feed, and so back to Gjendesheim. Altogether the walk was most enjoyable, and as we returned and gazed over Gjendin, the contrasts of storm and sunshine, tumbled clouds and rough waters, and occasional glimpses of the highest mountains gleaming through rifts in the surrounding blackness as the bright sunbeams lighted up their peaks of snow, formed the most striking picture of wild and desolate grandeur that can be imagined.

Esau's shooting is remarkably unerring, and we feel so annoyed with him sometimes when he *won't* miss even a palpably difficult chance, that we were quite glad a few days ago when he took such a long shot that it strained his gun, and the Skipper exclaimed, 'Ah, I told you you would, I've been expecting it all along.'

John had an unstrung kind of day. Starting down the river to fish soon after breakfast, he became so engrossed in his sport that he forgot all about lunch, and did not return till dinner-time, when he walked abstractedly into the room where we were sitting, and pulled out his watch; then after studying it and making calculations for a short time he remarked slowly, 'I left here at six minutes past ten, and hanged if it isn't ten minutes past six now; my watch must have stopped.' Then he wandered off upstairs to his room, still ruminating over this extraordinary occurrence to his watch; but in his absence Ragnild had changed all his things into another cabin without telling him anything about it, so that he found his old habitation swept and garnished, and began to think, like Clever Alice, 'This is none of I.' However, he got over this difficulty and came down to dinner, still looking a trifle abstracted, but with his usual appetite. Afterwards the Skipper paddled him across the river to fish, and when coming back, John upset the canoe and nearly drowned them both in the presence of Esau and every native in the district, who joined in mocking them in the Norwegian tongue from the bank.

Finally he informed us that during his wanderings he had composed a short poem, 'which,' said he, 'as you have not heard it, I will now proceed to recite.'

So we went to bed.

John and the Skipper upsetting in the Canoe

CHAPTER XXVIII

RAPID-RUNNING.

Sunday, September 5. – To-day the Skipper and Esau determined to try to run the canoes down the river to Sjödals Lake, where we intend to leave them during our stay at Rus Vand.

All things being ready, the Skipper started about eleven o'clock on his perilous voyage, closely follo-wed by Esau. The river is full of impracticable falls, some of them twenty or thirty feet high, but be-tween these places there are splendid rapids, and the excitement of running them is delightfully fascina-ting. When we came to a bad fall we carried the canoes round, and enlisted the services of our two men to help us in this part of the performance. Öla did not like this at all, for carrying a canoe of 80 lbs. weight over very rough ground is hard work, and Öla loveth the fireside and the odour of roasting coffee better than hard work on the Sabbath.

Presently we came to a place which the Skipper wanted to run, but which Esau declared to be too dangerous; it was a very swift and rocky rapid, with two extremely sudden turns, the lower of which was only a few yards above a high fall. Esau only ran past the first turn, which was quite nervous work enough, and then got to shore and waited on the bank for the result of the Skipper's exploit.

Down he came at about fifteen miles an hour, took the first turn most successfully, and then, by some extraordinary strokes of his paddle, which no man living but himself could have performed, and aided by a species of miracle, he got round the second; but then an eddy caught the canoe, and she became unmanageable, so that instead of stopping in a little creek of quiet water as he intended, he came straight on at a terrific speed, and ran high and dry on a ledge of rock just above the fall, losing his paddle at the shock. Wonderful to relate, the canoe was not a bit injured, but the paddle whirled over the abyss and disappeared for ever; and the Skipper was pleased because he had not done the same.

We spent five hours in this kind of amusement, and enjoyed it almost more than anything else we have done. The constant danger of a smash or an upset, the sensation of speed, the delight of the sudden rush to the gliding dip over a fall, with the water roaring past a rock on each side; the big waves below the fall, which catch the canoe and toss it from one to another till you feel as if you must be thrown out; and the curious appearance that the hurrying foam-flecked waters all round present, combine to make Sunday rapid-running a very popular pursuit.

While we were doing the last bit above Sjödals Lake, our men, instigated no doubt by Öla the Lazy, seized the opportunity given by a long rapid to go home, and as we were pretty well tired out with our exertions, we left the canoes above the lowest fall and walked back to Gjendesheim. But we cannot recommend this river to future voyageurs; there are too many places that cannot be run; and we hear that we are regarded as decidedly mad for having attempted it.

Making a Portage by the Sjoa River.

Öla, our stalker, is a man whom we do not much admire. He is a big, handsome fellow, with a light beard and moustache, and rather a weak face; and his good qualities are extreme cleverness at almost any kind of work – carpentry, smith's work, needle-work, and saddlery, all seem to come alike to him – and as a deer-stalker he is first-rate, and never makes a mistake. But we fear that his profession at home is to be an independent gentleman, and he is very lazy, and nearly always sulky. This sulkiness annoys us more than anything else, but we also get very angry with him for being afraid of everything. He is afraid to go in the canoes, and nothing has ever induced him to enter either of them. He is afraid of rowing against a wind, or going out stal-

king on two successive days, lest he should tire himself; and he is afraid of washing up plates and pans
lest he should lose dignity; but it does not bore him
to sit by and watch other people perform the operation.

The Gjende fly was a marvellous sight to-day; we
thought him numerous before, but we little knew
the accumulated villainy of which this noxious creature is capable. Every fly that we saw here a week
ago has now got a large and healthy family of some
hundreds, and a darkness which may be felt broods
over the river and its shores. And now that the cold
weather has set in, he begins to perceive that his
short but effectual career of annoyance draws near
to its close, and the whole face of nature is covered
with torpid crawling things, that make one turn in
disgust from everything one touches. May his end
come soon, for we love him not.

We are very comfortable here at night sitting
round the noble fireplace in the corner of the room.
These corner fireplaces are found in every sæter and
homestead in this part of the country, and are very
picturesque and cheery, vastly superior to the
modern stove, that may be seen standing up gaunt
and inhospitable in every house in more civilised
regions. Most of them have the chimney supported
by a crooked piece of birch wood coming down
from the roof and hooked underneath the projecting angle of stonework, but in some there is instead
an upright iron bar from the hearth. Generally
speaking, they are placed quite against the wall in
the corner, but we have seen several with a space

A Norwegian Fireplace.

behind large enough to walk through, and one which even had a bed behind it.

September 6. – The sea on Gjendin has organised something remarkably like a ground swell under the influence of the continuous storm, and its fury is more magnificent than ever; no boat here would have a chance of living in it.

Esau spent the morning packing his bird-skins in a wooden box for their journey home, as we hardly expect to get much more in the way of specimens. Then we had another afternoon at ryper, not quite so lucky as yesterday, but still satisfactory.

When we returned we found that Andreas had brought from Besse Sæter a vast pile of literature which had been accumulating at the Vaage post office for the last month. After dinner, when we were all buried in our respective letters and papers, occasionally reading out particularly interesting scraps of news, Ragnild came in and informed us that a certain Norwegian, whom we may call Mr. Fox, had come there to fish. This was a man who had done some business for us here two years ago, and we had had a little correspondence with him before coming out this year. Thinking we might have given him some trouble, and not having any great liking for his character, we naturally wished to be especially civil to him; so we asked Ragnild to bring him in and stay to interpret for us.

Presently he entered the room, and after greeting us sat down and refused to have anything to drink: this astonished us so much that it completely drove our small stock of smaller talk out of our heads. The commonplaces of polite conversation sound perfectly ridiculous when gravely uttered to an interpreter for transmission to the proper recipient, and so Ragnild seemed to think, for her translation always sounded much shorter than our flowery sentences. We tried a variety of feeble questions to which we already knew the answers, somewhat in the following style: −

'We presume, Mr. Fox, that you like Norwegian cheese?'

'Does your brother also like Norwegian cheese?'

'Do you speak German?'

'No? but your brother, we believe, plays the Norwegian german-flute ?'

'The friends of your sister's children are also our friends. They live in England, but we believe they still like Norwegian cheese.'

'We like much the cheese of the country, and have never suffered asphyxia from it.'

'We shall take a small quantity with us to England for the destruction of rats;' and so forth.

Presently Esau, getting impatient, suggested in a loud voice that we should 'ask him some questions out of Bennett's Phrase-book.' Then he was covered with shame, as he feared that Ragnild would immediately translate this to Mr. Fox; but fortunately she did not.

On reference later to the said Phrase-book we find that some very appropriate and useful sentences may be gleaned from its fertile pages. For instance, 'Who are you? What sort of weather is it to-day?' (these two remarks are introductory, as it were, and to inspire confidence in the person addressed). Then we come to the point: 'Will you lend me a dollar? Be quick! Thank you, you are very kind.' Here the speaker would turn to Ragnild and proceed thus: 'Put this in my carpet-bag. Make haste and bring me a light, open, four-wheeled phaeton carriage, drawn by one horse.' Then to Mr. Fox, 'Good morning; I must go, but I shall return in a month.' Then the speaker might wink at John and depart.

Now came the most awful pause that the history of the world in its darkest moments can yet point to. We coughed and glared at each other, and felt in our pockets as if we might find something to say there; and then the Skipper had a brilliant idea, and said, 'Ask Mr. Fox how long he intends to stay here.' But Ragnild at once replied, 'Only two days,' without referring the question to him at all; so that remark was wasted and our embarrassment became worse than ever; for now not only had we to invent subjects of conversation, but also to put them in such a form that Ragnild should not be able to answer them without taking Mr. Fox into her confidence. He all the time was most annoying, as he would do literally nothing to keep up his end of the conversation, and replied to our lengthiest and most brilliant efforts of exuberant verbosity by monosyllables and inarticulate grunts.

At last, in desperation, we presented him with a very nice new English knife, for which he did not seem to care at all; and so we parted, both sides feeling that the interview had been a failure.

The following note is extracted from one of the journals: – 'The common cheese of Great Britain is unknown in Norway, but in the roadside inn, the smallest sæter or farmhouse, and the humble cottage dwelling, the traveller can always obtain that excellent substitute, the goats'-milk cheese of the country.' The colour of this excellent substitute is that of Windsor soap; its consistency, leather; and its scent, decomposed glue, which causes the natives to keep it under a glass shade. If you eat it, your own dog will shun you; if you avoid it, you starve.

September 7. – Esau always wakes up in the most

boisterous spirits, and as the partitions between the cabins are only made of thin boards full of knotholes, he can be heard all over the house the first thing in the morning jeering at John, who sleeps next door, whistling and crowing like a baby in his cot: he continues these little games long after breakfast-time, and though he is wide awake, will not get up. All this sounds very pleasant and cheery to talk about, but the Skipper, who usually wakes in a temper the reverse of angelic, being influenced by an unequal liver, wishes that these walls were twice as thick, and that Esau was at Hong Kong.

Generally he tries little stratagems to induce Esau to get up, dressing operations having a tendency to quiet him. Sometimes he enters the room sniffing, and remarks, 'How deuced good the coffee smells roasting!' or 'We're going to have a tip-top fish for breakfast, but there's very little of that pie left; enough for two of us p'raps' (this would mean about eight pounds). Or he looks out of the window, and assuming an attitude of intense surprise, hanging on to the frame like Irving in 'The Bells,' says, 'By George, Esau! there's a fellow just below looking through a binocular that can give yours six lengths for mechanism.' If all these expedients fail, he gives in, and dresses quickly with his ears full of tow, leaving Esau aloft, and gets into the eating-room, where the floor and ceiling between put a soft pedal on operatic selections.

Esau says all this ill-feeling arises because the Skipper cannot whistle Berlioz's 'Faust,' and is jealous.

Andreas and Ragnild are making preparations for their departure, which takes place to-morrow; then Gjendesheim will be closed, the door fastened, the windows shuttered, and the place will be left to itself until next June. Very soon now Gjendin will be covered with ice and snow: most of the good folks in the sæters have already gone to the valleys for the winter.

We thought it would be more convenient for them if we took our departure to-day, so packed our goods on the pony and said 'Farvel' to Gjendesheim. Our last view of Gjendin, as we tur-

Jens and his Pony on their Way over Bes Fjeld.

ned to look from the top of the pass, was just as it appeared when we first saw it – black, gloomy, and forbidding, with the cold north wind sweeping in a hurricane over its waters, and heavy rain-clouds hanging over its mountain shoulders, making a scene as awfully lonely and desolate as it is possible to depict.

After the pony had gone with the last load we suddenly discovered that the tent had been forgotten: it and its appurtenances make a package weighing about 70 lbs. Now we *all* hate carrying 70 lbs., but fortunately at this crisis a *deus ex machiná* appeared in the person of a stranger. At first we thought it must be one of our own men returning for something after changing his coat, but on his nearer approach we found that he was the rest of the population of the district, whom we had not seen before, coming down in a body. This was Hans Kleven, who has the reputation of being the best hunter in the country.

He is a small sturdy man, with amazing shoulders and a pleasant, good-humoured face, and a most gorgeous cheek shooting-coat, of a pattern so enormous that there are only three squares on the whole of his back, which is a pretty broad one. This coat was given to him years ago, apparently about 1840, by an English sportsman, and he is as proud of it as ever Joseph was of his celebrated garment. To him we committed our tent, which he carried over to Besse Sæter, three miles away, without turning a hair. We rewarded him with a shilling, and from his profuse gratitude we conjecture that he only expected fourpence for the job.

Our first step at Besse Sæter was, as usual, to demand food; and John asked for a dish called 'Tuk melk,' which had been recommended to him as

264

very Norwegian and very good. A woman at once went to fetch it from the other sæter, a quarter of a mile away, and presently brought it in a large wooden milktub about the size and shape of a sitz bath. How that poor woman carried it we know not; it occupied half the table, and was so scrupulously clean that we feared to touch it with our sordid hands.

John and Esau at last attacked it in the orthodox manner, which is to sit on opposite sides of the table, and to draw a line across the surface of the milk with a spoon before beginning, and then to 'eat fair' up to that line. It would have amused some of our friends at home if they could have seen these two young men of fashion at the moment when both of them were engaged with abnormally large wooden spoons, silently ladling down 'Tuk melk' out of a tub as big as a drawing-room table.

They reported that it was on the whole good; something like curds, but with a sourer taste, and it was much improved by sugar; but though they ate a large quantity of it, being men of great courage and determination, they could not persuade the Skipper to risk his life in experiments with untried articles of food. He, however, gave utterance to the following refined expression of his sentiments: – 'I wouldn't touch that beastliness if you gave me fourteen pence a spoonful to swallow it.' No one offered the reward.

Out shooting on the other side of the lake, we put up a snipe just at evening, which went down again close to us. This species of game is not com-

mon up here, although we find his cousin the
woodcock fairly often; consequently we were much
excited, and advanced upon the foe with insidious
step, and bloodthirsty weapons almost at our shoulders in order to slay him as soon as he should rise.
All went well, and at the right moment up he got,
and promptly did the Skipper fire and miss him;
while Esau's gun for the first time on record missed
fire, and left him using language that ought to have
ignited any cartridge. So the happy bird zigzagged
off into the dim shades of sheltering night, and we
went on our way, full of thought and sorrow.

Arriving again at the sæter after narrowly esca-
ping shipwreck in the passage, we found that Jens
had come to meet us, and as he will enter our service from this date, we shall no longer need Ivar,
and paid him off, arranging, however, that he is to
come to help us home when we leave Rus Vand.

We like Ivar very much now, though we did not
by any means dote upon him at first. Ivar is a good
fellow, but an idiot, perfectly willing to do anything
in the world, but not understanding *how* to do anything. His budding reputation was blasted in our
eyes the first time that we left camp and entrusted
everything to his care; we were away for three days,
and in that time he consumed nearly four pounds of
our best butter; on our return we decided that he
was a knave, but we have since learnt that it was
only his natural impulsiveness that led him to commit such an outrage; and now that we have found
how eager he is to oblige us in everything, we like
his strange nature better than Öla's awful laziness of

character. He came into the room this morning to stand for his portrait, and the easy, graceful attitude that he assumed for the occasion was inimitable. His waistcoat and boots were perhaps his greatest charm, but his open countenance and genial smile (six inches in diameter), played no small part in causing him to become beloved by us as he was.

Ivar always laughed like a nigger on a racecourse, and whenever we took him out ryper-shooting he was exactly like an unbroken retriever: if a bird was killed, he *would* rush in to gather it, and we had to shout, 'Back, Ivar, back! Lie down! Down charge!' to prevent him disturbing any birds that might have chanced to remain during the yells and convulsions of Christy Minstrel mirth into which the death of a ryper always sent him. His behaviour usually made us laugh so much that we attributed any missing to the unsteadiness caused by constant hilarity. We gave him our spade as a parting present, and dismissed him with our blessing.

CHAPTER XXIX.

RUS VAND.

September 8. – This morning we crossed the fjeld to Rus Vand in a gale of wind. Waving a 'Farvel' to the kindly folk at Besse Sæter, we have a stiff climb up by the side of the torrent which comes gadareneing[1] down from Bes Lake, high above our heads, and presently we stand on the open fjeld above the sæter. Below lie the green waters and birch-clad banks of Sjödals Lake; far away to the east the great fall and larger trees that mark the outlet of the lake; and still further, glimpses of lower Sjödals Lake, with its forests of pine, haunt of the black game and capercailzie. But we cannot stand long to look, for the side of a Norwegian mountain, though eminently suited to hurricanes, is extremely *un*suitable for human beings while the stormy winds do blow. En avant, Messieurs, en avant! and we fight our way across the flat top to the opposite brow. Here we must pause, though Æolus himself say nay. 'What a glorious sight!' Straight in front, the cloud-girt peak of Nautgardstind, all glistening white with newly fallen snow, but of him only the top can be seen; his middle is hidden by a never-ending rush of scud-

---

1 Gadareneing, *i.e.* rushing violently down a steep place.

ding clouds. Higher still and westward the jagged summits of Tyknings Hö and Memurutind, also pure white where the snow can lie, but with huge black lines and chasms where the steep rocky face stands up gaunt and repellent, so sheer that snow can never lodge; nearer the tremendous mass of Bes Hö frowns above us; and far below in front the Russen River winds its way through barren rocks and patches of willow, to warmer and more hospitable regions, leaving with a leap of joy the cold storm-rocked Rus Lake, which has been its cradle since its birth in the mighty glaciers around.

Such was the scene lying before us on the north side of the mountain, grand beyond description, perhaps the finest in Norway, but not exactly inviting to shivering hungry mortals, so not much time was spent on it. Down we went, with the wind worse than on the other side, howling past our ears and screeching in the gun-barrels, and at last arrived at the lake to find Jens hauling for his life at the boat, which, though filled with water by the breakers, had fortunately not been battered to pieces on the rocky strand. He had left it dragged up on the beach out of the water, but the sea had increased so much in his absence, that if we had been a little later it would without doubt have been smashed.

However, we soon baled her out, and with Öla as Charon commenced the passage. Rusvasoset, as the outlet is called, is not more than 60 yards across, but the waves had had seven miles of very open water to get up in, and they came rolling down to this end in a very alarming manner. With great dif-

A Stormy Crossing at Rusvasoset.

ficulty we shoved off, and then with Öla sculling his hardest, and the Skipper keeping our head to wind, we at last got safe across with no mishap but the loss of Öla's hat and a thorough ducking for all of us.

Öla was very sorrowful about his hat, which was of pure Leghorn straw, double seamed, extra quality lining; and being further embellished with a black braid ribbon, it was a great source of pride to him; but we mocked when it flew away, and are inclined to bear its departure with equanimity, and hope it will be accepted as a propitiatory offering by the angry Lady of the Lake.

All the things were at last safely housed, and we soon made ourselves comfortable in our new abode, which is luxury itself in this weather when compared with a tent.

There are two huts, one by the edge of the lake, the other about 20 yards away, and it is the latter which we occupy. We enter by a door about five feet high, invariably knocking our heads against the lintel and swearing as we do so. The first room is about nine feet square, with a narrow dresser under the solitary window on the left, and an iron cooking stove in the nearest corner to the right, the more remote one being tenanted by a bed. Round the room at various heights are shelves and hooks adorned by cooking utensils of all kinds, very kindly left for us by their worthy owners; two or three stools complete the furniture; and on the floor are to be seen carved the effigies of departed trout of fabulous weight, with dates and the initials of their captors. Passing on through a still smaller doorway we find ourselves in another room of the same size, but with three beds instead of one, and an open Norwegian fireplace; the same kind of pegs and shelves, and hooks for guns on the wall; more profile fishes, and walls covered with records in pencil of game killed by former inhabitants, with occasional amusing notes. This is our dining, drawing, and bed room; the other is only used as kitchen.

The men's hut near the water is also divided into two rooms: the outer and much larger compartment is used as a cellar, larder, and general store-room, and presents, to say the least of it, a somewhat untidy appearance, as bottles, barrels, and boards, a grindstone, reindeer bones, a saw, a side-saddle, and old nets are piled together without any attempt at order. The inner room is very small, about nine feet by four, and there our two men sleep; and there also is a large oven built of stone, and heated by a fire inside it. As we had no bread, we proceeded to bake, and our ignorance of the manners and customs of this oven caused the bread to have a terribly trying time of it; for we did not make it hot enough at the first attempt, and the bread was left lying on the top covered by a cloth for over an hour while the oven was being heated a second time.

All's well that ends well, and this batch of rolls turned out the very best that frail man ever tasted, and consequently at supper we ate enough bread and butter and jam to supply a school feast of the hungriest description.

While the Skipper and John attended to the loaves Esau looked after the fishes, and very soon got a nice dish of half-pounders in the river. As he came back something in the middle of the stream caught his eye. 'It is, yet it can't be – yes, by George, it is, Öla's hat!' wedged in between two rocks, and slightly out of shape, but with the double-seamed, extra quality lining uninjured, and the pure Leghorn straw in very fair condition. The effusion with which Öla received it was a sight to be seen, but no one else exhibited much enthusiasm.

An inventory of our remaining stores reveals the fact that we have heaps of everything except coffee and bacon, which can only last about a week longer. In view of this happy state of things the Skipper proposed to spend a week of wild and reckless profusion and sinful extravagance.

Esau at once pictured himself seated on a grassy slope giving way to Epicurean indulgence, surrounded by three untouched pots of jam, and eating from a fourth with a table-spoon; at his side a cup of tea blacker than ink, and flavoured with condensed milk thicker than cream, while he flipped lumps of sugar into the water instead of pebbles, and commanded Öla to sand the floor of the hut with pepper.

John suggested as an amendment that we should make some exception to show that we possess the power of self-denial. 'Let us,' said he, 'deny ourselves in some one thing. Not in luxuries, which are getting scarce; in that there would be no merit. No; rather let us exercise our virtue in respect of what we have in the greatest abundance, and thereby show a great and shining example to the world. Let us abstain entirely from water.' (He had ascertained that there was plenty of whisky.)

Esau rose to oppose the remarks of the honourable gentleman. 'Such self-denial would be a good action, but the constant performance of virtuous actions tends to make one haughty. I dare say you fellows don't know this, but I do, because I've tried it. I prefer to be wicked and humble.'

The motion was not pressed to a division.

We are well provided with all kinds of food, for we found in the larder a shoulder of venison, and we have any amount of ryper, which, as John says, 'will save our bacon, though they could not save their own;' and so with a comfortable hut to live in, a river full of fish at our door, and a blazing fire to sit round, life assumes a rosy hue, and we go to sleep in real beds with bright hopes of the future.

The Skipper was heard to murmur as he turned

over to sleep, 'I say, what bread that is! When I get home I shall publish a pamphlet, and teach all the world to bake like that.'

It is rather rough on the Skipper's pamphlet to publish his recipe here, but this is copied from his journal:

'Take dough in large quantities and place it on a tin. Heat the oven till you are sick to death of piling on wood. Smoke a pipe, and remove the ashes. Place the dough in the oven, and leave home for an indefinite period. If you ever return, remove the decomposed particles, and let them get warm in the sun, or else freeze in the snow, it really don't matter a bit. Now heat the oven and recommit them. Brood over the oven, exhibiting the tenderest solicitude. They will soon be done, and perhaps will be good, perhaps not; nobody can tell.'

September 9. – Last night was very cold, and this morning there was ice on the lake, and the bilge-water in the boat was frozen solid. Esau and Jens went up the lake in the boat to stalk, and the Skipper accompanied them to fish, while John fished nearer home.

About six o'clock the boat was seen returning loaded with the head and skin of a very fine buck, and Esau gave us his history thus: –

'As soon as we landed halfway up the lake we found the spoor of two very large bucks and a smaller one which had swum across the lake in the night. They seemed to have gone towards the Tyknings glacier, so we went in that direction also. The wind was as bad as it could be in that valley, for we were obliged to walk exactly with it at first instead of against it, in order to get round a sufficiently large piece of country, and then work back against the wind. We walked a couple of miles without seeing anything, and at last got close to the Tyknings glacier and the iceberg lake at its foot. You know that lake well enough, Skipper, full of lumps of ice, some of them as big as this hut, which keep breaking off from the projecting glacier as it slides down; and I dare say you remember what an awful deathly stillness reigns there and what a dismal sight the lake is, cold and black under the shade of the crags which close in its sides.

'Well, we sat down there and used the glasses for a long time' –

'What do you mean by "using the glasses" interrupted John; 'drinking whisky and water?'

Esau withered him with a look and went on.

'Well, "spied," if you like, spied for a long time without seeing anything; and we had just walked on again a few yards, when the silence was suddenly broken by a cry from Jens of "Reins," and there, 300 yards in front of us, was a noble buck which had evidently been concealed from our view by some rocks, and had now smelt us and was departing at a stately trot, apparently despising undignified hurry.

'I fancy his intention was to trot away at that long swinging pace, and get into Asiatic Russia in time for tea; so I grabbed the rifle from Jens, as of course, now that he was alarmed, a long shot was our only chance; sat down on a stone, and with the fain-

test hopes of hitting him, fired twice, and, of course, missed.

'Now here was where my luck came in. If that
buck had not been so proud, he could have run
straight away from us to the glacier beyond the lake,
but we were "betwixt the wind and his nobility,"
and he wanted to get a clean breeze, and run against
it instead of down it. Consequently, when he was
about 350 yards away he turned to the right, apparently intending to make a circle round us, and so
get the wind in his face.

'Directly he turned broadside to us Jens gave a
shrill whistle, and the buck stopped short for a
moment, so that I had just time to make a careful
shot, and the bullet hit him in the ribs. At the shot
he stumbled, but recovered himself instantly, and
made off a good deal faster than before, evidently
perceiving that things were getting serious, and that
"this here warn't no child's play." Before I could
fire again he got into the ravine which runs down
towards Rus Lake, and was out of our sight.

We thought there was just a chance of cutting
him off in that extremely rough ground, though, of
course, we could not tell whether he was much hurt
or not; so we ran as hard as we could for about a
quarter of a mile, loading as we ran. Suddenly I
caught sight of him going very slowly, but luckily
he did not see us, so we dodged into a little gully,
and after another short run came in sight of him
standing still, no doubt owing to his wound, and
about 250 yards away.

'This time he saw us, and darted off as fleetly as

ever, no longer with his side to us, but straight away. I was dead beat, and Jens had thrown himself down, and was panting like – like' –

'A concertina?' suggested the Skipper.

'Yes, just so. Anyhow, we could not run another yard; you know what it is on those stones, so I sat down again, and with the rifle going like a pump-handle, fired, and, by the greatest luck, hit him close to the tail, and the bullet went clean through his body and smashed his shoulder. Down he went, and we raised a yell of triumph, whereupon he jumped up again and went off at a slapping pace in a most extraordinary manner. I believe if he could have reached the snow he would have done us even now but we were between him and the glacier, and he had nothing but rocks to go on, bad enough for a deer with the proper complement of legs and ribs, and very trying indeed to one crippled like this, I'm sure.

'However, he kept going at a great pace for a few hundred yards, and we lay in a state of exhaustion and watched him through the glass. Soon he began to move more slowly, and then to go round and round in a small circle, and at last he lay down. By that time I had partially recovered my wind, so I stalked him with great care and got within a hundred yards of him, took a steady aim for his heart, and pulled. To my horror he bounced up again, and ran like a hare for a dozen yards, and then rolled over and over as dead as Julius Cæsar.

'How Jens and I whooped and shook hands and laughed can be imagined by any one who has seen

Death of the 'Stor Bock' at the Iceberg Lake, Tyknings Hö.

a grand deer almost escape him, and then, by a bit
of luck and a breakneck run, just nailed him when
the chance seemed hopeless. After that we lay on
our backs and panted for some time, but after finishing the whisky and a large portion of the iceberg
lake we recovered sufficiently to skin our prize and
cut him up. He is a most splendidly fat "stor bock,"
Jens says by far the best that has been killed in these
parts this year; a beautiful skin, and, best luck of all,
his horns have got rid of the velvet, and are fit to
take home: and they have fourteen points. I measu-
red the fat on his loins, and it was two and a half
inches thick. Jens tried to bring home a hind quarter as well as the head and skin, but before he had
gone twenty yards he found that it was too much
for him, so turned back and buried it with the rest.'

'At this time of year the biggest bucks of a herd
seem to separate themselves from the rest and roam
about, either alone or perhaps a couple together.
We think they act wisely in this respect, as the calves are now old enough to run as fast as their mot-
hers in case of danger, and do not need any paternal
protection; and the bucks would no doubt become
horribly bored if they remained with their wives
and children all the year round; whereas by this system they are quite independent for a time, and
roam all over the country, seeing a lot of life and
living uncommonly well. Very much like a married
man, when he gets away on board a friend's yacht
for a couple of months, and comes back quite
brightened up at the end of his trip, and positively
agreeable and good-tempered to his wife and fami-

ly, insomuch that they are right glad to see him home again.

Of course the stalker's great object in life is to shoot one of these big bucks; but it is a desire seldom realised, as they are very restless, and only haunt the most secluded and difficult country. We have only met with two others in this expedition, and those the Skipper saw retiring at a good swinging trot over the heights of Memurutungen.

We have obtained some interesting information from Jens about the horns of the reindeer. As every one knows, both the bucks and does have horns, but they shed them at different times: those of the does and smaller bucks are now in velvet, and will not get properly hard until October; they will then remain on all through the winter, and be shed in the spring. But the large bucks have their horns hard now, and will shed them in the winter, and so be defenceless during the time when the snow lies thickest.

All this is undoubtedly true, for Jens is thoroughly trustworthy in his facts, but what is the reason?

Jens does not know, but he gives us another fact. In the winter, when the 'stor bocks' have no horns, the snow is often so deep that only the strongest deer can scrape it away to lay bare the moss which at that season forms their food. Then come the does and smaller bucks, and with their horns push away the unfortunate big ones, and so are saved from starvation, while the ill-treated 'stor bocks' have to work double tides in order to get anything to eat.

We present this fact in all humility to Mr. Darwin as a solution of the problem, 'Why has the female reindeer horns?' Evidently, they originally had none, but by constant pushing at their lords and masters they developed them by degrees; then, by the survival of the fittest, those does with the longest and sharpest horns prospered most, and soon there were none of the hornless does left, and all calves began to have horns as a matter of course.

Esau is inclined to the belief that, by the same line of reasoning, the big bucks, constantly being shot at through untold ages, have developed cast-iron ribs, and that that is the reason why they take such a lot of killing.

Possibly we have worked the theory in the wrong direction. It may be that originally all deer of every kind had horns, and the reindeer doe is the only female which now keeps them, because she alone has to fight for her living; but the snow and the horns together are cause and effect, of that we are convinced.

The *pièce de résistance* at dinner was a ryper curry, executed in the Skipper's best manner, and worthy of a place amongst the old masters, though providentially none of them were here to help us with it. John also contributed his share to the *menu*, a roley-poley pudding, which, when it came to table, looked a trifle doughy at the ends, as even the best of such puddings generally do.

John turned to Esau, and in his sweetest manner said, 'Do you like end, old fellow?'

He, a little astonished at this unwonted politeness, replied with equal courtesy, 'No, thank you, I don't think I care about end.'

'Ah,' said John, 'well, the Skipper and I *do*;' and thereupon cut the pudding into two portions, and was giving one to the Skipper and the other to himself, when the proceedings were interrupted by a brief but energetic scene of riot and bloodshed, which was terminated by a treaty of peace on the basis of the *status quo* as regards the pudding, and subsequent re-division of the same into three parts by a mixed commission.

Among the fish brought in to-day was one enormously long brute which ought to have weighed five pounds, but was only three pounds. The Skipper captured this prize at the outlet of the lake, which seems to be a favourite place for sick and dying fish like this.

Matters of food are generally referred to Esau, because he cares more about eating than the other two, as *they* say, or because he has got more sense than they have, as *he* says. The two explanations are probably identical.

When this fish was brought to him for judgment, he promptly said, 'Give it to the men.' The Skipper replied, 'My dear chap, whenever we collect any kind of food that isn't quite nice, you always "give it to the men."'

Esau became grave at once and answered, 'You forget we are not in England. At home, truly, we give the best of everything to our servants, and are thankful for the worst ourselves; but Norway is a country where the canker of civilisation has not yet crept in to taint everything it passes over, and where the noisome worm of increasing independence does not blossom in the heart of every tree. Our men would be proud and happy to chew this aged fish, and we have had instances to convince us that they would be prouder and happier if the aged fish were nearly putrid.'

CHAPTER XXX

LUCK.

September 10. – The Skipper caused great sorrow this morning at breakfast by announcing his intention of leaving Rus Lake on the day after to-morrow, which ought to be a Sunday, according to our reckoning. It seems that his conscience upbraids him for leaving a brother to be married without his assistance, and the House has sadly approved his decision.

While Esau was having a great day with the trout in the river, the Skipper went after deer, and came back cursing Fortune and all her emissaries and signs, which means ravens, horseshoes, spiders, and so forth. A few days ago, when he was starting on a stalk, he heard a raven croaking overhead, so refrained from looking up lest he should catch its eye, and have bad luck; but that raven was not to be balked of his victim, and obtruded himself so that the Skipper *had* to see him, and of course no deer came that day. The next day *two* ravens crossed his path, both cawing in the loudest and most jubilant manner; so he was greatly delighted, thinking that this was a sure precursor of good sport; but something was wrong, and again no deer resulted. But to-day two ravens came and cawed in a gentle, soothing, confident manner just outside the window before we got up: this gave the Skipper great belief in the turn of luck, and he started with a rope in his pocket to tie up the deerskins withal, his knife sharpened like a razor, and his bag full of cartridges. Once again he saw nothing, and was nearly withered away by the cold wind and rain. Coming home he picked up a horseshoe, probably the only one in the Jotunfjeld; but the times are out of joint, and these barometers of fortune have become depressed by the prevailing bad seasons and the state of the weather, so that they cannot be depended on.

In spite of the absence of sport he came back raving about the glorious views of the mountains, which quite repay any one for a long walk now that they are newly covered with snow. From Nautgardstind looking northwards, away from the glaciers, a splendid panorama is spread out – hill, forest, and lake, lighted up by the bright gleams of the September sun, still shining out bravely at intervals although winter has begun. Down to the right is the hilly woodland country through which we journeyed on our way hither, and on the left a vast plain of rolling ground. Far beyond this rises a towering cluster of high-peaked mountains, over whose heads float bands of fleecy clouds, while up their weather-worn sides the cloud-shadows drift and seem to nestle in sleep. They say these peaks are called Ronderne, but surely when seen on such a day, 'a dream of heaven' is a better name; for where else on earth can man be so near heaven as in a lofty solitude like this, where he can gaze his fill on natu-

Gloptind Rock, at the Western End of Rus Lake.

re's most beautiful loneliness untouched and undisturbed by human hand? Öla's ignorance of English enables one to gloat in silence over such a scene, without any danger of being rudely recalled to earth by a jarring exclamation of 'Ain't it lovely?' or 'That's about as good as they make 'em, eh?'

September 11. – The Skipper made a last stalk, with his usual luck, not seeing even a track, though he went into ground that we always considered a sure find, near the west end of the lake. Near there, and under the shelter of the curious sugar-loaf rock called Gloptind, there is a little ruined hut, which was built by a former occupier of Rus Vand for greater convenience in shooting near that part of the ground. When we were here before, Esau was obli-

ged to go home prematurely, and the Skipper and
Jens went to stay in this den after his departure, and
got several deer while there. This evening we persuaded the Skipper to tell us all about it, and after
he had put himself in what he considered a comfortable attitude on the bed, and lighted his pipe, he
began.

'Well, when Esau went home, Jens and I were
left up here, and got on very comfortably considering the disadvantages under which the human race
has laboured ever since that unlucky business of the
Tower of Babel.'

'What *does* he mean?' whispered John anxiously
to Esau. – 'How should *I* know?' replied the latter.
'Just listen a bit longer, and I daresay we shall find
out.'

The Skipper went on: 'We went out several days,
and walked enormous distances without seeing any
deer, so one day we decided to put a frying pan,
some firewood, and a change of clothes into the
boat, and row up to that little tumbledown stone
hut at the other end for a night or two, as it is in the
heart of the most unfrequented country and there is
nothing near to scare the most timid deer.

'We packed everything into the boat and rowed
off one fine morning, the clouds, however, beginning to hang ominously over the distant mountains.
Jens rowed slowly, so that I could fish on the way,
and our progress was further delayed by a head-
wind.

'Very soon the clouds closed in all round, and the
sky got very dark. Jens kept rowing on steadily,

from time to time looking up at the high mountain ridges that wall in the west end of the lake, while I devoted my attention to whipping the water from the stern, hoping to entice some unwary fish before the approaching rain should stop our chance of getting some fresh food. Suddenly he stopped rowing, and uttering the magic word "Reins," pointed up to an apparently deserted mountain slope on the Bes Hö side, and handed me the glass, by the aid of which I soon discovered two reindeer bucks feeding about a mile away, and almost straight above us.

'I had on a blue serge suit, so the first thing to be done was to change to my stalking suit then and there in the boat; meanwhile the threatened rain began to descend in torrents, and the wind swept by in such squalls that Jens had to work hard to keep the boat in her place. At last the change was completed, the serge suit stowed away under a mackintosh, and we got to shore and began our stalk.

'It was a difficult task to keep out of sight while advancing, and we could only move at intervals when the deer shifted for a few moments behind a rock or into a hollow in their search for food, so that we had first to run, when opportunity offered, for a quarter of a mile over very bad ground, then crawl another quarter over more broken ground; and at length, after an hour of this, being pretty close to the deer, they happened to come more into view, and we had to lie prone on our bellies for nearly twenty minutes (while they fed their way into the next hollow); and the heavy rain pelted

down on us till we were soaked, sodden, and nearly perished with cold.

'I thought that time of cramped penance would
never end, but at last the hindermost buck got his
head safe behind a welcome ridge, and then we
were soon up and after them.'

Here the Skipper stopped to strike a match on his
trousers and relight his pipe, and then resumed:
'Now we knew we must be close to them, and with
rifles cocked, and hearts beating uncomfortably,
advanced expectant. I forgot to tell you that after
Esau went home I allowed Jens to take his rifle out,
he was so desperately keen about it.

'Suddenly we came on the bucks only forty yards
away, conscious of danger, but not knowing what
they feared; too unsettled to feed, too uncertain to
move.

'I fired first, and immediately afterwards, as pre-
arranged, Jens fired, and both deer bounded into the
air and disappeared like lightning over a ridge
beyond them. We followed at our best pace, I
cramming in a couple of cartridges as we ran, and
saw them again directly, still running, and a good
deal further away. I fired two more shots, and one
buck fell dead at once, while the other galloped on
about twenty yards further, and then suddenly
stumbled and fell head over heels.

'I fancy that our first shots killed them, and that
one was really killed by Jens, but may I never know
for certain! The yell that we gave when we saw
them both lying dead woke the echoes of that dre-
ary solitude, and must have been worth hearing by

Good Sport, Bad Weather. The Skipper's two 'Stor Bocks'.

any student of human nature: in a wild shout of triumph there is only one language for all nations, and Jens and I joined our voices in the same glorious tongue for once.

'Both these deer were "stor bocks," six years old and fat. We skinned them there, and leaving the bodies as usual safe under stones, returned to the boat with the heads and skins. By the way, John, you must have seen the horns of these two deer on the wall of Besse Sæter, for I had no means of getting them home, and Jens put them up there.

'The day was drawing to a close when we reached the little stone hut which was to be our lodging: its roof was full of holes, and let the rain through like a sieve; but we stretched the two deerskins over it, and so made it habitable for a time. Inside there is, as you know, only just room for two men to lie side by side touching each other; and here, after a liberal meal and a contemplative pipe, we turned in and slept like honest men.

'Next morning after breakfast, while I was making up a fresh cast for my rod, I saw a man approaching the hut. As this was the only intrusion from human beings that we had suffered for more than a month, I was not a little surprised. Where the deuce could a man come from? and what the dickens could he want? It soon proved to be old Tronhúus with a note for Jens.

'I must explain that Besse Sæter where Jens lives belongs to a man who comes from Christiania, and Jens is only his tenant there. This man had arrived at his sæter two days before this with a young

The Old Stone Hut near Gloptind.

English nobleman, whom he was proud to have as his guest, and to whom he naturally wished to show some sport; but he had been unable to do so for want of a good stalker. This was of course very unfortunate for him and his guest, but it by no means justified his present conduct. He had addressed a letter to Jens, but written it in English, so that I should read it, sending merely a verbal message to Jens by his father, to ensure our both knowing the purport of the letter, which was to the following effect: – "Jens. If you do not return with the bearer of this letter to Besse Sæter to show myself and Lord — some deer, you will at once lose your tenancy of Besse Sæter." I could not keep Jens and thus cause him to be unfairly ejected from his home, so having no paper with me, I wrote in pencil on the back of the note that Peter had brought: "As you must be aware that Jens is acting as my servant this summer, and that by calling him away you leave me absolutely alone at the stone hut on Rus Vand, I hope that you will not detain him after receiving this note."

'With this missive Jens departed, and soon old Peter followed him, and left me, like Robinson Crusoe, alone on my desert highland. I am bound to say that I felt inclined to inquire with Selkirk, "solitude, where are the charms?" as I turned to perform the duties of the day, absolutely deserted in that desolate spot, with no companions but the lake and solemn mountain heights around me; so after a short time I put the Lares and Penates' –

'Hullo, what's that?' broke in Esau; 'you never said anything about bringing that with you before.'

'You duffer!' said the Skipper; 'it's Norwegian for the frying-pan and tea-kettle: do you mean to say you've been all this time in the country without learning that?'

'Oh, all right,' grunted Esau, 'go on.'

'Well, I put them into the boat and sculled the seven miles back to this hut, as I did not feel inclined to remain alone in that little stone hutch for the night.

'Three days passed before they let Jens return to me; and during that time I was certainly rather dull, and at night felt a trifle creepy, but the days did not pass as slowly as you might have imagined; for being without assistance my time was fully occupied in catching my daily supply of fish, chopping firewood, cooking, washing, and so on. At night the wind howled dismally round the cabin walls, but after the hard work of the day I soon fell asleep, and at last began almost to like the solitary life. Still I longed for Jens to come back, as I could not go out stalking alone; the season was far advanced, and the weather very cold.

'How I cursed that Englishman' (gentle murmurs of 'Bet you did' from the other two) 'as I cleaned out the tea-pot and scoured the frying-pan! and how I pictured him to myself wandering with my faithful Jens over the best reindeer-fjeld, and scaring away all the deer with *his* loud-sounding Bond Street express!'

'I say, Skipper,' put in Esau, 'did his Bond Street express make any more row than *yours*? because if –

'My dear fellow,' said the Skipper, 'you always put that kind of expression into narrative; it's Homeric an educated man would be pleased with it.

'I was always expecting Jens; every sound, real or imaginary, caused me to look up over the deserted lake, and hold my breath while I listened to make out his voice in the distance; and when I went down the river I heard his cheery shout in the rush of every rapid and the roar of every fall.

'After all it was only three days, and then one afternoon I found him waiting for me at the hut. I was glad to see him – gladder than I am to hear the dinnerbell at home, as glad as a bee is to get into the open air after bunting its head against a window-pane for three days' ('Beautiful simile!' from John),

294

'and especially glad to see how pleased old Jens was to return to me again. I was also not particularly sorry to hear that he had found a herd of deer and taken Lord — within shot; and the only result was a calf, which Jens himself shot after the Englishman had missed.

'After this I had a good time with grand fishing and more deer, but we did not stay much longer at Rus Vand; as you know, I was back in England by the end of September.'

The story ended, we called the men in and had a great settlement of wages and milk bills, and arranged how the Skipper's baggage should be transported tomorrow, and the rest next week.

Then we filled up glasses round with whisky and drank a solemn Skaal (pronounced Skole) to every

A Night at Rusvasoset, after a Day at Haircutting.

one, and then to Gammle Norgé, and finished the evening with 'Auld Lang Syne.' It must have been a ludicrous sight as we stood tightly packed in that tiny room, with heads all bent towards the centre to avoid the rafters, our hands crossed in orthodox fashion, and roaring at our highest respective pitches as much of the words as we knew, while we swayed our arms up and down in the manner essential to the proper rendering of the good old song.

When the men cleared out, Esau produced a gorgeous counterpane which he had commissioned Peter to buy in Vaage six weeks ago, and which the old man brought over from Besse Sæter to-day. Its manufacture is peculiar to this district; it is woven in most tasteful colours, red, magenta, blue, and green being the most prominent, with a kind of diamond pattern in white running diagonally across it; but, from the 'What's the next article?' air with which Esau exhibited it, we began to suspect that he was rather disappointed with it, and wanted to induce some one to buy it. Suffice it to say that its introduction was received with coldness.

This was a bad dayf or sport; we caught very little, and shot less. We did spy a reindeer directly after breakfast, but as he was about six miles away, close to the top of one of the highest mountains, and running as if Loki were after him, no one cared about pursuing him.

John fishing in the lake managed to lose a 'twa and saxpenny' minnow, trace, and twenty yards of reel line, and was quite discontented.

At night the wind had increased to a storm, and

the clouds were right down on the water, and hur‐
rying past in endless wreathing drifts like witches
trooping to their nocturnal Sabbath.

CHAPTER XXXI

NOT LOST, BUT GONE BEFORE.

September 12. – Early this morning we sorrowfully packed the Skipper's things on the pony, and then we three and Öla marched off down the river towards civilisation. The Skipper hoped to get over about twenty-five miles before night; Esau wanted to try the river a long way down; and John said he 'always liked a stroll on Sunday,' and with that object accompanied the Skipper for the first eleven miles of his journey, returning to Rusvasoset in time for dinner.

About four miles below Rus Lake, the river, which is there about thirty yards wide, suddenly disappears into a narrow cleft in the rocky bed, and runs in this curious rift for several hundred yards, and then again emerges into daylight. The sides of this rocky prison are just over a yard apart at the narrowest place, though the gap only appears to be a few inches wide; but the force with which the immense body of water is squeezed through the tortuous passage far down below, whirling huge boulders along with irresistible force, and covering the surrounding rocks with moisture from the ever-rising misty spray, makes it a severe trial to the nerves to step across the cleft; the ceaseless din of the rushing water is of itself sufficiently appalling.

This channel has evidently been gradually worn down through the solid rock, which here appears to be a reef of softer nature than the usual formation of this country. On the top and in niches all the way down are still to be seen the turn holes caused by stones working round and round in an eddy; but the curious fact is that while at the top the cleft is only a yard across, it widens regularly out as it gets deeper, and at the bottom is fully ten yards in width. Now it seems unlikely that the Russen river could ever have been content to run in a bed so much narrower than its present one, and from the appearance of the strata we imagine that as it worked down and undermined the cliffs at each side, they have gradually toppled forward to meet each other. Probably soon they will actually touch, after which a very short time will see the natural arch so formed covered with vegetation, and the river will run in a subterranean passage.

Through this channel no fish could pass alive, so there Esau bade 'farvel' to the Skipper, and, encumbered with rod and fishing bag, leaped like a goat across the intervening Devil's Dyke, and was soon lost to view as he fished his way up stream.

The other two pursued their journey steadily, and found it pleasant to gradually walk down from the Scotch mist which overhung everything up at Rus Vand, into, firstly, dull dry weather just below the clouds, and then a little further into real sunshine and warmth. About one o'clock they reached Hind Sæter, the tenants of which were still there, but just in the act of removing to the valley. Here they feasted together on fladbrod, and then the things were packed on a cart, and the Skipper, following them as they jolted away under Öla's guidance through the pine forest, was seen no more by his disconsolate comrade.

When John returned to Rusvasoset a little before dinner-time, we found it necessary to bake bread and a pie, our invariable rule 'when in doubt.' This was not a case that admitted of any hesitation, for the Skipper had taken all the food that he could annex for his sustenance on the journey, as he did not expect to find any people in the sæters on his path.

The evening was spent in general tidying, and mending various articles which had gone wrong; holes in landing-nets, rents in trousers and coats, and inserting new screws in Esau's boots for the stalk he hoped, but hardly expected, to make on the morrow. At night the outlook was anything but encouraging, dense clouds folding all nature in their cold embrace, and the pitiless rain beating down on our poor little hut as if it took a pleasure in the occupation.

September 13. – Rain, and nothing but rain.

September 14. – We never knew when sunrise and daybreak took place to-day, or whether they happened at all, for the prospect was more hopeless than ever, and the rain still fell with unabated vigour.

We were at the end of our indoor resources, but fortunately Öla returned with some English papers

Cheerful! the Huts at Rus Lake.

which he had found waiting for us at Ransværk, the sæter at which he and the Skipper passed the night, and at which this bundle of literature had been deposited about a fortnight ago by the latest traveller from Vaage. But for this, there would certainly have been bloodshed in this remote spot, our tempers not being equal to the strain of two days in succession without being able to see ten yards in front of us, or to stir out without becoming waterlogged.

Even the fish were apparently at last disgusted at not being able to get into a dry corner by jumping out of the water, and our efforts to persuade them to try the interior of a waterproof bag only met with indifferent success.

The stubborn resistance of our well-tried roof has at last been overcome, and soon after turning in last night we had to turn out again to rig up various hydrostatic appliances with a view to diverting the course of some of the superfluous rainfall, and irrigating the floor therewith instead of letting the beds get it all. The latter really needed it much less than the boards, which were somewhat dusty; but probably the mistake arose from John sitting on one of them while he mixed the dough, so that it might have been taken for a flour-bed.

September 15. – At last we were relieved by a change in the wind, soon followed by a cessation of rain, and then the mist began to lift, and by noon the sun was actually beginning to glimmer feebly, and the mountains to be visible for half their height.

John went on a general tour of mountaineering and prospecting in search of scenery, and came back

Rus Lake from the Western End: Nautgardstind in the Distance.

delighted with himself, having made a higher climb
than usual, and seen Nautgardstind in all the perfect
beauty with which the newly fallen snow had endo-
wed him.

It has already been mentioned that John does *not*
like walking uphill, and when he makes a self-sacri-
ficing and voluntary ascent as he did to-day, he
comes home brimming over with an excess of conscious virtue which does not pass away until the
genial influence of a good meal and a pipe has reduced him to the level of all humanity.

On his way home he heard a feeble squeak in a
bush, and peering in discovered a small animal
which he at first took for a guinea-pig; but soon,
perceiving that it must be a lemming, his natural

303

impulse was to poke it with a stick. This was his first
interview with one, though they are common
enough up here; and he is disposed to think them
morose in disposition; but really he ought to have
recognised the fact that the thin end of a walking-
stick is not a means of intercourse at all likely to
arouse the sympathy of any animal, least of all that
of a juvenile lemming, who is obviously overcome
with drowsiness, and wants to be let alone.

The winter is now coming on apace, and already
every fall of rain down here is a snowstorm in the
mountains, and every clear night means a biting
frost up there. Esau, scaling the heights of Bes Hö
with Jens in search of deer, found none on account
of the mist, and in addition to the danger of getting
lost, a new peril was added by the snow. It appeared that during the night a severe frost had immediately followed the rain and coated everything with
ice, then snow had fallen to the depth of three inches, and on the top of that rain and sharp frost again.
The result was that at every step they broke through
the crust of ice on the top, and sank through the
three inches of soft snow on to the lower stratum of
ice. This was all very well as long as they were on
rough ground; but the snow making every place
look the same, in one instance they got on to one
of the steep little glaciers which are common on Bes
Hö, without knowing that they had done so: and
suddenly Jens lost his footing and began to slide
downwards at a terrific speed. It seemed to Esau
that he would shoot straight down into Rus Vand,
looking very blue and cold three thousand feet

below; but a friendly boulder intervened, and by its assistance, and by spreading himself out like a gigantic spider, he managed to arrest his wild career, and they got safe across the treacherous glacier.

They had to cross another on their return, which was done with fear and trembling; but although the difficulties of this kind of stalking when unaccompanied by deer may seem to outnumber the pleasures, still occasionally they were on fairly safe ground, and could get their hearts out of their mouths for a few brief moments. At such times the splendid view of all our old Gjendin mountains rising tier after tier behind each other, a boundless sea of peaks and domes and jagged crags, all robed in purest white, with the sun lighting up the virgin snow almost too brightly for the eye to rest on; the

Glissading Home after a Black Day.

305

keen frosty air; and the solemn stillness, only broken now and again by the twittering of a flock of snow buntings, amply repaid them for the arduous climb.

Then a few minutes of glorious excitement as, by the aid of glissades, they shot down the steeps that it had needed hours of hard labour to surmount, and they were back on the shores of Rus Vand, where at present the snow had hardly begun to lie.

In spite of the cold we had some first-rate fishing, and Esau caught a trout which he asserted to be the very best fish for shape, condition, and colour, that ever came out of Rus Lake, or anywhere else. Though not as large as many we have caught, being only 2 1/2 lbs., it certainly was a beauty, and resembled the perfect fish that are occasionally seen in an oil painting, but very seldom encountered in tangible, edible form.

The Rus trout, like those of Gjendin, are quite silvery, almost as bright as a salmon, but with a few pink spots instead of black ones, and uncommonly pretty they look when fresh out of the water.

Rus Lake from the Eastern End: Tykning Hö
and Memurutind in the Distance.

Too soon evening put an end to our sport, and when the last rays of the setting sun had tinted the distant snow with a delicate pink hue which lingered, paled, and faded as the cold silvery light of the moon began to assert its sway, the keen air drove us home, and made us content to enjoy from the hut door the lovely clear night which succeeded so bright a day.

CHAPTER XXXII.

A LAST STALK.

September 16. – The morning did not belie its fair promise, but opened as brightly as the most exacting hunter could require.

Esau and Jens made a last laborious and fruitless stalk, trying not only the whole Rus Valley, but

Off! a Reindeer Recollecting an Engagement.

crossing the mountains northwards into Veodalen and traversing all the slopes of Glitretind, a most splendid sight just now with his towering pyramid, 8140 feet high. Such a walk would have been impossible but for the snow, which had been reduced by the wind to the consistence of hard sand, and made the going as good as it could be.

Esau, who saw nothing all day, was a little annoyed on his return to hear that John had wandered but a short distance up Nautgardstind to gloat over the view, and there walked almost into a reindeer buck; which, as John was armed with no more deadly weapon than a double-barrelled field glass, had escaped uninjured. 'Twas ever thus.

However, the mention of this buck opened on John's devoted head the floodgates of Esau's memory, and he insisted on telling about his last stalk here two years ago, as follows: –

'By George! I shall never forget how Jens and I turned out that morning across the same precipice that you passed to get up Nautgardstind: we started pretty early because it was my last day, and I had sworn to catch something or perish.

'About ten o'clock we saw four deer, a fine buck and three does, on a long narrow snow-drift on the east side of the mountain: they were about a mile off and moving away, with the wind blowing straight from them to us; so we went after them as fast as we could, without much attempt at concealment at first.

'Presently they left the snow and turned to the left, as if to skirt round the mountain, we still following and getting rather nearer to them. They seemed very restless and kept moving, and at last began to trot, and soon got out of our sight.

'We were half an hour without seeing them again, and at last Jens discovered them far down below us in the large valley where you saw that one to-day. The place where they were was quite un-approachable, but Jens pointed out a sort of pass by which he thought it was likely they might leave the valley, and so we went and hid ourselves in a con-venient nook fifty yards to the leeward of that place.

'There we lay in a bitterly cold wind for an hour, and then the deer began to come in our direction. Now was the critical moment: there were two practicable routes in the pass; would they choose the nearer one, which would give me a shot, or the other? They stopped a little time to look for food, and provokingly grazed their way very slowly towards the wrong one, and then all of a sudden seemed to make up their minds and tur-ned to the right one. The cold and cramp were forgotten as the deer came within three hundred yards and were nearing us quickly, and, with rifle cocked, I was already wondering whether the buck's horns were in velvet or not, and thinking what a splendid coat he had; when without any warning a storm of sleet swept down upon us, and a dense mist drifted over the mountain and shut out from our gaze the rocky pass and deer alike wrapped in impenetrable gloom.

'For fully half an hour this lasted, and then the mist cleared as quickly as it had come, the sleet stop-ped, and the sun shone out, making the ground fair-ly smoke: but, alas! the deer were gone. We looked for their tracks, and found that they had actually passed within forty yards of us during the storm; but our chance was missed, and there was nothing for it but to renew the search.

'Another hour of walking, and Jens' quick eye caught sight of them, this time high above our heads on some snow near the top of Nautgardstind, and at last, thank goodness, lying down. There seemed to be a possibility of getting to them, and we spent another hour crawling like serpents in the attempt, only to find our way barred when we were within four hundred yards by a ridge over which we could not pass unseen.

'However, from there we saw plainly that we could approach them by going up the mountain, and then coming quite straight down above them, with hardly any difficult ground to traverse. So we performed that weary crawl back again until we were safely out of sight, and then went up Nautgardstind at a speed that has never been equalled.

'Half an hour took us to the top, and then Jens made the only mistake in a stalk that I ever saw: he got his bearings wrong somehow, and thought that the deer were on one bit of snow, the top end of which we could see, while I thought they were on another. Of course I had much more confidence in Jens' opinion than in my own, but it turned out that he was wrong, and in crawling to the place where he expected them to be, we unluckily came into full view of the snow where they really were – a fact which was made unpleasantly apparent to us by our suddenly catching sight of four deer galloping down the drift two hundred yards away.

'I took a careful aim at the buck, but fired too low, and the bullet broke his fore-leg, which did not prevent him from following the does, though at a reduced pace. Now I think our best chance would have been to remain perfectly still, and trust to his stopping in time in some place where I could get to him: but Jens was terribly excited, begging me to shoot, and my own head was by no means as cool as it should have been, so I sat on a rock and fired away all my remaining cartridges except two, at the gradually receding form of the reindeer: I suppose at the last shot he was five hundred yards away, and l don't think I ever hit him again.

'Presently he got round the corner to the right, and into the next valley, where a few days before I had killed two deer; and as I ran to the right above him an astonishing sight met my gaze. The valley was full of deer, about fifty altogether, in three distinct herds, and they were all running about frightened by the firing, and not sure in which direction it would be safe to go.

'While we watched them from our peak a mile above, a buck and two does with a calf left the herd, and began to come towards the very snowdrift on which the four deer were lying when we made the fatal mistake. What became of the rest we never knew, nor whither our wounded buck went; for when we saw this fresh four making for the drift, it occurred to us to run towards the top and try to intercept them if they should attempt to ascend the mountain on the snow, as we expected they would.

'Off we ran at top speed over terribly rough

ground, and before we got nearly in shot of the top of the long drift we saw the deer get on to it at the bottom, and begin to gallop up with their untiring stride. It was simply a race, with long odds on the Running Rein; and soon we saw them standing at the top, while we were still over two hundred yards from it. Then for the first time they saw us (for the drift was in a ravine, and out of our sight as we ran), and they turned to flee, but Jens somehow managed to find breath enough to whistle, and the deer stopped for a moment.

'I fired my last two cartridges, but in the condition to which I was reduced by the run I could not have hit a haystack, and no damage was done. So we turned homewards with deep and abiding sorrow in our hearts, too despondent to look again for our wounded buck, or to see what became of the other herds.

'In those days I always took out seven cartridges, which I fondly imagined to be a lucky number; but after this I solemnly registered two vows: firstly, never to go out with so few again; and secondly, never to shoot them all away at absurd distances in the forlorn hope of killing a wounded deer.' Esau here paused for a moment or two, and then resumed: 'By Jove, I did make myself agreeable to the Skipper when I got home that night. I remember he said' –

But John thought it was his turn to have a few weeks' conversation, and rudely interrupted Esau's reminiscences by calling his attention to some writing which, like Belshazzar, he had detected on the wall above his bed. It was in pencil, and seemed to have been written in prehistoric times, for it was all illegible except the first two lines, and even those required a great deal of deciphering by the aid of a dripping candle, while Esau knelt on his bunk and flattened his nose against the log wall, before he could read them. Then after licking the tip of a pencil for a long time in meditative silence, he scrawled the remainder of the poem underneath, so, that the whole composition read as follows: −

> A reindeer three miles off you spy,
> And to shoot that reindeer you will try.
> First a mile at the top of your speed you go,
> Then you climb a mile up loose rocks and snow,
> Then a mile on your hands and knees you crawl,
> And −

(when you have executed these little manæuvres and arrived at the place with your garments all in tatters and your whole body a mass of bruises, in all probability you will either find that the insidious animal has removed himself to the uttermost ends of the earth five minutes before your appearance on the scene, or else you do get a shot at him and)

> − you miss that reindeer after all.

CHAPTER XXXIII

HOMEWARD BOUND.

September 17. – Our ears were gladdened by the sound of Ivar's hoarse cachinnation some time during the night or early morning, and on turning out he informed us that he should have been here yesterday, but his cart had been smashed on the road beyond Hind Sæter; however, he had patched it up and got it to the sæter; so we distributed our goods on the two ponies, after seizing our last chance of a 'square meal,' by eating an enormous breakfast of venison pie, cutlets, and trout.

All our stores came to an end yesterday, except candles and soap. The latter article has for some time been lying in great bars on a shelf as a reproach to us, and we were glad to get it out of our sight to-day, and 'give it to the men,' as we would anything else that is repulsive to our feelings. There were a few scraps of other delicacies which we divided among the retainers, and then taking with us a fore-quarter of 'stor bock' for our own consumption on the journey, and a hind-quarter carefully sewn up in the sail of Esau's canoe, and intended as a present for Mr. Thomas, we regretfully took leave of the little hut, and started for Besse Sæter.

315

Öla and Jens were sent down the Russen River, which is the nearest way to Hind Sæter; and Ivar was to meet us at the eastern end of Sjödals Lake as soon as he could get there.

We paused at the brow of the hill to have a last look at the beautiful lake and quaint little huts, and to take off our hats to grand old Nautgardstind, to whom we hoped we were not bidding an eternal 'farvel;' and then we turned across the fjeld, and, losing sight of the Rus valley, were soon looking forward again to the change and uncertainty of the homeward journey.

From Besse Sæter, which was reached at noon, we launched our craft into the lake with a nasty sidewind blowing, which delayed our progress considerably, so that we took an hour to reach the lower end of the lake, a distance of not quite four miles.

There we found Ivar with his pony and sleigh, on which the canoe was conveyed to the junction of the Sjoa and Russen Rivers, where Esau launched her again and ran the rapids down to Ruslien Sæter, a very fine bit of stream, in which the canoe could only just manage to live.

Finding that the sæter girls were still here, we went in and asked for milk. They suggested cream: amendment carried without a division. A huge bowl of the thickest and most delicious cream was set before us, which we, armed with two enormous spoons, attacked and soon consumed titterly, with an indefinite amount of fladbrod and cheese. Charge for the whole, sixpence! We have no hesitation in saying that the cream alone would have been worth its weight in gold in Piccadilly.

We then regained our craft, and had a delightful cruise down to Hind Sæter, the stream going at millrace speed all the way, so that we did the two and a half miles in fifteen minutes, arriving long before our cavalcade of men and ponies, who started twenty minutes before us, while we were discussing the cream.

The sæter was deserted for the winter, but Ivar produced his cart from the bed of a stream where he had left it to improve the wheels, and at half-past five we, with Jens and one cart, resumed our journey, leaving the other two men with the canoe to follow us.

We had originally intended to make the journey to Lillehammer from here entirely by canoe down the Sjoa until it joined the Laagen, but the premature departure of the Skipper knocked that little scheme on the head.

It would have been a tremendous enterprise, for the Sjoa is such a turbulent river that there would have been a great deal of portage to be done; but we had agreed to allow a fortnight for it, and were looking forward to it with great delight. The Laagen is a fairly navigable river all the way, with the exception of a few very large falls; but there is a good road by its side, so that we should have had no difficulty if we had been lucky enough ever to reach it. However,

> 'The best laid schemes o' mice an' men
> Gang aft a-gley;'

and we were reduced to the prosaic necessity of walking, and helping to hold our luggage on to a jolting cart.

As we gradually descended into the birch-woods we were much struck by the beautiful effects of the variegated autumn tints, and soon the brilliant reds and yellows of the birches began to contrast with the dark green of the fir trees, the light greyish green of the lichen, and rich brown and purple of the ground and undergrowth. It was so long since we had seen any trees, that their beauty seemed to come to us quite as a new sensation.

Below Hind Sæter the road lay through dense forests of pines for mile after mile, with hardly any change except where we got occasional glimpses of the Sjoa tearing madly along far beneath us – so far that only a faint murmur came up from the leaping, hurrying waters. Hour after hour we walked, and still the same dark forest gloomed above us, so remote from the busy haunts of men that it seems not to be worth any one's while to cut the trees except for use in the immediate neighbourhood, and hundreds of them lie naked and dead as they have fallen before the fury of the gale, and slowly rot or are devoured by insects until their place is ready for a successor.

As the shades of evening began to close, we were several times startled as the huge body of a caper-cailzie darted across the road at a pace which seem-ed impossible to such an enormous bird, and with an absence of noise that appeared equally unnatural.

About half-past eight we came to a more open

part of the forest, and soon we saw a glimmering light ahead: Jens cheerily said, 'Ransværk;' and in a few more minutes we pulled up at the door of a large sæter.

Without knocking Jens opened the door, and we walked in and struck a light. There the usual fireplace and table, and in the further corner a bed, which, as we presently perceived, was occupied by two girls. This discovery embarrassed us a little; but no one else, least of all the girls themselves, appeared to be at all disconcerted.

In our favoured land a woman would probably be slightly concerned if she were aroused from sleep by the unceremonious entrance into her room of three men, two of them ruffianly-looking strangers of foreign exterior; but not so these artless beings. The elder one at once got out of bed and proceeded to dress, while her sister remained where she was and soon fell asleep.

When the dressing commenced, we, being innocent young bachelors, retired and remained outside till it was finished, but we do not believe she appreciated our delicacy at all.

Then this poor girl, no doubt very tired after a hard day's work at cheese-making, proceeded to relight the fire, prepare coffee, and broil some venison for us. And just as we finished a hearty meal, Öla and Ivar arrived, so that she had to begin all over again for them. Finally, in spite of our remonstrances, she dragged her sister out of the bed, and insisted on our having it, while they went and slept in another building a few yards away. So John took the bed they had vacated, while Esau made a couch for himself in the cheese-room, and we slept the sleep of the hardworked, virtuous, penniless wanderer.

Verily they have a better idea in Norway of true hospitality than in any other country under the sun.

September 18. – How strange that our return to the haunts of men should be chiefly marked by the sparseness of the fare provided for breakfast! A tin of sardines took the place of the usual trout; and although Ransværk consists of a group of several sæters, and almost attains to the dignity of a village, and our quarters were in the largest and most imposing mansion, there were no forks or spoons to be obtained, and we had to fish our sardines out of their native oil with a Tollekniv, assisted by a finger, and convey them to our mouths with the same implements.

After breakfast Esau and Jens turned out in pursuit of capercailzie, which abound in the forest here; but though they persevered until three o'clock, and got several shots, the annoying birds all 'went on,' as an English keeper generally says when you ask, 'Did you see if I killed that rabbit?'

Esau had used up all his large shot at ducks up at Gjendin, and his cartridges were perfectly ineffectual at such a strong bird as the capercailzie. Besides this, they are extremely wary, and always rise about thirty yards from the shooter; they fly quite straight, and so are very easy to hit; but though Esau knocked clouds of feathers out of them at every shot, and did bring one to the ground which, from the closeness of the underwood, could not be gathered, he was obliged to submit to disappointment for once.

In one part of the forest they heard a raven shrieking angrily ('skriking,' Jens called it, which has the same meaning in North country dialect), and going to the place were in time to see a goshawk gliding swiftly away with some victim in its grasp. In another place there were a lot of squirrels, which Jens induced Esau to shoot for some purpose of his own. What that purpose was we could only guess by seeing him gather a bunch of beautiful wild cur-rants and some flowers just before reaching the sæter, and then brush his hair and march out with his bouquet, berries, and squirrel-skins to some place unknown.

Soon after three o'clock we resumed our march, and almost directly quitted the good Vaage road along which we travelled last night, and took to a cow track on the right. The cart with the canoe had a very rough time of it for the first five or six miles, jolting and bumping in and out of holes, bogs, and ruts, and over boulders and logs in a most appalling manner; then we had a piece of decent road again, and at the finish another mile of rough track.

Soon after starting we passed the sæter where Jens lives when he is not hunting in the mountains, and Esau wishing to see what kind of snow-shoes they use in this part of the country, Jens ran up to the house and fetched his 'skier.' To give an idea of the absurd honesty which prevails here, we noticed that though Jens had been absent from home for the last two months, and the windows were shuttered up, yet the door was only latched; and after the inspection of the snow-shoes, Jens would not trouble to take them back, but simply left them by the side of the road, to wait his return three or four days hence.

Another instance illustrating the same simplicity occurred to us once when travelling in quite a different part of Norway. When changing carioles at a station our baggage was all heaped together on the roadside, and as we wanted to stay there an hour or so for dinner, and this was a main road with a fair amount of traffic, we suggested to the landlord that our goods had better be brought inside the station. He merely looked up at the sky with a weather-wise eye, and replied, 'Oh no, I'm sure it won't rain.'

Our route to-day through the forest was most beautiful, at one time descending to the level of the Sjoa, and even struggling along its bed where the going on the bank seemed to be inferior, at another climbing up and up and ever higher, until we stood on the summit of the range of hills which confine this valley on the northern side. It is called Hedalen, and is one of those strikingly beautiful half-cultivated Norwegian dales which occupy the space between civilisation and the untouched realms of nature.

This evening, the setting sun throwing a rich golden glow over the scene, and lighting up the brilliant autumnal colours of the trees, gave us an opportunity of seeing it quite at its best.

Gradually the forest began to get more open, and the road to improve. Several peasants in picturesque garb were seen on the wayside: rough buildings became more frequent, and fields and fences quite common; at first only pasture land, but soon corn-fields and patches of potatoes.

Then at last in the twilight we make a swift descent from the ridge along which the road runs; a short plunge through a thicket, down a grassy track; a bridge over a little stream; and as we breast the opposite bank, a pile of buildings looming in front and looking perfectly gigantic to our eyes, so long accustomed to the tiniest of huts; and Jens points up, cracks his whip, and says, 'Bjölstad.' The pony boils up something like 'a trot for the avenue,' and rattles the cart into a large square courtyard, tenanted only by two huge dogs; and as a cheery old Norseman rushes out in great excitement to welcome us and lead us into a bright, clean, curtained room, we feel that we have said farewell to the delights of savage life, and will probably have to put on a necktie to-morrow.

Here we parted with our faithful Jens, and very sorry we were to do so, as we think him a first-rate fellow: a man with a bright eye and stolid demeanour; naturally silent, but game for anything; a keen sportsman and wonderful stalker, and without a particle of the laziness and sulkiness which characterised Öla.

Here, for the first time since leaving Lillehammer in July, we slept between sheets.

Our own and only Ivar has volunteered to what he calls 'transportare' all our baggage in his cart down to Lillehammer, distant about eighty miles hence, for the sum of twenty-two shillings. This sounds unreasonable, but it was his own suggestion, so we did not argue the point, only stipulating that he should be there by noon on Tuesday, to-day being Saturday, and leaving the details to him.

Our thoughts were here recalled to the Skipper and his adventures by finding the following note from him: –

'DEAR ESAU, – I have left bebind me here certain of what the Romans so appropriately called "impedimenta," and hope that you will be able to bring them home for me. I got an old, old man with a small cart to bring my luggage down from Ransværk. It was a wet day. I walked the first nine miles while the old man and the rain were both driving. This ancient driveller seemed to imagine it was a fine day, and had hung on his best coat and hat, further aggravating his appearance with a spotted kerchief and a light heart. He seemed remarkably cheerful, as carolling he drove his carjole and cajoled his horse through the dripping pine forests. I arrived here at midday, and the owner, Ivar Tofte, came out to meet me. He took a great fancy to me, and we finished together a bottle of the most delicious aquavit, which he produced from a cellar where it had been laid down in the time of the Vikings. It is a pity neither of you can speak the language! –

Yours haughtily,

'THE SKIPPER.'

We found that the 'impedimenta' of which the Skipper had spoken were 147 loaded cartridges wrapped up in a flannel shirt, the whole being enveloped in a partially cured reindeer-skin.

We were further reminded of our lost one by looking in the Day-book (or traveller's name-book), where his was the last English name. This was not surprising, for though Bjölstad is a posting station, it is a very out-of-the-way place; but we looked back for two years without finding that any other Englishman had been here, and then the Skipper's name occurred again. Between these dates the names were all Norwegian, and there were not very many even of them.

CHAPTER XXXIV

BJÖLSTAD.

Sunday, September 19. – Bjölstad is an ancient Norwegian homestead, and consists of several separate buildings surrounding a central rectangular court. The house that we slept in bears the date of 1818, and is the most modern as well as the largest of the group; it is really a suite of state apartments for the use of the King on the rare occasions when he visits this part of his dominions.

On the left-hand side of the courtyard, as we stand at the door of our state apartments, is a very quaint and picturesque old house with a handsome porch, built in the Byzantine style, date 1743, and in this the owner lives whenever he comes to this farm.

Opposite to us is another building even more curious in its architecture, and considerably older than the other; and the remaining side of the yard is occupied by another more modern edifice used chiefly as a storehouse. Besides these there are several other detached outbuildings, in which sleighs, ploughs, spare cooking utensils, rugs, and various other useful and useless articles are kept, including all the fittings and even the weathercock of an ancient church which used to stand close to the farm, but which is now demolished and partly reduced to firewood.

The owner of all this grandeur is one Ivar Tofte, a wealthy yeoman who has several other farms in other parts of the country, one of which is much larger and more important even than Bjölstad; and we were lucky enough to find this Northern

Old Buildings in the Courtyard at Bjölstad.

Cræsus at home, for it turned out that he was the cheery old man in the shocking bad hat who had run out to welcome us last night.

This morning he came into our room after breakfast, with a bottle of aquavit in his hand wherewith to drink our health. Now to refuse this ceremony is an unpardonable insult, but we had tasted aquavit before, and had a wholesome dread of the nauseous compound, reeking of carraway seeds and aniseed, which we were accustomed to expect out of an aquavit bottle. So we poured out very small glasses, clinked them in approved manner, and raised them to our lips as we uttered the magic word Skaal, more with a feeling of disgust than any other sensation. And then it was beautiful to see a heavenly smile steal over Esau's ingenuous countenance; while John, softly murmuring, 'Chartreuse, by George!' reached for the bottle, and with a shout of 'Skaal Ivar Tofte,' proceeded to fill himself a bumper. It was a perfect liqueur, soft, delicate, and mellow, as probably age alone could have made it; and we drank Skaal to 'Gammle Norgè,' and England, and Kong Oscar, and Queen Victooria, and Ivar Tofte again, and then ourselves again; whereupon the old man perceived that we appreciated his 'cuvée de réserve,' and went for another full bottle, which he left in our room, so that we could 'put it to our lips when we felt so dispoged.'

After this, John, feeling at once genial and liberal, announced his intention of buying a sheenfelt (sheepskin rug) for importation into England; and Tofte with an aged retainer volunteered to show us his stores of sheepskins.

First our guide procured a bunch of enormous keys, such as Bluebeard would have hanging from his waist in a pantomime, labelled 'Key of the Wine-cellar. Umbrella stand. Fowl-house. Potted shrimps. Cupboard where the jam's kept,' &c., &c. Then he marched off to one of the buildings, followed by us and the other old man, whose profession was apparently to exalt Bjölstad sheenfelts, and to debase – as far as extreme volubility and strict inattention to the elements of truth would enable him to accomplish that object – an ancient one which John wished to give in part payment.

Bluebeard led us up some stairs to the Blue Chamber, where we saw hanging in a row the skins, not of his deceased wives, but of many 'timid-glancing, herbage-cropping, fleecy flocks,' to use the beautiful and touching language of the Greek poet. Then the two accomplices selected the sheen-felt which they intended us to buy, and began to expatiate on its beauties in terms of undisguised admiration; and after half an hour's huckstering and haggling, of course they persuaded John to take that and no other. However, it was a beautiful specimen of this kind of rug, of a dark grey colour, and very thick, warm, and heavy; so both sides were highly satisfied, and proceeded to the drinking of more aquavit in celebration of the bargain.

The weather was so unpleasant, and Bluebeard and his aquavit were so engaging, that we decided not to leave here till to-morrow. Our host was delighted to hear this, and at once went for more aquavit, which he appears to consider the first necessity of life; and then he proceeded to show us round his ancestral halls, as though he were a sober old verger of Westminster Abbey.

There was a sort of old-world Rip van Winkle sleepiness about Bjölstad very soothing to men who like us have lived in the nineteenth century for some few years. All the varlets and handmaidens were dressed in the old native costume, so appro-priate to the ancient wooden buildings with quaintly carved eaves and doorways, about which they hovered. In the courtyard were two enormous dogs, that barked loudly whenever we appeared, but at the same time wagged their tails and looked imbecile and good-natured. There were also four geese, who meant to be sitting basking in the rain, but as soon as anybody came to one of the numerous doors, or crossed the yard, they all stood up and quacked solemnly fourteen times each, then hissed once, and sat down again; and as some one was always moving about the court, the quiet rest of those birds was more anticipatory than real; but they alone of all the living creatures at Bjölstad appeared to have any fixed employment which demanded constant attention.

Bluebeard first took us through the state apartments, which contained many curious and interesting things of all ages, from an axe nearly a thousand years old, to a Birmingham plated teapot won at the Christiania horse show in 1860.

The Toftes boast themselves descended from Harald Haarfager, and are so proud of their ancestry, that from time immemorial they have never married out of their own family. If dear old Bluebeard may be accepted as an ordinary result of this system, it must be confessed that it has its advantages.

The things that he chiefly delighted to show us were those which had been used by the King during his occasional visits, the most curious being a large stone table made of one enormous slab not more than three-quarters of an inch thick, but very hard

and elastic, more like a steel plate than stone; gor-
geously embroidered counterpanes and chairs; some
very old ploughs and sleighs; and a brass-bound box
with a marvellous representation of Adam and Eve,
very evidently before the Fall, and the most remarkable thing in serpents which the wildest flight
of human imagination has yet conceived. There
were some very nice silver utensils and ornaments,
but not many, as most of his plate is kept at his largest farm. All that he had here was in a cupboard
with a rubbishy unlocked deal door, standing in
Johns bedroom; a fact which speaks volumes for the
trusting simplicity and total inability to read a man's
character from his appearance, caused by a millen-
nium of marrying your cousin once removed. Poor
Bluebeard! he little thought what a viper he was
nurturing in his bosom, or rather in his chest (his
plate-chest), and that in that room lay one who
could perhaps, if he would, answer the questions –

Who took the Gainsborough?

Who has the Dudley diamonds?

Who stole the donkey? and

Where's the cat?

N.B. – John has now a large collection of ancient Norwegian silver, counterpanes, belts, tankards,
knives, and ornaments to dispose of at very low pri-
ces if no questions are asked. – ADVT.

September 20. – We left Bjölstad in carioles on a
real road about nine o'clock, Bluebeard himself
assisting in the operation of harnessing the ponies
and packing the baggage. Just as we were driving
off, a brilliantly original idea occurred to him, and

he said, 'Come in and taste my aquavit.' We did not like to refuse an old grey-haired man's simple request, so descended and drank another Skaal to all the usual loyal, patriotic, and festive toasts, and then we drove off murmuring somewhat indistinctly, 'Shkaal Iva' Tofte Shhkaal Iv Toffic Shko Toffy. Jolly good fler-ole-shole-Toffy.'

All day we drove, and ever as we descended the Hedalen valley with the noisy Sjoa on our right hand, the farming kept improving, and the country becoming more populous; and we saw many families digging potatoes, many pigs roaming free and unmolested as they do in Ireland, and a few men bringing up stores from the town for the long season of snowed-up dreariness now so near at hand. Jens told us that in winter, even so far to the south as Vaage, the sun only rises about eleven, and sets at one o'clock, giving barely three hours of daylight in midwinter; though he said that in the mountains where he spends his time hunting, there is rather more light than in the valleys.

It may be well to explain in what manner so much information was obtained from men whose language was unknown to us, and to whom ours was equally incomprehensible.

The glorious principle of co-operation did it all. The Skipper spoke Norse with great elegance and fluency, but did not understand it at all. Esau could understand it perfectly, but was unable to express himself in that tongue to even a limited extent; and John could neither speak nor understand a word. Consequently our united accomplishments were equal to meeting any emergency that might arise, even to the disentanglement of such a coil as —

Brandforsikringsselskabet, or —

Sommermaandernepassagerbekvemmeligheder,

or any other of the little complex words that an educated Norwegian can construct. It is wonderful to hear the natives launch out into one of these cataracts; they do it fearlessly, and steer through the whole with unflagging fortitude and very seldom with any fatal results.

The hay harvest seemed to be quite finished except on the roofs of the houses, where some people were still cutting and carrying their crops. The barley had just been reaped, and was now being dried by the process of impalement, a dozen sheaves, one above the other, being transfixed by a pole stuck into the ground, just as a naughty boy sticks a row of moths on a long pin, or as the unfortunate Bulgarians were supposed to be exhibited during the 'atrocity' scare. Can it be possible that those stories arose from the distant contemplation of a barley-field?

The Norwegians also dry their hay in a different manner from that usually practised in England. They erect high hurdles made of larch poles in lines at intervals all over the field, and on these they hang the hay to dry as we hang towels on a horse, and it is by this means so well exposed to both air and sun that it dries very quickly. No doubt the hurdles are also very useful in spring as a shelter for the young lambs.

The weather kept improving so much that we grew quite jubilant, and the ever-changing scenes that opened before us seemed full of life and bright-

A Norwegian 'Atrocity'

ness, and we looked with a certain amount of pleasure on even the magpies, which sat on the fences
in scores, pluming their black-green feathers, and
talking things over quietly to themselves. So different from the wary magpie of England, who, knowing that he is an Ishmael, glories in the fact, and
shrieks defiance to mankind at the top of his voice
and a tree.

For three hours we followed the brawling Sjoa
through scenery that would bear comparison with
Switzerland, and then we reached the spot where it
joins the mighty Laagen, and crossing the latter by a
picturesque but discouraging bridge, soon struck

the main road, and pulled up for our first change of ponies at Storklevstad, nineteen miles from Bjölstad.

At another place further on we found a shop kept by a Norwegian Yankee, and entered it to buy some sugar-candy, wherewith to appease our cariole-boy. This storekeeper informed us that the emigration from Norway to the States was enormous just now, especially to Minnesota and Wisconsin, and that no less than sixteen men had gone this year from the little village of Vaage – a place which does not strike one as being likely to contain that number of ablebodied men at one time. Öla had told us that five of his brethren were in Minnesota, but that he himself had no intention of leaving his native country; and this we thought to be well, for if he were to join them we are convinced that any enterprise in which they might be engaged would inevitably fail with his invaluable co-operation and assistance – unless perhaps the Skipper could be induced to go out there and occasionally exhort him.

At Listad we lunched off a real white tablecloth; that is to say, we ate not the cloth, but everything eatable that was placed on it.

We also found a note from the Skipper asking us to bring along one or two little things that he had been obliged to leave behind in his hurried flight, just as the allied armies kept finding Napoleon's belongings at different places after Waterloo. The present loot consisted of a coat, sleeping rug, and a towel.

At Kirkestuen we quitted the track for the night, having made fifty miles in about ten hours. This, according to our experience, is a fair rate of progression in Norway; in fact, the traveller is more likely to find the average below this than above, unless he drives the good little ponies faster than they like to go, which is wrong.

Here the three women who kept the station were immensely amused because we asked for coffee with our food, and one of them took upon herself the task of rebuking us for such dissipated habits, and explained at great length that no respectable people ever did such a thing. 'Coffee,' she said, 'should only be drunk during the day, gruel after sunset.' But we persisted in our reckless demand, and they finally gave in, and produced the delicious compound that may be expected at any wretched little dwelling throughout the country.

This was the first place where the papered rooms and iron stoves of modern Norway obtruded themselves on our notice; but in spite of these we were very comfortable, and think that Kirkestuen deserves all the praise which we cannot find lavished upon it in any of the guide-books: it is cheap, comfortable, and clean, and the food is excellent. If the three young ladies who preside over its arrangements wish to send us any little remuneration for this advertisement, we are agents for several Central African Missions, to which we could hand it over; or, as 'best aquavit' is a good deal appreciated by the missionaries themselves when they are suffering from certain diseases peculiar to the Central African climate, we would receive that liqueur in cases of not less than three dozen in lieu of money.

CHAPTER XXXV

DOWN TO CHRISTIANIA.

September 21. – The steadily improving weather of our homeward journey is very pleasant, and already we are beginning to almost forget those 'Miseries in Cold and Grey' which were so conspicuous during our last few days at Rus Vand.

To-day we noticed that the whole population of the country appeared to be engaged in the seductive pastime of potato-digging. One family that we passed consisted of papa, mamma, and eight children of different ages, all absorbed in this pursuit. The parents had gardening tools, the elder children were using pickaxes and trowels, the younger ones fireshovels and wooden baking spades, and the mere babies were hard at work with spoons and toasting-forks.

Here and there we detected a few people still making hay, presumably because they had no potatoes. In Norway the hill-sides are so steep and rocky that there is not overmuch room for the cultivation of grass, so they have to collect it from every available corner where a few sprays of anything green can contrive to exist. As we have mentioned, they are now curing grass on the house-tops, and to-day we saw a man with a scythe about eighteen inches long, mowing in amongst the stones on the river bank, and in some of the places where he went the scythe blade was the only blade visible to the naked eye. One thing seems certain, that a Norwegian will make hay while the sun shines, even if he can only find rocks out of which to make it.

On this part of our journey we passed a great many spotted black and white pigs: these pigs move with a greater dignity of bearing than the ordinary white pig of Scandinavia, and altogether seem to consider themselves superior to him, although they have not a curly tail. Personally we think there is a certain subtle charm about the curly tail of the white pig, a something that sets him off and renders him more pleasing to the eye of the beholder than is a spotted pig with a straight tail. However, our humble opinion does not seem at all to affect the swagger of the spotted pig.

Near Formö we overtook a rosy-cheeked girl of about eighteen, astride a bare-backed pony: the pony was seized with a spirit of emulation, and insisted on accompanying the carioles for some distance in spite of her efforts to stop it.

The weather was now delightful; the roads were dry and dusty, and the sun was so hot that the long cool shadows of the pine woods which at frequent intervals hedge in the road were quite a welcome relief both to us and our shaggy steeds.

Ever as we followed the almost imperceptible descent of the road, the great river Laagen became wider, deeper, and bluer, as it gathered increased volume from the numberless tributaries which flow into it from every hill, till at length at Fossegaarden it plunged over a series of ledges in a splendid succession of falls, and after winding awhile amid firc-lad islands and shaded grassy banks, it flowed into the Mjösen Lake and was lost, while we on the road above, rounding the last corner and turning to the east, soon found ourselves in Lillehammer, which really looked quite a towny little town.

Esau stopped at Fossegaarden a couple of hours to throw a fly in the tempting-looking water below the falls, and was rewarded at the first cast by a rise from a fish whose peculiar wriggling and rolling soon showed him to be a grayling; and before leaving, the bag was filled with some very fine specimens of this beautiful and delicate fish.

We were greeted as old friends at the Victoria Hotel, where Ivar had already arrived with our things. Then we ordered our own dinner, and told the host to supply Ivar with whatever he wanted regardless of expense (the result of this reckless munificence was a bill for nearly two shillings); and in the happy frame of mind produced on both sides by this course we settled our accounts with him, and giving him all our worn-out garments and some candles and matches, we parted with the last of our henchmen.

By the way, we here found a note from the Skipper asking us to bring home a pair of shooting boots, three socks, and the remains of what had apparently been a pocket handkerchief; but the obvious course that suggested itself was 'give 'em to the men,' and we insisted on Ivar taking these valuables.

September 22. – With the utmost difficulty, by threats and coercion Esau was induced to leave his bed, and dragged to the steamer in time for her departure, as, if left to his own inclinations, he would have remained in his insidious couch until this globe had performed its diurnal revolution.

As it was, the 'Skiblädner' was indulging in a final premonitory shriek before leaving the pier when we came hurrying and stumbling down the hill at all paces, and we only stepped aboard just as she threw off the last detaining rope.

The steamer was at first very empty, but more people joined us at every stopping-place, of which there are about a dozen on the lake. Some of these are little villages, with only the bright roofs and church spire peeping out from among the fir trees; others no more than a landing-stage projecting into the blue waters, and no other indications of life save perhaps a couple of idle fishing boats and a flagstaff.

The morning was so calm and fine, that the grayling playing under the shore made the only break in the otherwise unruffled surface of the lake, and it seemed strange to find ourselves back in summer again, having left winter with its snow and frosts far above us up at Rus Vand only a few days ago.

At Hamar some English people came aboard, so that we had some one to talk to. At every place where the steamer stopped and fresh passengers came off in boats to meet us, it seemed to be customary that they should take off their hats to the captain on the bridge as they pulled up alongside: even when we passed the smallest places without stopping, merely throwing the mail bag into a boat as we darted by, the fresh-water sailors on the steamer all took off their hats to the fresh-water sailors ashore, the latter always returning the salutation; and considering the fact that two steamers pass every day, this indicates no small degree of politeness.

There is a great amount of character to be noticed among the natives during a voyage on the lake, and although they are badly and even grotesquely dressed (for the pretty old costume has quite disappeared in this part of the country, and its modern substitute is hideous), still their old-fashioned manners and simple courtesy are very striking; and in spite of their love of a little mild ostentation they are so quiet and well behaved, that they would appear to great advantage if contrasted with the crowd that may be found say on a Greenwich steamer.

At Eidsvold we left the steamer for the train which was waiting to receive us, and about nightfall were once more in Christiania, and after a sumptuous supper went to rest in sumptuous beds, thinking ere we fell asleep of how to-morrow we should again have to submit ourselves to the yoke of civilisation, to discard our flannel shirts for linen ones and stick-up collars, to throw aside our shooting boots, and again bite off our nails, which have grown to their natural length under the soothing influence of a long spell of unworried conscience.

September 23. – We found Christiania this morning almost as hot as we left it, the streets all dry and dusty, and the trees parched for want of rain; and the sunshine was very pleasant as we wandered about the town into the various shops, purchasing articles by the assistance of which we hoped to attain popularity among our relatives on our arrival in England.

The shopkeepers were almost all very slow; in fact, the transaction of any business is not the hardy Norseman's strong point. We copy this extract from the Skipper's journal: −

'I went to the bank this morning to get some circular notes changed, and they kept me there fussing over them for fifty minutes before I got the money. During this time of expectation I read two letters from home through, and had a chase after a torpid fly on the floor with my stick: considering his languid condition this fly showed great spirit, but after following him about three feet along the floor and nine inches up the wall, I made a fortunate dash at him, and concluded his existence. Then I thought for a while and stared all round the room, and cut my nails with my knife. Then I counted how many boards there were in the floor, and how many nails there were on an average in each board, and made a little calculation on these figures to discover how many nails there were in the whole room, and what they weighed, how much they cost, how many miles they would reach if laid end to end, and how many men at how much an hour for how long it had taken to drive them all in. Then again I thought for a while, but still the money did not come, and my moral reflections on men and things had just led me to the conclusion that all mortals were but desolate creatures, and that I of all men was most desolate and abandoned, when at the end of forty minutes an official arrived with a sort of cheque. And after that it took ten minutes more to change the cheque into money in a lower room, where the clerks had their hair so beautifully brushed and were so haughty, that instead of being angry I could only thank them profusely for giving me the money at all.'

After finishing our hunt for curios, it occurred to us that we ought to see the viking's ship recently unearthed somewhere on the fjord, so we walked down to the University, where we were told by a student that it was not yet open to the public, but that if we would ask the Professor of Archæology, whom John profanely designated 'the boss that runs the antiquity show,' he had no doubt that, being strangers, we should be allowed to see the ship.

Would the fact of a man being a foreigner obtain his admission to a private view of an English curiosity, save perhaps the plans and mechanism of an ironclad or torpedo? Probably not.

Revolving these thoughts within our minds we sought the professor, and he at once left the work upon which he was engaged and took us to the ship, which was locked up inside a wooden building that has been erected for it.

Very interesting it was, the preservation of the wood and also the ironwork being wonderful. Unfortunately, some archæologists of earlier date than the present had also made some excavations in search of memorials of the past. They had cut a large hole in the side amidships, for the purpose of carrying off the ornaments and other valuables by which the dead viking was surrounded, in the chamber constructed for his body right in the centre of the boat. The modern archæologists call their predecessors 'sacrilegious robbers,' but we are averse to the use of strong language among men of science.

However, the rest of the ship was perfect, even to the shields which used to adorn the gunwale, which are now seen to have been made of thin wood, and were probably only ornamental. She was a good big boat, rather flat-bottomed and low in the water, but with great breadth of beam, and built on lines that left no room for doubt as to her seagoing qualities.

The whole day was occupied by this shopping and sight-seeing, and we went to bed more exhausted than by a hard day's stalking at Gjendin, and not half so much satisfied with our achievements.

It is almost unnecessary to mention that we found at the hotel a note from the Skipper, begging us to bring home a waterproof sheet and a few clothes that he had been obliged to leave there. We think that this young man must have shed nearly all his raiment before leaving Norway, and gone home clad in a yellow ulster which we know he had left at the hotel in July; for, judging from the fragments that we have picked up from time to time on our homeward route, he cannot have much other property with him except his gun, rifle, and fishing-gear.

CHAPTER XXXVI.

HOME AGAIN.

September 24. – To-day our Norwegian friends who lent us the hut at Rus Vand came to dine with us, and then saw us safely aboard the 'Angelo,' and at five o'clock, in the presence of an immense crowd which covered the whole quay, some of the people cheering, but many more weeping, we steamed out of the harbour.

As the sound of the last bell died away, and the last gangway fell with a crash on to the landing-stage, a hatless, breathless man rushed up the companion and darted at the spot where he supposed the gangway to be: seeing that he was too late, he yelled to the people on shore, and made as though he would have cast himself into the water, but was restrained by the passengers. Meanwhile a fleet of little boats endeavoured to catch a rope and be towed until he could be lowered into one of them; but all failed, and the unfortunate man was carried off to Christiansand, so that on his involuntary voyage he would have leisure to meditate on the folly of a too prolonged farewell.

With a gentle breeze we steamed down the fjord, which never looked more lovely than on this eve-

345

ning; and so beautiful was the night, so warm, so radiant, and with such a depth of glorious colouring from the departed sun, that people crept away into the shade out of the *moonlight*, from pure force of habit, after the heat of the summer.

The influence of such a night, together with a certain sense of something completed; the calm ocean all round us, and the soothing, monotonous throbbing of the untiring screw, produced a longing for confidence in John's bosom, so that he gave utterance to his sentiments as he leant with Esau over the rail of the hurricane deck, and watched the ever-sparkling phosphorescent lights caused by the passage of the vessel through the quiet water.

'Yes, I'm sorry to be leaving Norway, for, you know, there's something delightful to me about the simplicity of the people' (Esau's mind reverted to Ivar Tofte and his plate cupboard); 'they seem to place a childlike confidence in a stranger, which is quite incomprehensible to me. Then there is an unwordable calm, an indescribable tranquillity, which seems to cling both to the country and its inhabitants; even the houses seem to possess an imperturbable serenity of demeanour which you will not find on any other island in Europe. In fact, y'know, Esau, it's a country where one might live quietly and die in peace, where "moths do not corrupt, neither do worms break through and steal," don't you know, Esau? And I'm deuced sorry to have to count among past memories the time we have spent here, where the unbroken harmony of existence is that repose for which my soul has longed these many years; but never until now, no, by George! never, has it been able to discover the most uncertain tracings of its ideal.'

Here Esau, who had his deck shoes on, seeing what sort of a mood John was in, stole away quietly towards the cabin, and left him prosing on to the German Ocean. He paused, however, a moment before descending the companion stairs, and caught a few more words which, as the moon had now set, John was confiding to the darkness.

A couple more days, and we shall be back in England, where, y'know, I think civilisation is overdone. My existence there is a perpetual state of toadying and being toadied: you see, it's a place where the serpent of social emulation creeps into our very beds, and hangs suspended over our heads by a mere thread when we least expect him; and, y'know, Esau — ' But Esau had slunk down the stairs, and the rest of this impassioned outburst is, we fear, lost to humanity.

September 25. – We woke up to find ourselves just leaving Christiansand, and soon reached the lighthouse at, what the Skipper calls 'the bottom left-hand corner of Norway,' but remained in bed while we glared at it through the port.

We were taking out a great number of emigrants for America, fine, sturdy-looking young fellows, probably as hard as nails, and quite equal to coping with the difficulties of a new country. They all looked so cheery and full of hope and expectation, that we could not help thinking rather sadly of the day when they will wake up to some of the unpleasant realities of Yankee life, and wish themselves back again in their native hills among their own simple-minded friends.

The day passed in the manner usual at sea when the water is smooth and the ship goes merrily homeward bound. Hardly any one missed a meal – rather a difference from the ordinary state of affairs in the wild North Sea; and at evening the sun went down in a blaze of scarlet and gold, which was reflected from the perfectly calm surface; and we turned in with tranquil minds, even Esau being now reasonably hopeful of seeing the Humber without suffering the pangs of starvation.

Esau is not a good sailor. On the last occasion of our return from Norway he crossed by the 'Angelo' a fortnight before the Skipper; and the latter, on arriving on board prepared for the voyage, saw the steward, and asked him, 'What sort of a passage did you have last trip, George?'

'Beautiful, sir. I never see a smoother sea.'

Then the Skipper went on, 'Did you see anything of Mr. Esau on the voyage?'

To which George replied, 'I seen him come aboard.'

And this brief remark of George's conveyed a world of untold fact.

September 26. – We dropped anchor outside Hull at half-past five this evening, in the remainder of the very same drizzling rain that was going on when we left England in July. Hull on Sunday in a soaking rain is not a place to grow romantic about, so we omit all reference to our first sensations and maledictions on our return to our native climate, and proceed to a more agreeable subject – dinner.

It was a merry meal in company with four of our fellow passengers, who were likewise returning from sport in Norway – two from salmon fishing, two from red-deer stalking, and with whom there was consequently a bond of sympathy.

With these kindred spirits, after British beef had been washed down with British beer, a Skaal drunk in British champagne, and tongues were loosened by the confidential pipe and British cigar, we chatted long and pleasantly; wandering again with rod and gun among the rugged mountains of that wild north land, recalling exploits performed, and perhaps indulging in those mild and harmless exaggerations of doughty deeds which no traveller or sportsman can resist. Already we found ourselves forgetting the few disagreeable incidents that occurred during our trip, and viewing everything through that rosy mist which happily arises before all past hours of pleasure and discomfort alike. Too soon bedtime put an end to our retrospect, and we slept the sleep of the wearied traveller, with dreams of trout, ryper, and reindeer – steamboat, cariole, and sleigh – mountain, lake, and river – tent and sæter – paddle and pony – hurrying through our brains in wild confusion.

To-morrow, alas! we commence again a life of gilded misery and gloomy magnificence. Give to us the untrammelled freedom of 'Gammle Norgé,' and the humble crust of fladbrod – *with* JAM.

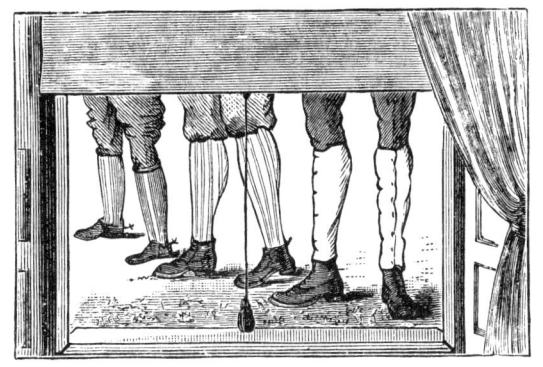

'FARVEL.'

Part of
NORWAY

English Miles
20 40   80   120

NORTH

SEA

Throndhjem

Vaage
Skeaker° Lom
Nystuen   Lillehammer
Bergen   Lake
           Mjösen
Eidsvold
KRISTIANIA

Stavanger

Flekkefjord
Kristiansand
        Skagerrak

Skeaker   Vaage

Lom

Yeodalen

Gjetvetind

Galde-
piggene
8160
                Hestlagaho
                7500
        Leir Hö
        7660
        Memuratind Iceberg
        7000   Lake
Heilstagu
Hö 7550
Uledals-   Memuru Glaciers
tinderne   Old Hut
                Drevers   Bes Hö
                                7400   Besse
                                        Sæter
                Gopit
                Ice Camp   Besseggen
                                Gjendesheim
Snello   Memurutungen   Huts
Melkedals   Gjendinstungen   Gjendin Lake
tinderne   Very high & steep
        Svartdal Snow Mountains
Eidsbugaren Sletmarkho
                        Glaciers
                Mugna Kalvaahogda

BYGDIN   LAKE

TYEN LAKE

Author's Route
Roads
△   Camps
○   Sæters & Posting Stations.